SILVER ON THE TREE

SUSAN COOPER

SILVER
ON
THE
TREE

A MARGARET K. MCELDERRY BOOK

AN ALADDIN BOOK
Atheneum

AUTHOR'S NOTE: In Chapter Three, I have taken the liberty of transplanting Sir Mortimer Wheeler's excavation of the Roman amphitheatre at Caerleon from 1928 to the present day. In Part Four, the five lines attached to the sword Eirias are those once proposed by Robert Graves as an envoie to the ancient Irish "Song of Amergin."

Non-Welsh readers please note that Aberdyfi is pronounced "Aberduvvy."

Published by Atheneum
All rights reserved
Copyright © 1977 by Susan Cooper
Published simultaneously in Canada by
McClelland & Stewart, Ltd.
Manufactured by Fairfield Graphics, Fairfield, Pennsylvania
ISBN 0-689-70467-4
First Aladdin Edition

FOR MARGARET

On the day of the dead, when the year too dies,
Must the youngest open the oldest hills
Through the door of the birds, where the breeze breaks.
There fire shall fly from the raven boy,
And the silver eyes that see the wind,
And the Light shall have the harp of gold.

By the pleasant lake the Sleepers lie,
On Cadfan's Way where the kestrels call;
Though grim from the Grey King shadows fall,
Yet singing the golden harp shall guide
To break their sleep and bid them ride.

When light from the lost land shall return,
Six Sleepers shall ride, six Signs shall burn,
And where the midsummer tree grows tall
By Pendragon's sword the Dark shall fall.

*Y maent yr mynyddoedd yn canu,
ac y mae'r arglwyddes yn dod.*

CONTENTS

PART ONE

WHEN THE DARK COMES RISING

CHAPTER ONE

MIDSUMMER'S EVE

WILL SAID, turning a page, "He liked woad. He says
—listen—*the decoction of Woad drunken is good for wounds
in bodies of a strong constitution, as of country people, and
such as are accustomed to great labour and hard coarse fare.*"

"Such as me, and all other members of Her Majesty's
Navy," Stephen said. With great precision he pulled a tall,
heavy-headed stem of grass out of its sheath, and lay back in
the field nibbling it.

"Woad," said James, wiping a mist of sweat from his plump
pink face. "That's the blue stuff the Ancient Britons used to
paint themselves with."

Will said, "Gerard says here that woad flowers are yellow."

James said rather pompously, "Well, I've done a year's
more history than you have and I know they used it for blue."
There was a pause. He added, "Green walnuts turn your
fingers black."

"Oh, well," said Will. A very large velvety bee, overloaded
with pollen, landed on his book and waddled dispiritedly
across the page. Will blew it gently on to a leaf, pushing back
the straight brown forelock that flopped over his eyes. His
glance was caught by a movement on the river beyond the
field where they lay.

"Look! Swans!"

Lazy as the hot summer day, a pair of swans sailed slowly

by without a sound; their small wake lapped at the riverbank.

"Where?" said James, clearly with no intention of looking.

"They like this bit of the river, it's always quiet. The big boats stay over in the main reach, even on a Saturday."

"Who's coming fishing?" said Stephen. But he still lay un-moving on his back, one long leg folded over the other, the slender stem of grass swaying between his teeth.

"In a minute." James stretched, yawning. "I ate too much cake."

"Mum's picnics are as huge as ever." Stephen rolled over and gazed at the grey-green river. "When I was your age, you couldn't fish at all in this part of the Thames. Pollution, then. Some things do improve."

"A paltry few," Will said sepulchrally, out of the grass.

Stephen grinned. He reached out and picked a slender green stalk with a tiny red flower; solemnly he held it up. "Scarlet pimpernel. *Open for sun, closed for rain, that's the poor man's weathervane.* Granddad taught me that. Pity you never knew him. What does your friend Mr. Gerard say about this one, Will?"

"Mmm?" Will was lying on his side, watching the weary bumblebee flex its wings.

"Book," James said. "Scarlet pimpernel."

"Oh." Will turned the crackling pages. "Here it is. Oh lov-erly. *The juyce purgeth the head by gargarising or washing the throat therewith; it cures the tooth-ach being snift up into the nosethrils, especially into the contrary nosethril.*"

"The contrary nosethril, of course," Stephen said gravely.

"He also says it's good against the stinging of vipers and other venomous beasts."

"Daft," said James.

"No it's not," Will said mildly. "Just three hundred years old. There's one super bit at the end where he tells you very seriously how barnacle geese are hatched out of barnacles."

"The Caribbean might have foxed him," Stephen said. "Millions of barnacles, but not one barnacle goose."

James said, "Will you go back there, after your leave?"

"Wherever their Lordships send us, mate." Stephen

4

threaded the scarlet pimpernel into the top buttonhole of his shirt, and unfolded his lanky body. "Come on. Fish."

"I'll come in a minute. You two go." Will lay idly watching as they fitted rods together, tied hooks and floats. Grasshoppers skirled unseen from the grass, chirruping their solos over the deep summer insect hum: it was a sleepy, lulling sound. He sighed with happiness. Sunshine and high summer and, rarer than either, his eldest brother home from sea. The world smiled on him; nothing could possibly be improved. He felt his eyelids droop; he jerked them apart again. Again they closed in sleepy content; again he forced them open. For a flicker of a moment he wondered why he would not let himself fall harmlessly asleep.

And then he knew.

The swans were there on the river again, slow-moving white shapes, drifting back upstream. Over Will's head the trees sighed in the breeze, like waves on distant oceans. In tiny yellow-green bunches the flowers of the sycamore scattered the long grass around him. Running one of them between his fingers, he watched Stephen standing tall a few yards off threading his fishing-line through his rod. Beyond, on the river, he could see one of the swans moving slowly ahead of its mate. The bird passed Stephen.

But as it passed, it did not disappear behind Stephen. Will could see the white form clearly through the outline of Stephen's body.

And through the outline of the swan, in turn, he could see a steep slope of land, grassy, without trees, that had not been there before.

Will swallowed.

"Steve?" he said.

His eldest brother was close before him, knotting a leader on his line, and Will had spoken loudly. But Stephen did not hear. James came past, holding his rod erect but low as he fastened the hook safely into its cork handle. Will could still see, through him, the forms of the swans as if in a faint mist. He sat up and stretched out his hand to the rod as James went by, and his fingers moved through the substance of the wood as if there had been nothing there.

And Will knew, with dread and delight, that a part of his life which had been sleeping was broad awake once more.

His brothers walked off to the river, moving diagonally across the field. Through their phantom forms Will could see the only earth that in this elusive patch of time was for him solid and real: the grassy slope, its edges merging into mistiness. And on it he saw figures, running, bustling, driven by some urgent haste. If he stared at them too hard, they were not there. But if he gazed with sleepy eyes, not quite focussed, he could see them all, sun-dappled, hurrying.

They were small, dark-haired. They belonged to a very distant time. They wore tunics of blue, green or black; he saw one woman in white, with a string of bright blue beads about her neck. They were gathering bundles of spears, arrows, tools, sticks; packing pots into wrappings of animal skin; putting together packages of what he supposed was meat, in dry rippled strips. There were dogs with them: full-haired dogs with short pointed muzzles. Children ran and called, and a dog lifted his head to bay, but no sound came. For Will's ears, only the grasshoppers chirruped, over the deep insect hum.

He saw no animals but the dogs. These people were travellers; not belonging here, but passing through. He was not even sure whether the land on which they stood, in their own time, lay in his own part of the Thames Valley or in some totally different place. But he knew one thing very clearly, suddenly: they were all very much afraid.

Often they raised their heads, fearfully, and gazed away to the east. They spoke seldom to one another, but worked on, hastily. Something, someone, was coming, threatening them, driving them on. They were running away. Will found himself catching the sense of urgency, willing them to hurry, to escape whatever disaster was on its way. Whatever disaster . . . he too stared eastward. But it was hard to tell what he saw. A strange double landscape lay before him, a firm curving slope visible through the phantom misty lines of the flat fields and hedges of his own day and the glimmering half-seen Thames. The swans were still there, and yet not there; one of them dipped its elegant neck to the surface of the water, ghostly as an image reflected in a window-pane. . . .

. . . and all at once, the swan was real, solid, opaque, and Will was no longer looking out of his own time into another. The travellers were gone, out of sight in that other summer day thousands of years before. Will shut his eyes, desperately trying to hold some image of them before it faded from his memory. He remembered a pot glinting with the dull sheen of bronze; a cluster of arrows tipped with sharp black flakes of flint; he remembered the dark skin and eyes of the woman in white, and the bright luminous blue of the string of beads about her neck. Most of all he remembered the sense of fear.

He stood up in the long grass, holding his book; he could feel his legs trembling. Unseen in a tree over his head, a song-thrush poured out its trilling twice-over song. Will walked shakily towards the river; James's voice hailed him.

"Will! Over here! Come and see!"

He veered blindly towards the sound. Stephen the purist fisherman stood casting delicately out into the river, his line whispering through the air. James was threading a worm on his hook. He put it down, and triumphantly held up a cluster of three small perch tied through the gills.

"Goodness," Will said. "That's quick!"

Before he could regret the word, James was raising an eyebrow. "Not specially. You been asleep? Come on, get your rod."

"No," said Will, to both question and command. Stephen, glancing round at him, suddenly let his line go slack. He looked hard at Will, frowning.

"Will? Are you all right? You look—"

"I do feel a bit funny," Will said.

"Sun, I bet. Beating down on the back of your neck, while you were sitting there reading that book."

"Probably."

"Even in England it can get pretty fierce, matey. Flaming June. And Midsummer's Eve, at that . . . go and lie down

7

in the shade for a while. And drink the rest of that lemonade."

"All of it?" said James indignantly. "What about us?"

Stephen aimed a kick at him. "You catch ten more perch and I'll buy you a drink on the way home. Go on, Will. Under the trees."

"All right," said Will.

"I told you that book was daft," James said.

Will crossed the field again and sat down on the cool grass beneath the sycamore trees, beside the remains of their picnic tea. Sipping lemonade slowly from a plastic cup, he looked uneasily out at the river—but all was normal. The swans had gone. Midges danced in the air; the world was hazy with heat. His head ached; he put aside the cup and lay on his back in the grass, looking up. Leaves danced above him; the branches breathed and swayed, to and fro, to and fro, shifting green patterns against the blue sky. Will pressed his palms to his eyes, remembering the faint hurrying forms that had flickered up to him out of the past; remembering the fear. . . .

Even afterwards, he could never tell whether he fell asleep. The sighing of the breeze seemed to grow louder, more fierce; all at once he could see different trees above him, beech trees, their heart-shaped leaves dancing agitated in a wilder swirl than sycamore or oak. And this now was not a hedge-line of trees stretching unbroken to the river, but a copse; the river was gone, the sound and smell of it, and on either side of him Will could see the open sky. He sat up.

He was high over the wooded valley of the Thames on a curving grassy slope; the cluster of beech trees around him marked the top of the hill like a cap. Golden vetch grew in the short springy grass at his side; from one of the curled flowers a small blue butterfly fluttered to his hand and away again. There was no more heavy hum of insects in valley fields; instead, high over his head through the stirring of the wind, a skylark's song poured bubbling into the air.

And then, somewhere, Will heard voices. He turned his head. A string of people came hurrying up the hill, each darting from one tree or bush to the next, avoiding the open slope.

The first two or three had just reached a curious deep hole
sunk into the hill, so closely overgrown by brush that he
would not have noticed it if they had not been there, tugging
branches aside. They were laden with bundles wrapped in
rough dark cloth—but so hastily wrapped that Will could see
the contents jutting through. He blinked: there were gold
cups, plates, chalices, a great gold cross crusted with jewels,
tall candlesticks of gold and silver, robes and cloths of glimmering silk woven with gold and gems; the array of treasure
seemed endless. The figures bound each bundle with rope,
and lowered one after another into the hole. Will saw a man
in the robes of a monk, who seemed to be supervising them:
directing, explaining, always keeping a nervous watch out
over the surrounding land.

A trio of small boys came hurrying up to the top of the hill,
despatched by the pointing arm of the priest. Will stood up
slowly. But the boys trotted past him without even a glance,
ignoring him so completely that he knew he was in this past
time only an observer, invisible, not able even to be sensed.

The boys paused on the edge of the copse, and stood looking out keenly across the valley; they had clearly been sent to
keep watch from there. Looking at them huddled nervously
together, Will let his mind dwell on hearing them, and in a
moment the voices were echoing in his head.

"No one coming this way."

"Not yet."

"Two hours maybe, the runner said. I heard him talking
to my father, he said there's hundreds of them, terrible, ram-
paging along the Old Way. They've burned London, he said,
you could see the black smoke rising in great clouds—"

"They cut off your ears if they catch you. The boys. The
men they slit right open, and they do even worse things to
the women and girls—"

"My father knew they'd come. He said. There was blood
instead of rain fell in the east last month, he said, and men
saw dragons flying in the sky."

"There's always signs like that, before the heathen devils
come."

"What's the use of burying the treasures? Nobody'll ever come back to get them. Nobody ever comes back when the devils drive them out."

"Maybe this time."

"Where are we going?"

"Who knows? To the west—"

Urgent voices called the boys back; they ran. The hiding of bundles in the hole was finished, and some of the figures already scurrying down the hill. Will watched fascinated while the last men heaved over the top of the hole a great flat flint boulder, the largest he had ever seen. They fitted it neatly inside the opening like a kind of lid, then unrolled over the top a section of grassy sod. Branches growing from surrounding bushes were tugged across the top. In a moment there was no sign of any hiding place, no scar on the hillside to show that the hasty work had ever taken place. Crying out in alarm, one of the men pointed across the valley; beyond the next hill a thick column of smoke was rising. At once, in panic, all the group fled down the grass-skinned chalk slope, slipping and leaping, the monkish figure as hasty and helter-skelter as the rest.

And Will was swept by a wave of fear so intense that it turned his stomach. For a moment he knew, as vividly as these fugitives, the animal terror of cruel violent death: of pain, of hurting, of hate. Or of something worse than hate: a dreadful remote blankness, that took joy only from destruction and tormenting and others' fear. Some terrible threat was advancing, on these people just as on those others, shadowy forms he had seen in a different, distant past a little while before. Over there in the east, the threat was once more rising, roaring down.

"It's coming," Will said aloud, staring at the column of smoke, trying not to envision what might happen when its makers came over the brow of the hill. *"It's coming—"*

James' voice said, full of a curious excitement, "No it isn't, it's not moving at all. Are you awake? *Look!*"

Stephen said, "What an extraordinary thing!"

Their voices were above Will's head; he was lying on his back in cool grass. It was a moment before he could recollect himself, and stop shaking. He heaved himself up on to his elbows, and saw Stephen and James standing a few paces away, their hands full of rods and fish and bait pails. They were staring at something in a kind of wary fascination. Will craned his head round to the hot humming meadow, to see what held them. And he gasped, as his mind was half torn apart by a great wave of that same blind terror that had swamped him a moment before, a world and ten centuries and yet no more than a breath away.

Ten yards off in the grass, a small black animal was standing motionless, facing him: a lithe, lean animal perhaps a foot and a half long, with a long tail and sinuous, curving back. It was like a stoat or a weasel and yet it was neither. Its sleek fur was pitch black from nose to tail; its unwinking black eyes were fixed unmistakably on Will. And from it he felt a pulsing ferocity of viciousness and evil so strong that his mind rebelled against believing it could exist.

James made a sudden quick hissing sound.

The black creature did not move. Still it stared at Will. Will sat staring back, caught up in the unreasoning shout of terror that twanged on through his brain. Out of the corner of his eye he was aware of Stephen's tall form standing at his side, very still.

James said softly, "I know what it is. It's a mink. They've just started turning up round here—I saw it in the paper. Like weasels, only nastier, it said. Look at those eyes—"

Impulsively breaking the tension, he yelled wordlessly at the creature and slashed at the grass with his fishing rod. Swiftly, but without panic, the black mink turned and slid away through the field towards the river, its long back undulating with a strange unpleasant gliding movement like a large snake. James bounded after it, still clasping his rod.

"Be careful!" Stephen called sharply.

James shouted, "I won't touch it. Got my rod. . . ." He disappeared along the riverbank, past a clump of stubby willow.

"I don't like this," Stephen said.

"No," Will said. He shivered, looking at the place in the field where the animal had stood, staring at him with its intent black eyes. "Creepy."

"I don't mean just the mink, if that's what it was." There was an unfamiliar note in Stephen's voice that made Will abruptly turn his head. He moved to get to his feet, but his tall brother squatted down beside him, arms resting on knees, hands fiddling with the wire leader on a piece of fishing-line.

Stephen wound the line round his finger and back again, round and back again.

"Will," he said in this strange taut voice. "I've got to talk to you. Now, while James is off chasing that thing. I've been trying to get you alone ever since I came home—I hoped today, only Jamie wanted to fish—"

He floundered, stumbling over his words in a way that filled Will with astonishment and alarm, coming from the cool adult brother who had always been so much his symbol of everything fulfilled, complete, grown-up. Then Stephen brought his head up and stared at Will almost belligerently, and Will stared nervously back.

Stephen said, "When the ship was in Jamaica last year, I sent you a big West Indian carnival head, for a Christmas and birthday present put together."

"Well of course," Will said. "It's super. We were all looking at it only yesterday." .

Stephen went on, ignoring him. "I'd got it from an old Jamaican who grabbed me one day in the street, out of nowhere, in the middle of Carnival. He told me my name, and he said I was to give the head to you. And when I asked how on earth he knew me, he said, *There is a look that we Old Ones have. Our families have something of it too.*"

"I know about all that," Will said brightly, swallowing the foreboding that hollowed his throat. "You sent a letter, with the head. Don't you remember?"

"I remember it was a damn funny thing for a stranger to say," Stephen said. "Old Ones, we Old Ones. With capital letters—you could *hear* them."

"Oh not really. Surely—I mean, you said he was an old man—"

"Will," Stephen said, looking at him with cold blue eyes, "the day we sailed from Kingston, that old man turned up at the ship. I don't know how he talked them into it, but someone was sent to fetch me to him. He stood there on the dock, with his black, black face and his white, white hair, and he looked quietly at the rating who'd fetched me, until the boy left, and then he said just one thing. *Tell your brother,* he said, *that the Old Ones of the ocean islands are ready.* Then he went away."

Will said nothing. He knew there would be more. He looked at Stephen's hands; they were clenched, and one thumb was flicking automatically to and fro over its fist.

"And then," Stephen said, his voice shaking a little, "we put in at Gibraltar on the way home, and I had half a day ashore, and a stranger said something to me in the street. He was standing beside me, we were waiting for a traffic light—he was very tall and slim, Arab I think. Do you know what he said? *Tell Will Stanton that the Old Ones of the south are ready.* Then he just disappeared into the crowd."

"Oh," Will said.

The thumb abruptly stopped moving on Stephen's hand. He stood up, in one swift movement like a released spring. Will too scrambled to his feet, blinking up, unable to read the suntanned face against the bright sky.

"Either I'm going out of my head," Stephen said, "or you're mixed up in something very strange, Will. In either case you might have a little more to say to me than *oh*. I told you, I don't like it, not one bit."

"The trouble is, you see," Will said slowly, "that if I tried to explain, you wouldn't believe me."

"Try me," his brother said.

Will sighed. Of all the nine Stanton children, he was the youngest and Stephen the oldest; there were fifteen long years between them, and until Stephen had left home to join the Navy, a smaller Will had shadowed him everywhere in silent devotion. He knew now that he was at the ending of something he had hoped would never end.

He said, "Are you sure? You won't laugh at me, you won't
. . . judge?"

"Of course not," Stephen said.

Will took a deep breath. "Well then. It's like this. . . .
This where we live is a world of men, ordinary men, and
although in it there is the Old Magic of the earth, and the
Wild Magic of living things, it is men who control what the
world shall be like." He was not looking at Stephen, for fear
of seeing the changing expression that he knew he would certainly see. "But beyond the world is the universe, bound by
the law of the High Magic, as every universe must be. And
beneath the High Magic are two . . . poles . . . that we call
the Dark and the Light. No other power orders them. They
merely exist. The Dark seeks by its dark nature to influence
men so that in the end, through them, it may control the
earth. The Light has the task of stopping that from happening. From time to time the Dark has come rising and has been
driven back, but now very soon it will rise for the last and
most perilous time. It has been gathering strength for that
rising, and it is almost ready. And therefore, for the last time,
until the end of Time, we must drive it back so that the world
of men may be free."

"*We?*" Stephen said, expressionless.

"We are the Old Ones," Will said, strong and self-
confident now. "There is a great circle of us, all over the
world and beyond the world, from all places and all corners
of time. I was the last one to be born, and when I was brought
into my power as an Old One, on my eleventh birthday, the
circle became complete. I knew nothing about all this, till
then. But the time is coming closer now, and that is why you
were given the reassurances—warnings, in a way—to bring to
me, I think from two of the three oldest of the circle."

Stephen said, in the same flat voice, "The second one didn't
look very old."

Will looked up at him and said simply, "Nor do I."

"For God's sake," Stephen said irritably, "you're my little
brother and you're twelve years old and I can remember you
being born."

"In one sense only," Will said.

Stephen stared in exasperation at the figure before him: the stocky small boy in blue jeans and battered shirt, with straight brown hair falling untidily over one eye. "Will, you're too old for these silly games. You sound almost as if you believed all this stuff."

Will said calmly, "What do you think those two messengers were, then, Steve? You think I'm smuggling diamonds, maybe, or part of a drug ring?"

Stephen groaned. "I don't know. Perhaps I dreamt them . . . perhaps I really am going out of my head." The tone tried to be light, but there was unmistakable strain in his voice.

"Oh no," Will said. "You didn't dream them. Other . . . warnings . . . have begun coming too." He fell silent for a moment, thinking of the anxious hurrying figures looming misty out of a time three thousand years past, and the Saxon boys, after that, watching terrified for the marauding Danes. Then he looked sadly at Stephen.

"It's too much for you," he said. "They should have known that. I suppose they did. The messages had to come by word of mouth, that's the only way secure from the Dark. And after that it's up to me. . . ." Quickly he seized his brother's arm, pointing, as the incomprehension on Stephen's face began changing unbearably to alarm. "Look—there's James."

Automatically Stephen half-turned to look. The movement made his leg brush against a low bramble clump growing out into the field from the trees and hedge behind. And out of the sprawling green bush rose a flickering, sudden cloud of delicate white moths. They were an astonishing sight, feathery, exquisite. Endlessly flowing upward, hundred upon hundred, they fluttered like a gentle snow-flurry round Stephen's head and shoulders. Startled, he flapped his arms to brush them away.

"Stay still," Will said softly. "Don't hurt them. Stay still."

Stephen paused, one arm raised apprehensively before his face. Over and around him the tiny moths flurried, round and around, wheeling, floating, never settling, drifting down.

They were like infinitely small birds fashioned of snowflakes; silent, ghostly, each tiny wing a filigree of five delicate feathers, all white.

Stephen stood still, dazed, shielding his face with one hand. "They're beautiful! But so many . . . what are they?"

"Plume moths," Will said, looking at him with a strange loving regret, like a farewell. "White plume moths. There's an old saying, that they carry memories away."

In one last whirl the white cloud of moths flowed and fluttered round Stephen's uncertain head; then the cloud parted, dispersing like smoke, as in the same curious communion the moths disappeared into the hedge. The leaves enfolded them; they were gone.

James came thudding up behind them. "Gosh, what a chase! It *was* a mink—must have been."

"Mink?" Stephen said. He shook his head suddenly, like a dog newly come out of water.

James stared at him. "The mink. The little black animal."

"Yes, of course," Stephen said hastily, still looking dazed. "Yes. It was a mink, then?"

James was bubbling with triumph. "I'm sure it was. What a piece of luck! I've been watching out for one ever since that article in the *Observer*. It told you to, because they're a pest. They eat chickens, and all kinds of birds. Someone brought them over from America, years ago, to breed them for the fur, and a few escaped and went wild."

"Where did he go?" said Will.

"Jumped into the river. I didn't know they could swim."

Stephen picked up the picnic basket. "Time we took the fish home. Hand me that lemonade bottle, Will."

James said promptly, "You said you'd get me a drink on the way back."

"I said, if you caught ten more fish."

"Seven's pretty close."

"Not close enough."

"Stingy lot, sailors," said James.

"Here," said Will, poking him with the bottle. "I didn't drink all the lemonade anyway."

"Go on, Sponge," said Stephen. "Finish it." One corner of the basket was fraying; he tried to weave the loose ends of wicker together, while James gulped his lemonade.

Will said, "Falling to bits, that basket. Looks as though it belonged to the Old Ones."

"Who?" said Stephen.

"The Old Ones. In the letter you sent me from Jamaica, with that big carnival head, last year. Something the old man said, the one who gave you it. Don't you remember?"

"Good Lord no," said Stephen amiably. "Much too long ago." He chuckled. "That was a crazy present all right, wasn't it? Like the stuff Max makes at art school."

"Yes," Will said.

They strolled home, through the long feathery grass, through the lengthening shadows of the trees, through the yellow-green flowers of the sycamore.

CHAPTER TWO

BLACK MINK

THE WAY HOME was a winding way: first through fields and along towpaths, to the place where they had left their bicycles; then along curving small green-shaded roads. Oak and sycamore and Lombardy poplar reached high on either side; houses slept behind hedges fragrant with honeysuckle and starred with invading bindweed. In the distance they could hear the hum of a hurrying, more preoccupied world, and see the cars flicking by on the motorway that straddled the valley of the Thames. It was late afternoon now; the horizons were lost in haze, and clouds of gnats danced in the warm air.

They were cycling along Huntercombe Lane, half a mile from home, past Will's favorite flint-walled, brick-trimmed cottages, when James braked suddenly.

"What's up?"

"Back tire. I thought it would last, but it keeps getting softer. I can pump it up enough to get home."

Will and Stephen waited, while he unhitched his pump. Faint voices drifted towards them from further up the road; the road crossed a small bridge, up there, over a stream that meandered through the farm fields on its way to join the Thames. Generally the stream moved so sluggishly that it hardly deserved the name, though on just one wild day of his life Will had seen it in spate. He scooted his bicycle idly up towards it. No sound of running water today; the stream glimmered shallow and still, scummed with green weed like a pond.

Voices came nearer; Will leaned over the side of the little bridge. Below on the bank a small boy came running, panting, with a shiny leather music-case that looked half as big as himself banging against his legs. Three others were in pursuit of him, yelling and laughing. Will was about to turn away, thinking it a game, when the first boy, finding his way blocked by the side of the bridge, twisted, skidded and then turned at bay in a movement that somehow spoke not play but desperation. He was dark-skinned, neatly dressed; the boys following were white, and scruffier. Will could hear them now. One was yelping like a hound.

"Pakkie—Pakkie—Pakkie! Here boy, here boy! Here Pakkie—"

They slid to a halt in front of the small tense figure. Will recognized two of them as boys who went to his own school, a tough troublesome pair much given to gang-rumpus on the playground. One of them smiled a thin nasty smile at the boy they had been chasing.

"Don't want to say hallo, Pakkie-boy? What you scared of, eh? Where you been?"

The boy jerked to one side and lunged, trying to slip past and away, but one of the others stepped swiftly sideways and blocked him. The music-case fell to the ground, and as the small boy leaned to pick it up a large dirty foot came down on its handle.

"Been to piano lesson, has he? Didn't know Pakkies played the piano, did you, Frankie? Only those funny little plinky-plink instruments, *wheee-eeeee-eeeee*—" He capered about, making sounds like a bad violinist; the others gurgled with unpleasant laughter, one of them picking up the music-case and whacking it for applause.

"Please give me back my case," said the small boy, in a precise, unhappy little voice.

The bigger boy held it high over the water of the stream. "Come and get it, Pakkie, come and get it!"

Will shouted indignantly, "Give it back!"

Their heads turned sharply; then the bully's face relaxed into a sneer as he recognized Will. "Mind your own mucking business, Stanton!"

The other boys hooted derisively.

"You brainless oiks!" Will yelled. "Always picking on little kids—give it back to him, or—"

"Or what?" said the boy, and he looked at the smaller boy and smiled. He opened his hand, and let the music-case fall into the stream.

His friends guffawed and cheered. The small boy burst into tears. Will, spluttering, thrust his bicycle aside; but before he could move further a whirl of limbs shot past him and Stephen's tall rangy form was bounding down the slope.

The boys scattered, too late. In only a few paces Stephen had grabbed the ringleader. Holding him by the shoulders, he said softly, "Get that case out of the water."

Will watched, motionless, caught by the controlled fury in the quiet voice, but the other boy was riding too high on his own confidence. He twisted in Stephen's grasp, snarling at him. "You crazy? Get meself all wet for some bleedin' nignog? That little cat-food eater? You think I'm—"

The last word had no chance. With a quick shift of grip Stephen suddenly heaved the boy off his feet and into the air, and dropped him into the scummy green water of the stream.

The splash left a silence. A bird chirruped gaily overhead. The two boys on the bank stood motionless, staring at their leader as he slowly hoisted himself up, dripping weed and muddy water, to stand knee-deep in the nearly stagnant stream. He looked at Stephen, his face empty of expression; then bent, picked up the flat leather music-case and held it out, dripping, at arm's length. Stephen handed it to the little boy, and he took it, dark eyes saucer-wide; then turned and fled without a word.

Stephen swung round and climbed back up to the road. As he stepped long-legged over the wire fence, the boy standing in the water came suddenly to life as if released from a spell.

He splashed back to the bank, muttering. They heard a few scattered obscenities, then a furious shout: "You think you're so great, just because you're bigger'n me!"

"The pot is speaking to the kettle," said Stephen peacefully, swinging his leg over his bicycle.

The boy yelled: "If my Dad ever catches you, you just wait—"

Stephen paused, propelled himself to the edge of the bridge and leaned over. "Stephen Stanton, at the Old Vicarage," he said. "You tell your Dad he can come and discuss you with me any time he likes."

There was no answer. James came up at Will's side as they rode away; he was beaming. "Lovely," he said. "Beautiful."

"Yes," Will said, pedalling. "But—"

"What?"

"Oh, nothing."

"That must have been little Manny Singh," Mrs. Stanton said, digging a large knife into the treacle tart. "They live at the other end of the village, in one of the houses on that new estate."

"I know them," Mary said. "Mr. Singh wears a turban."

"That's right. They aren't Pakistani, as it happens, they're Indian—Sikhs. Not that it's relevant. What horrible boys those three are."

"They're horrible to everybody, that lot," James said, hopefully watching the size of the piece of tart about to be cut for him. "No relation to race, colour or creed—they'll bash anyone. So long as he's smaller than them."

"They seemed a little more . . . selective today," Stephen said quietly.

"I'm not sure you should have dropped him in the water, though," his mother said placidly. "Pass the custard round, Will."

"Richie Moore called the little boy a cat-food eater," Will said.

Stephen said, "Pity that stream wasn't ten feet deep."

James said, "There's an extra piece of tart there, Mum."

"For your father," Mrs. Stanton said. "Eyes off. He doesn't work late for you to pinch his dinner. Don't *stuff*, James. Even Mary's eating more slowly than you." Then she raised her head suddenly, listening. "What's that?"

They had all heard the faint noise outside; it came again, louder. Distant squawking sounds rose from the chickens in their yard behind the house; not ordinary squawks of protest or demand, but high cackles of alarm.

Instantly the children stampeded, James even forgetting his treacle tart. Will was first out of the back door—and then instantly, abruptly, he stopped, so that Stephen and James blundered round him and almost fell. They ran on. But Will could feel the sense of malevolence, of immanent undiluted ill-wishing, so strong all around him that he could scarcely move. He stood, shaking. Thrusting against the sensation as against a high wind, he stumbled on after the others. His mind felt thick and slow. He thought, *I have felt this before.* . . . But there was no time to remember.

He heard shouting from the yard, and scuffling feet, through the cackling of the frightened birds. In the half-light of the hazy evening he saw Stephen and James dodging to and fro as if chasing something; closer, he thought he saw a small twisting dark body, lithe and swift, darting between them. Stephen grabbed for a stick; whacked at the shape; missed. The stick hit the ground, splintering. A garden fork stood against the fence of the hen run; Will seized it, moving closer. The animal ran past his feet. It made no sound.

"Get it, Will!"

"Hit it!"

Feet flurried, birds squawked, the yard was full of colliding bodies, grey shapes in the dim light. For an instant Will saw the full moon, an enormous yellow arc beginning to rise over the trees. Then James was bumping into him again.

"Over here! Catch him!"

Will had one quick clear glimpse. "It's another mink!"

"Of course! Over *here!*"

Twisting in its urgent search for flight, the mink was suddenly between Will and the fence, cornered. White teeth flashed. It stood taut, staring, and screamed suddenly, a high angry screech that pierced Will's mind and brought flooding into it the overwhelming awareness of evil he had felt when stepping outside the door. He flinched.

"Now, Will, now! Hard!"

They were both yelling at him. Will swung the garden fork high. The mink stared at him, and screamed again. Will looked at it. *The Dark is rising; killing one of its creatures will not stop the Dark from rising.* He let the fork drop.

James groaned loudly. Stephen leapt to Will's side. The mink, teeth bared, ran straight at Stephen as if to attack him; Will gasped in horror, but at the last minute the creature veered aside and darted between Stephen's legs. Even then it did not run at once for freedom; it dived at a frightened huddle of chickens, seized one by the neck and bit hard at the back of its head, so that the bird went instantly limp. The mink let it drop, and fled into the night.

James was stamping in angry frustration. "The dogs! Where are the dogs?"

A beam of light wavered outside the kitchen door. "Barbara took them to Eton to be clipped," his mother's voice said. "She's late because of picking up your father."

"Oh *damn!*"

"I agree," said his mother mildly, "but there it is." She came forward with the light. "Let's look at the damage."

The damage was considerable. When the boys had sorted noisy hysterical pullets from their dead companions, they had six fat corpses lying in a row. Each bird had been killed by a vicious bite at the back of its head.

Mary said, bewildered, "But so many? Why so many? It didn't even try to take a single one away."

Mrs. Stanton shook her head in bafflement. "A fox will kill one bird and run off with it, quickly. Which makes more sense, I must say. You say this thing was a *mink?*"

"I'm sure," James said. "There was a piece in the paper. Besides, we saw one this afternoon by the river."

Stephen said drily, "Looks as though it just enjoyed killing our chickens."

Will was standing a little way off, leaning against the wall of the barn. "Killing for the love of it," he said.

James snapped his fingers. "That's what the paper said. Why they were pests. It said the mink was the only animal besides the polecat that killed for the sake of killing. Not just when it was hungry."

Mrs. Stanton picked up a pair of dangling dead chickens. "Well," she said with brisk resignation, "bring them in. We'll just have to make the best of it and hope the wretched animal didn't choose the best layers. And just let him try to come back. . . . Steve, will you tuck up the rest of them?"

"Sure," Stephen said.

"I'll help," said James. "Wow—you were lucky, Steve. I thought it was going to bite you. Wonder what stopped it?"

"I taste bad." Stephen looked up at the sky. "Look at that moon—we hardly need a torch at all. . . . Come on. Wood, nails, hammer. We'll make that hen-run eternally mink-proof."

Will said, "It won't come back." He was looking at the pimpernel flower drooping wilted and forgotten from Stephen's buttonhole. *"Good against venomous beasts.* It won't come back."

James peered at him. "You look funny. You okay?"

"Of course I am," Will said, fighting the turmoil in his mind. "Course I am. Course. . . ."

His head was whirling; it was like giddiness, except that it seemed also to be destroying his sense of time, of what was now and what before or after. Had the mink gone, or were they still chasing it? Had it yet come at all; were they shortly to be attacked, the hens to begin a dreadful frightened clamour? Or was he . . . somewhere else . . . entirely . . . ?

He shook his head abruptly. *Not yet. Not yet.* "Dad's tool chest is in the barn now. He moved it," he said.

"Come on, then." Stephen led the way into the wooden outbuilding that was known, more romantically than it deserved, as the barn. Their house had once been a vicarage, never a farm, but the chickens and rabbits that their farm-bred mother kept were enough to change its mood.

James snapped on the electric light, and they paused, blinking; then collected hammer, pliers, stout nails, some chickenwire and several pieces of left-over half-inch board.

"Just right," Stephen said.

"Dad made a new rabbit-hutch last week. Those are the bits."

"Leave the light on. It'll shine out."

A shaft of light from the dusty window beamed out into the night. They began cutting chicken-wire and fitting together boards, on the far side of the hen-run where the mink had wriggled its way in.

"Will—see if there's another piece of board in there, about a foot longer than this one."

"Righto."

Will crossed the moonlit yard towards the stream of yellow light reaching out from the barn. Behind him the sound of Stephen's hammer rang rhythmically over the still-restless murmur of the hens.

And then the whirling took hold of his mind again, and caught his senses into confusion, and the wind seemed to blow in his face. Tap-tap-tap . . . tap-tap-tap . . . the hammering seemed to change, to a hollow metallic sound as of iron striking iron. Staggering, Will leaned against the wall of the barn. The shaft of light was gone, and the moon. The alteration came with no more warning than that: a time-slip so complete that in an instant he could see no trace of Stephen or James, nor any familiar thing or animal or tree.

The night was darker than it had been. There was a creaking sound that he could not identify. He found he was standing against a wall still, but a wall of different texture; his fingers, which had been touching wood, discovered now large blocks of stone, mortared together. The air was still warm as in his own time. From the other side of the wall, he could hear voices. Two men. And both voices were so familiar to Will, out of the other side of his life that his family had never touched or seen, that the small hairs rose on the back of his neck and joy swelled in his chest like pain.

"Badon, then." A deep voice, expressionless.

"It will have to be."

"Do you think you can drive them back?"

"I don't know. Do you?" The second voice was almost as deep, but lightened by a warmth of feeling, like a profound amusement.

"Yes. You will drive them back, my lord. But it will not be forever. These men may be driven back, but the force of nature that they represent has never yet been driven back for long."

The warm voice sighed. "You are right. This island is doomed, unless. . . . I know you are right, my lion. I have known it since I was a boy. Since a day—" He stopped. There was a long pause.

The first man said gently, "Do not think about it."

"Do you know, then? I have never spoken of it to anyone. Well, of course you must know." He laughed softly; the sound held affection rather than amusement. "Were *you* there, Old One? You? I suppose you must have been."

"I was there."

"All the best men of Britain slaughtered. Every one. Three hundred leaders at the one gathering, *three hundred!* Stabbed, strangled, clubbed, at one sign—I even saw him give the sign, do you know that? I, a boy of seven. . . . All dead. My father amongst them. The blood flowed and the grass was red, and the Dark began its rising over Britain—" He choked on the words.

The deep voice said, grim and cold, "It shall not rise for ever."

"No, by heaven it shall not!" He had collected himself again. "And a few days from now Badon shall show that. *Mons Badonicus, mons felix.* So let us hope."

"The gathering is begun, and men come from every corner of your loyal Britain," said the first. "And this night the Circle shall be summoned, the Circle of the Old Ones, to meet this great need."

Will stood straight, as if someone had called his name. He was so deep in this time now that he had no need of calling. There was no thought, even; only awareness. He turned, and saw light glimmering round the doorway in the stone wall;

walked forward to the doorway, jumped suddenly at the sight of two figures armed with sword and spear in front of him, at either side of the door. But neither moved; they stood stiff, at attention, staring ahead.

Will reached out to the heavy, thick-woven curtain that hung over the entrance, and pulled it aside. Bright light blazed into his eyes; he brought up his arm to cover them, blinking.

"Ah, Will," said the deeper voice. "Come in, come in."

Will stepped forward, opening his eyes. He stood there, smiling at the tall robed figure with its fierce proud nose and springing shock of white hair. It was a long time since they had met.

"*Merriman!*" he said. They moved to one another, and embraced.

"How do you, Old One?" the tall man said.

"Well, I thank you."

"Old One to Old One," said the other man softly. "The first and oldest of them, and the last and youngest. And I too greet you, Will Stanton."

Will looked at the clear blue eyes in the weather-brown face; the short grey beard; the hair still brown but streaked with grey. He went down on one knee, and bent his head. "My lord."

The other bent forward in his creaking leather chair and touched Will's shoulder briefly in greeting. "I am glad to see you. Rise now, and join your master. This part of time is for you two alone, and there is much to do."

He stood, pushing a short cloak back over one shoulder, and strode to the door, soft-shod feet noiseless on the patterned mosaic floor. Though he was a head short of Merriman's great height, there was an authority in him that towered over any man. "I will go and hear the new count of men," he said, turning at the door, over the clatter and scrape of spears as the guards presented arms. "A night and a day. Be swift, my lion."

Then he was gone, as if the swirl of the cloak had carried him away.

Will said, "Those guards didn't challenge me."

"They had been told to expect your coming," Merriman said. There was a wry smile on his bleak bony face as he looked down at Will. Then suddenly he put his head back with a quick intake of breath and a sigh. "Eh Will—how is it with you, in the second great rising? For this now, here, is the first, and I tell you it does not go well."

"I don't understand, you know," Will said.

"Do you not, Old One? After all my teaching, and the learning of the Book of Grammarye awhile ago, do you still not understand how time must elude the consciousness of men? Perhaps you are still too close to men yourself. . . . Well." He sat down abruptly on a long couch with curved arms. There was little furniture in the high square room; on its painted plaster walls bright pictures of country summer glowed, sunshine and fields and harvest gold. "Within the time of men, Will," he said, "there are two great risings of the Dark. One is in the time into which you were human-born. One is here and now, fifteen centuries before that, when my lord Arthur must win a victory that can last long enough to detach these invading ravagers from the Dark that drives them on. You and I have a part to play in the defence against each of these two risings. In fact, the same part."

"But—" Will said.

Merriman raised one bristling white eyebrow, looking at him sideways. "If you dare to ask me, *you*, how it is that someone from the future can take part in something that has, in that foolish phrase, already happened. . . ."

"Oh no," Will said. "I shan't. I remember something you said to me once, a long while ago—" He screwed up his face, groping in his memory for the right words. *"For all times co-exist*, you said, *and the future can sometimes affect the past, even though the past is a road that leads to the future."*

A small smile of approval flickered in Merriman's grave face. "And therefore, now, the Circle of the Light must be called, by Will Stanton the Sign-seeker, who once on a time achieved the joining of the Six Signs of the Light into a circle. It must be called, so that from the one and the same calling it may help the men of this world, both in the time of Arthur and in the time from which you come."

"So," Will said, "I must take the Signs from their refuge, through that most complicated spell we laid on them after they had been joined. I only hope I can find the way."

"So do I," said Merriman a trifle grimly. "For if you do not, the High Magic which guards them will take them outside Time, and the only advantage the Light holds in this great matter will be lost forever."

Will swallowed. He said, "I must do it from my own century, though. That was when they were joined and hidden."

"Of course," Merriman said. "And that is why my lord Arthur asked us to be swift. Go, Will, and do what you have to do. A night and a day: that is all the time we have, by the measure of the earth."

He stood and crossed the floor in one swift movement and grasped Will's arms in the old Roman salute. Dark eyes blazed down from the strange craggy face, with its deep lines. "I shall be with you, but powerless. Take care," Merriman said.

"Yes."

Will turned away, to the door, and pulled aside the curtain. Outside in the night there still faintly rang out the metallic hammering, the striking of iron upon iron.

"Wayland Smith works long, this day," said Merriman behind him, softly. "And not on shoes for horses, in this time, for horses are not yet shod. On swords, and axes, and knives."

Will shivered, and without a word went out into the black night. His head whirled, a wind blew into his face—and once more the moon was floating like a great pale orange before him in the sky, and in his arms was a wooden board, and the sound of hammering before him was that of a hammer driving nails into wood.

"Ah," Stephen said, looking up. "That looks perfect. Thanks."

Will came forward and gave him the board.

CHAPTER THREE

THE CALLING

U P I N Will's attic bedroom the air was warm and still, furry with summer heat. He lay on his back, listening to the late-night murmur and chink below as the last waking Stantons—his father and Stephen, he thought, from the rumbling voices—made ready for bed. This had been Stephen's bedroom once, and Will had carefully packed up his belongings to let the rightful owner take residence again for the length of his leave. But Stephen had shaken his head. "Max is away—I'll use his room. I'm a nomad now, Will. It's all yours."

The last door closed, the last glimmer of reflected light went out. Will looked at his watch. Midnight had passed; Midsummer Day was here now, a few minutes old. Half an hour's wait should be enough. He could see no star through the skylight in his slanting roof, but only a moon-washed sky; its muted brightness filtered down into the room.

The house was muffled in sleep when finally he crept down the stairs in his pyjamas, gingerly treading the furthest corners of those steps that he knew would creak. Outside the door of his parents' room he froze suddenly; his father, snoring in a gentle crescendo, half-woke himself, grunted, turned rustling over and was lost again in soft-breathing sleep.

Will smiled into the darkness. It would have been no great matter, for an Old One, to put the household away into a pause of Time, caught out of reality in a sleep that could not be broken. But he did not want that. There were likely to be enough ways, tonight, in which he would have to play with Time.

Softly down the lower staircase into the front hall he went. The picture he had come to find hung on the wall just inside the big front door, beside the hat-rack and umbrella-stand. Will had brought a small flashlight with him, but he found he did not need it; the moonlight silvering the air through the hall windows showed him all the familiar figures the picture held.

He had been fascinated by it since he was very small, so small that he had to clamber up on the umbrella-stand to peer inside the dark carved wood of the picture-frame. It was a Victorian print, done all in murky shades of brown; its great attraction was the enormous complicated clarity of its detail. In flowing script it was entitled *The Romans at Caerleon*, and it showed the construction of some complex building. Everywhere crowds of figures tugged ropes, led oxen straining on sturdy wooden yokes, guided slabs of rock into place. A paved central floor was finished, smooth and elliptical, flanked by columned arches; a wall or staircase seemed to be rising beyond. Roman soldiers, splendidly uniformed, stood overseeing the bands of men unloading and tugging the neatly cut stones into place.

Will looked for one soldier in particular, a centurion in the far right-hand corner of the foreground, leaning against a pillar. He was the only still figure in the whole panorama of busy construction; his face, drawn in clear detail, was grave and rather sad, and he was gazing out of the picture, into the distance. That sad remoteness was the reason why Will, when small, had always found himself more intrigued by this one odd figure than by all the rest of the scurrying workers put together. It was also the reason why Merriman had chosen the man for the concealing of the Signs.

Merriman. Will sat down on the stairs, chin on hands. He must think, think hard and deep. It was simple enough to remember the way in which he and Merriman had managed the hiding of the linked circle of six Signs, the most powerful—and vulnerable—weapons of the Light. Back into the time of this Roman they had gone, and there among the stones whose picture hung before him now, he, Will, had slipped the Signs into a place where they could lie safe and unseen, buried by Time. But to remember that was one thing, to reverse it quite another. . . .

He thought: The only way is to live through that all over again. I have to go again, to go once more through everything we did in hiding the Signs—and then, instead of stopping, I shall have to find a way to take them out again.

He was beginning to be excited now. He thought: Merriman can be there but I shall have to do it. *I shall be with you, but powerless,* he said. So he won't be able to show me the moment when I have to say something, or do something, whatever it is; he may not even know when it comes. Only I can choose it, for the Light. And if I fail, we can go no further forward from here. . . .

Excitement dwindled beneath the appalling merciless weight of responsibility. There was one key only to the spell that would release the Signs, and only he could find it. But where, when, how?

Where, when, how?

Will stood up. The way out of the spell could be found only by going back into it. So, first he must re-enact the casting of it; turn Time so that once more he could live through the hours, more than a year earlier, when with Will at his side Merriman had—

What had Merriman done? It must be an exact echo.

Putting down his flashlight, Will stood before the picture on the wall, remembering. He reached out and put one hand on its frame. Then he stood very still, gazing in total concentration at a group of men in the picture's middle distance: men straining at a rope that was pulling a slab of rock towards some point that could not be seen. He emptied his mind of all thought, his senses of all other sight or sound; he gazed and he gazed.

And very gradually, the sound of creaking rope and rhythmic shouts and the grinding of rock against rock began to grow in his ears, and he smelled dust and sweat and dung—and the figures in the picture began to move. And Will's hand was no longer on the wooden picture-frame, but on the wooden side-support of an ox-cart laden with stone, and he stepped forward into the world of the Romans at Caerleon, a boy of that time, cool in a white linen tunic on a warm summer's day, with square stone cobbles uneven beneath his sandalled feet.

"*Heave*-two-three . . . *heave*-two-three. . . ." The stone inched forward on its rollers. In other rhythms, the same shouts rang through the air from other groups, soldiers and labourers working together, skins olive or dusty pink, hair curly black or lank blonde. Stone crashed and squealed against stone; men and animal grunted with effort. And Merriman said into Will's ear, from behind him, "You must be ready to slip the link, when the moment comes."

Looking down, Will saw the six Signs of the Light, joined by links of gold, clasped about the waist of his tunic like a belt. Bright and dark they lay between the gleaming links, each of the six the same shape, a circle quartered by a cross: dull bronze, dark iron, blackened wood; bright gold, glittering flint, and the last that he would never forget, seeing it sometimes even in dreams—the Sign of water, clear crystal, engraved with delicate symbols and patterns like a circle of snowflakes caught in ice.

"Come," Merriman said.

He swept past Will, tall in a dark blue cloak that fell almost to his feet, and drew level with the pillar beyond the steaming oxen, where a centurion stood watching a team of workmen lace straps and ropes round the topmost slab of granite on the wagon. Will followed, trying to be inconspicuous.

"The work goes well," Merriman said.

The Roman turned his head, and Will saw that it was the same sombre figure whose image he had passed almost every day of his life. Bright dark eyes regarded Merriman from a lean, long-nosed face.

"Ah," the man said. "It is the Druid."

Merriman inclined his head in a kind of mock-formal greeting. "Many things to many men," he said, smiling slightly.

The soldier looked at him reflectively. "A strange land," he said. "Barbarians and magicians, dirt and poetry. A strange land, yours." Then he snapped suddenly taut; part of his attention had been all the while on the ox-cart. "Careful, there! You, Sextus, the rope at that end—"

Men scrambled to balance the descending slab, which had tipped perilously to one side; it came down in safety and the man in command of the team saluted, calling his thanks. The centurion nodded and relaxed, though still watching them. Another wagon rumbled past, laden with long beams of wood.

Merriman looked out at the rising structure before them; their wider view now showed that it was a half-built amphitheatre, stone-walled, with tiers of wood-topped seats rising in a great curving sweep from the central arena. "Rome has many talents," he said. "We have some skill with stone, here, and none can match our great stone circles, with their homage to the Light. But the skill of Roman builders for the daily life of men as well as for worship—your villas and viaducts, your pipes and streets and baths. . . . You are transforming our cities, friend, as you have begun transforming the pattern of our lives."

The soldier shrugged. "The Empire grows, always." He glanced at Will, who hovered at Merriman's side watching the team of men swinging the long stone slowly to one side, down from the wagon.

"Your boy?"

"He learns a little of what I know," Merriman said coolly. "I have had him a year now. We shall see. He has the old blood in him, from the years before your fathers came."

"No fathers of mine," the centurion said. "I am not Empire-born. I came from Rome seven years back, commissioned into the Second. A long time gone. Rome is the Empire, the Empire is Rome, and yet, and yet. . . ." He smiled suddenly at Will: a kind smile, lightening the severe face. "You work hard for your master, boy?"

"I try, sir," Will said. He enjoyed following the formal patterning of the Latin; it came without effort to an Old One, as did any language of the world, but brought somehow a particular pleasure because of the echoes of it in his own native tongue.

"The building interests you."

"Marvellous, it is. The way each piece of stone is cut to fit exactly to the next, or to hold a beam of wood. And the putting them together, so carefully, precisely—they know just what they are doing—"

"It is all planned. Just as anywhere in the Empire. This same amphitheatre has been built in a score of legionary fort towns like this one, from Sparta to Brindisium. Come, I will show you."

He took Will by the shoulder, with a beckoning glance at Merriman, and led him across the sandy central floor of the arena to a half-finished vaulted arch, one of eight entrances through the rising tiers of seats. "When my third team brings up that next slab, it will fit here, so—and lock in place, there—"

A column of stone slabs was beginning to rise at the side of the arch. Will peered at the next as it drew close on its rollers, tugged by four sweating soldiers. A grunting, straining team hoisted it into place in the rising arch. It was much larger than the rest: irregular with a large hollow depression in the top, but with one broad, unusually flat surface for the front side. Will saw the incised letters: COH. X. C. FLAV. JULIAN

"Built by the tenth cohort, the century of Flavius Julianus," Merriman said. "Excellent." And silently, in the Old Ones' manner of speaking into the mind, he said to Will, *"In there. Now."* At the same moment, he stumbled, knocking clumsily against the centurion's elbow; the Roman turned courteously to catch him.

"Is anything wrong?"

Swiftly Will slipped the belt of linked Signs from his waist and dropped it into the hollow irregularity in the slab's top side over which the next slab of stone would be placed; he pushed earth and stones hastily over it to keep the gleaming metals from view.

"I beg your pardon," Merriman was saying. "Foolish—my sandal—"

The soldier turned back; the team came straining up; Will

moved quickly aside and the stone slab groaned and squeaked into place. And the Circle of Signs was shut into a coffin of stone, to lie hidden for as long as this work of the Roman Empire should survive.

The detached part of Will's mind, aware of everything as a spell-brought echo of things he and Merriman had done before, came jolting now into his consciousness. *Now!* it said. *What next?* For this was as far as those first actions had gone. After this point, on the day of the hiding of the Signs, he had very soon found himself back in his own century, flicked forward in Time with the precious circle hidden safe behind him. So the secret that he must now urgently find, the precious key to their recovery, must lie somewhere in these next moments of Roman time. What could it be?

He looked desperately at Merriman. But the dark eyes over the high curved nose held no expression. This was not Merriman's task, but his own; he must do it alone.

All the same there might be a reason why Merriman was there, for this half of the spell as for the other; even unwittingly, he might have some part to play. It was for Will to discover that part, if it were so, and take hold of whatever might be there for him to take.

Where, when, how?

The centurion shouted commands, and his nearest team of workers swung round and marched back for the next stone. Watching them, the Roman shivered suddenly, and drew his cloak tighter round his shoulders.

"Britain-born, all of them," he said wrily to Merriman. "Like you, they find no horror in this climate."

Merriman made a formless, murmuring sound of sympathy, and for no reason that he could imagine Will found the small hairs rising on the back of his neck, as if in a warning from senses that had no other speech. He stood tense, waiting.

"These islands," the Roman said. "Green, I grant you. Well might they be green. Always the clouds, the mist and damp and rain." He sighed. "Ah, my bones ache. . . ."

Merriman said softly, "And not the bones only . . . it must be hard, for one born in the sun."

The centurion stared out over the wooden seats and stone columns, looking at nothing, and shook his head helplessly.

Will said, in a small clear voice that seemed to him to belong to somebody else. "What is it like, your home?"

"Rome? A great city. But my home is outside the city, in the country—a quiet life, but good—" He glanced at Will. "I have a son who must now be as tall as you. When last I saw him I could throw him in the air and catch him in my hands. Now my wife tells me he has learned to ride like a centaur, and swim like a fish. Swimming now, perhaps, in the river near my land. I wanted him to grow up there, as I did. With the sun hot on the skin, and the air shrill with cicadas, and a line of cypress trees dark against the sky . . . the hills silver with olive trees and terraced for the vines, with the grapes filling out, now. . . ."

The homesickness was a throbbing ache like physical pain, and suddenly Will knew that the answer was here in the air, in this moment of simple unprotected longing with a man's deepest, simplest emotions open and unguarded for strangers to hear and see. This was the road that would carry him.

Here, now, this way!

He let his mind fall into the longing, into the other's pain, as if he were diving into a sea; and like water closing over his head the emotion took him in. The world spun about him, stone and grey sky and green fields, whirling and changing and falling down into place not quite the same as before, and the yearning homesick voice was soft in his ears again; but the voice was a different voice.

The voice was a different voice and the language was changed, to a soft accented English with long slanting vowels. And it was evening now, with a moon-washed silver-dark sky above and shadows all around, shapes and shadows indistinguishable one from the next.

But in the new voice, the ache of longing was exactly the same.

". . . it's all sun and sand and sea, that part of Florida. My part. Flowers everywhere. Oleander and hibiscus, and poinsettia in big wild red bushes, not shut up in skinny little

Christmas pots. And down on the beach the wind blows in the coconut palms and the leaves make a little rattling noise, like a shower of rain. I used to swing on those leaves when I was your age, like swinging on a rope. If I were down there now I'd be out fishing with my dad—he's got a forty foot Bertram, a beauty. Called *Betsy Girl* after Mom. Out through the channel in the mangroves, you go—dark green, like forests in the water. The water's green too till you get way out in the Gulf, and then it's a deep, deep blue. Beautiful. And you swing the outriggers up with the lines over, and ballyho on, and you'll catch bonita or dolphin, or if you're lucky, pompano. The tourists all want sailfish or kingfish. Day before I left home, I got a sixty pound king. Ginny, that's my girl, she took a picture of it."

Will could see him outlined against the sky, bright and dark by turns now as gathering clouds crossed the moon: a lean young man with long hair caught back in a stubby ponytail. The soft, remembering voice went on.

"Haven't seen Ginny for eight months. Man, that's a long time. I've got our first day all planned out for when I get home. Keep thinking about it. Long lazy day in the sun, swimming, lying on the beach, surfing maybe. And beer and hamburgers at Pete's. His burgers are just out of this world, big and juicy on a homemade bun, with this special sour pickle relish. Ginny loves them. . . . She's so pretty. Long blonde hair. Great figure. She writes me every week. Didn't come over here because her old man's got a weak heart and she felt— ah, she's just a great girl." He paused, and slowly shook his head. "Hey, I'm sorry. You really got me going. I guess I didn't know how much I'd been missing . . . people. It's been fun here on the dig, but I'll sure be glad to get home."

Behind him, a rounded grassy slope rose as skyline; yet although this seemed totally strange, Will had the conviction that somehow he was in the same place as before. Perhaps it was only that linking emotion, the ache in the American's voice, and yet. . . .

Merriman's voice said in the dim night, cheerful, breaking the mood, "He seems to have pressed a button, asking you about home. Have you been here a long time?"

"It'll be a year, by the time I'm through. Not so long really, I guess." The young man became self-consciously brisk. "Well, hey, let's show you. I wish this wasn't such a quick visit, professor—there's so much you could see better in the morning."

"Ah well," Merriman said vaguely. "I have appointments. . . . Over here, you said?"

"Just a minute, I'll get a lamp. Better than a flashlight—" The American vanished into a boxlike structure that seemed to be a small wooden shed; a light flared in a window, and then he was back again with a hissing hurricane lamp un-expectedly held aloft, casting a bright pool around them in which Will could see grass at their feet, and Wellington boots on Merriman's trousered legs. Beyond, poles and ropes and small drooping marker-flags jutted from an excavation made into the grassy mound that he had thought a natural slope, as if a giant slice had been cut from an earthen cake. At the inside of the excavation, where it cut furthest into the mound, he could see stones. He could see a stone-paved floor like a stretch of square cobbles; the scattered stones of a fallen arch; rising tiers of stones where once wooden benches had stood. . . .

The whirl of others' emotions cleared from Will's mind, and instead wonder and relief and delight flooded into him like a spring tide, and he knew, looking at the stone, that the secret releasing the Signs from their enchantment had been caught at the proper moment indeed.

"You know the background, of course, Professor Lyon," the young American said. "Always the mound was known as King Arthur's Round Table, with absolutely no justification of course. And no one could get permission to dig. Or funds for that matter, until this Ford Foundation deal. And now that we finally get inside it, what do we find inside King Arthur's so-called Round Table but a Roman amphitheatre."

"You'll find a Mithraeum, too, before you're done, I shouldn't wonder," Merriman said, in a strange brisk profes-sional voice Will had not heard before. "Caerleon was a major fort, after all—built for keeping down the barbaric British in their mists and fog."

The American laughed. "I don't really mind the mists and fog. It's the rain—and all that mud afterwards. They sure knew how to work with stone, those old Empire-builders. Look, here's the inscribed slab I was telling you about—Centurion Flavius Julianus and his boys."

The lamp hissed, the shadows danced; he led them to a shoulder-high column of great slabs of rock. Will saw the highest, the largest, with its inscribed letters battered now by age. It was newly excavated; an inch of earth still lay over it, where the stone above had slipped to one side.

Merriman took a small flashlight from his pocket and shone it, quite unnecessarily Will thought, on the inscribed block of stone. "Very neat," he said fussily, "very neat. Here Will, my boy, have a look." He handed Will the light.

"We think there were eight entrances," the American said, "all vaulted, with this kind of stonework. This must have been one of the two main ones—we only started clearing it this afternoon."

"Excellent," Merriman said. "Now just show me that other inscription you mentioned, would you?" They moved away to one side of the cave-like dig, taking the pool of yellow lamplight with them. Will stood still. He snapped on the light for a second, to be sure of his step, then turned it off. Putting his hand forward in the darkness of what he knew now was his own time, Midsummer Day a matter of seconds after he had first left it, he reached scrabbling into the earth that had lain since the decay of Rome's Empire, some sixteen centuries before, in the hollow of the big rock of the broken arch. And his fingers met a circle of metal quartered by a cross, and putting down the flashlight to scrabble with both hands in the earth, he drew out the linked circle of Signs.

Very carefully he shook off the dirt, with the circles and their gold links spread wide to keep the metal from rattling. He glanced up. Merriman and the young archaeologist were no more than a glimmer of light, yards away across the excavation. Excitement tight in his throat, Will clipped the belt-like chain of Signs round his waist, tugging his sweater down to cover them. He went forward to the lamplight.

"Ah, well," Merriman said blandly. "Time we were going, I'm afraid."

"It's very exciting," Will said, bright and enthusiastic.

"I'm so glad you stopped by." The young American led them to a car parked behind a fence. "It's been a privilege to meet you, Dr. Lyon. I only wish the others had been here— Sir Mortimer will be real sorry—"

In a flurry of farewells he handed them into the car, pumping Merriman's arm in a kind of hearty reverence. Will said, "You made Florida sound lovely. I hope you see it soon."

But archaeology had driven his earlier emotion quite out of the young American's mind. Nodding, smiling vaguely, he disappeared.

Merriman drove slowly down the road. He said, his voice changed utterly, "You have them?"

"I have them safe," Will said, and a strong hand clenched his shoulder briefly, hard, and was gone. They were no longer master and boy, nor ever would be again; they were Old Ones only, caught out of Time in a task both were long-destined to fulfill.

"It must be tonight, and quickly," Will said. "Here, do you think? Now?"

"I think so. The times are linked, by our presence and by the place. Above all by your good work. I think so." Merriman stopped, turned the car, and drove back towards the excavation. They got out and stood in silence for a moment.

Then they went together into the darkness, skirting the cleared arch and walls, climbing to the top of the grassy mound. There they stood, under a sky dark now with scudding clouds that hid the moon; and Will took from his waist the linked belt of crossed circles that was the symbol of the Circle of the Light, and held it up in both hands. And time and space merged as the twentieth and the fourth centuries became for a Midsummer's instant two halves of a single breath, and in a clear soft voice Will said into the night, "Old Ones! Old Ones! It is time. Now and for always, for the sec-

41

ond time and the last, let the Circle be joined. Old Ones, it is time! For the Dark, the Dark is rising!"

His voice ran strong; he held the Signs high, and a glimmer of starlight flashed on the circle of crystal like white fire. And all at once they were no longer alone on the silent grassy mound. From all the world over, from every point of time, the shadowy forms of men and women from every kind and generation crowded there in the night. A great glimmering throng was gathered, the Old Ones of the earth come together for the first time since, six seasons earlier, the Signs had in their presence been ceremonially joined. The darkness rustled; there was a formless murmuring in the place, a communication without speech.

Merriman and Will stood there together on the hill in the night full of beings, and waited for the one last Old One whose presence would weld this great gathering into an ultimate instrument of power, a force to vanquish the Dark.

They waited, and the night grew brighter with starlight; but she did not come.

The glimmering forms murmured and rippled as though the land blurred, and Will's consciousness, at one with the minds of all his fellows there, was filled with unease.

Merriman said, low and husky, "I was afraid of this."

"The Lady," Will said helplessly. "Where is the Lady?"

"The Lady!" Indistinct as the wind, a long whisper ran through the darkness. *"Where is the Lady?"*

Will said softly to Merriman, "She came at the turn of the year, the year before last, for the Joining. Why does she not come now?"

Merriman said. "I think she has not the strength. Her power is worn by resisting the Dark—you and I know well how she has spent herself, in the past. And though she managed the effort for the joining of the Signs, you remember that then she had no strength even to take her leave."

"Yes," Will said, remembering a small, fragile old figure, delicate as a wren, standing beside him overlooking a great throng of Old Ones as Merriman stood now. "She simply . . . faded. And then she was gone."

"And it seems that she is gone still. Out of reach. Gone until a helping magic may come from the sum of the centuries of this spell-ridden island, to bring her to our need. For the first time, for the only time, the help of mere creatures is needed for the Lady."

Merriman drew himself up, a tall shadowy hooded figure in the night, dark as a pillar against the sky. He spoke without effort or great force, yet his voice filled the night and seemed to echo to and fro over the unseen heads of that enormous throng.

"Who knows?" he said. "Who can tell? Oh all you Circle of the Old Ones, who can tell?"

And one voice came out of the night, a deep beautiful Welsh voice, rich and smooth as velvet, speaking with a rhythm that gave it the lilt of singing.

"*Y maent yr mynyddoedd yn canu,*" the voice said, "*ac y mae'r arglwyddes yn dod.* Which means, being translated, The mountains are singing, and the Lady comes."

There was a great stir among the aery crowd, and before he could help himself Will let out a cry of joyful recognition at the words. "The verse! Of course! The old verse from the sea." He sobered suddenly. "But what does it mean? We all know that line, Merriman—but what does it mean?"

The question echoed in many voices, whispering and susurrating like the sea when a small breeze rises. The deep Welsh voice said, reflectively, "When the mountains are singing, the Lady will come. And remember one thing. It is not in the Old Speech, which we all use, that those words have come down to us, but in a younger language—that is nevertheless one of the most ancient used by men."

Merriman said softly, "Thank you, Dafydd my friend."

"Welsh," Will said. "Wales." He stared into blank dark space, where clouds once more were drifting over the moon. He said hesitantly, his mind feeling for the right word, the right idea, "I am to go to Wales. To that part where I have been once before. And there I must find the moment, the right way. . . . Somewhere in the mountains. Somehow. And the Lady will come."

"And we shall be complete and singly-bound," Merriman said. "And the end of all this questing will begin."

"*Pob hwyl,* Will Stanton," said the rich Welsh voice gently in the darkness. "*Pob hwyl.* Good luck. . . ." And it faded and died into the soft whine of the wind, and all the gathering around them faded too, vanishing away to leave them standing, two lone figures, there in the darkening night on the grass-smooth mound, in the Midsummer Day of the time into which Will had been born.

Will said, "But for that first time, to which I was called, the rising of the Dark in the time of Arthur. . . . We are allowed only a night and a day to bring help there. And I cannot keep to that limit now. So what of the great king, and the battle that is to come at Badon? What will—" He stopped himself, cutting off words that belonged not to Old Ones but to men.

Merriman said, completing it, "What will happen there? What will happen, what has happened, what is happening? A battle, won for a little while. A respite gained, but not for long. You can see, Will. Things are as they are, and will be. In Arthur's time, we have the Circle to help us, for they have been gathered, and much can therefore be accomplished. But without words from the Lady, the last height of power cannot be reached, and so the peace of Arthur that we shall gain for this island at Badon will be lost, before long, and for a time the world will seem to vanish beneath the shadow of the Dark. And emerge, and vanish again, and again emerge, as it has done through all the length of what men call their history."

Will said, "Until the Lady comes."

"Until the Lady comes," Merriman said. "And she will help you to the finding of the sword of the Pendragon, the crystal sword by which the final magic of the Light shall be achieved, and the Dark put at last to flight. And there will be five to help you, for from the beginning it was known that six altogether, and six only, must accomplish this long matter. Six creatures more and less of the earth, aided by the six Signs."

Will said, quoting, *"When the Dark comes rising, six shall turn it back."*

"Aye," Merriman said. Suddenly he sounded very weary. "Six, for a hard turning."

On impulse Will quoted again, a whole verse this time, from the old prophetic rhyme that had come gradually to light —a world ago, it seemed to him—with the growing of his own power as an Old One.

> *"When the Dark comes rising, six shall turn it back,*
> *Three from the Circle, three from the track;*
> *Wood, bronze, iron; water, fire, stone;*
> *Five shall return, and one go alone."*

He spoke the last line more slowly, as if he were hearing it for the first time. "Merriman? That last part, what does it mean? It has never put anything into my mind but a question. Five shall return, and one go alone . . . Who?"

Merriman stood there in the quiet night, his face obscured by shadow; his voice was quiet too, and without expression. "Nothing is certain, Old One, even in the prophecies. They can mean one thing, or they can mean another. For after all, men have minds of their own, and can determine their actions, for good or ill, for going outward, or turning in. . . . I cannot tell who the one may be. None shall know, until the last. Until the . . . one . . . goes . . . alone. . . ." He gathered himself, and stood straighter, as if pulling them both back out of a dream. "There is a long road to tread before that will come, and a hard one, if we are to triumph at the end of it. I go back now to my lord Arthur, with the Signs, and the power of the Circle which only they can call."

He held out his hand, barely visible in the star-washed darkness, and Will gave him the linked belt of crossed circles, gold and crystal and stone glittering between dark wood, bronze, iron.

"Go well, Merriman," he said quietly.

"Go well, Will Stanton," Merriman said, his voice tight with strain. "Into your own place, at this Midsummer hour,

where affairs will take you in the direction you must go. And
we will strive at our separate tasks across the centuries,
through the waves of time, touching and parting, parting and
touching in the pool that whirls forever. And I shall be with
you before long."

He raised an arm, and he was gone, and the stars spun
and the night whirled about, and Will was standing moonlit
in the hall of his home, his hand on the frame of a sepia Victorian print that showed the Romans building an amphitheatre at Caerleon.

CHAPTER FOUR

MIDSUMMER DAY

AT A TRIUMPHANT TROT Will mowed the last patch of grass, and collapsed, panting, draped over the lawn-mower handle. Sweat was trickling down the side of his nose, and his bare chest was damp, speckled with tiny cut stems of grass.

"Ouf! It's even hotter than yesterday!"

"Sundays," James said, "are always hotter than Saturdays. Especially if you live in a village with a small stuffy church. James Stanton's Law, you can call that."

"Go on," said Stephen, passing with his hands full of twine and clippers. "It wasn't that bad. And for two horrible little boys you still sound pretty angelic in the choir." He dodged neatly as Will flung a fistful of grass cuttings.

"I shan't be there much longer," James said, with some pride. "I'm breaking. Did you hear me croak in the canticle?"

"You'll be back," Will said. "Tenor. Bet you."

"I suppose so. That's what Paul says too."

"He's practising. Listen!"

Distant as a fading dream, from inside the house the soft clear tone of a flute rippled up and down in scales and arpeggios; it seemed as much a part of the hot still afternoon as the bees humming in the lupins and the sweet smell of the new-cut grass. Then the scales gave way to a long lovely flow of melody, repeated again and again. Halfway across the lawn Stephen stood caught into stillness, listening.

"My God, he's good, isn't he? What is that?"

"Mozart, First Flute Concerto," Will said. "He's playing it with the N.Y.O. this autumn."

"N.Y.O.?"

"National Youth Orchestra. You remember. He was in it for years, even before he went to the Academy."

"I suppose I do. I've been away so long. . . ."

"It's a big honour, that concert," James said. "At the Festival Hall, no less. Didn't Paul tell you?"

"You know Paul. Old Modesty. That's a lovely-sounding flute he's got now, too. Even I can tell.

"Miss Greythorne gave it to him, two Christmases ago," said Will. "From the Manor. There's a collection that her father made, she showed us."

"Miss Greythorne. . . . Good Lord, that takes me back. Sharp wits, sharp tongue—I bet she hasn't changed a bit."

Will smiled. "She never will."

"She caught me up her almond tree once when I was a kid," Stephen said, grinning reminiscently. "I came climbing down and there she was out of nowhere, in her wheelchair. Even though she hated anyone seeing that wheelchair. 'Only monkeys eat my nuts, young man,' she said—I can still hear her—'and you'll not even make a powder monkey, at your age.' "

"Powder monkey?" James said.

"Boys in the Navy in Nelson's day—they used to fetch the powder for the guns."

"You mean Miss Greythorne knew you were going into the Navy?"

"Of course not, I didn't know myself then." Stephen looked a little taken aback. "Funny coincidence though. Never occurred to me before—I haven't given her a thought for years."

But James's mind had already taken off on a tangent, as it frequently did. "Will, whatever became of that little hunting horn she gave you, the year she gave Paul the flute? Did you lose it? You never even gave it one good blow."

"I still have it," Will said quietly.

"Well, get it out. We could have fun with it."

"One day." Will swung the lawn-mower round, shoving its handle at James's unready hands. "Here—your turn. I've done the front, now you do the back."

"That's the rule," said their father, passing with a weed-loaded wheelbarrow. "Fair's fair. Share the burden."

"My burden's bigger than his," James said dolefully.

"Nonsense!" said Mr. Stanton.

"Well it is, actually," Will said. "We measured, once. The back lawn's five feet wider than the front, and ten feet longer."

"Got more trees in it," said Mr. Stanton, unclipping the catch-box of grass cuttings from the front of the mower, and emptying it into his barrow.

"That makes more work, not less." James drooped, more dolefully still. "Going round them. Trimming afterwards."

"Go away," said his father. "Before I burst into tears."

Will took the box and clipped it back on the mower. "Good-bye, James," he said cheerfully.

"You haven't finished yet, either, matey," Mr. Stanton said. "Stephen needs some help tying up the roses."

A muffled curse came from the front garden wall; Stephen, embraced by the sprawling branches of a climbing rose, was sucking his thumb.

"I believe you may be right," Will said.

Grinning, his father picked up the wheelbarrow and prodded James and the lawn-mower up the driveway; Will was starting over the lawn when his elder sister Barbara came out of the front door.

"Tea's nearly ready," she said.

"Good."

"Outside, we're having it."

"Good, better, best. Come and help Steve fight a rose bush."

Rambler roses, spilling great swathes and bunches of red blossom, grew along and over the old stone wall that bordered the road. Gingerly they untangled the most wildly sprawling arms, drove stakes into the gravelly earth, and tied the branches to keep the billowing sprays of roses off the ground.

"Ouch!" said Barbara for the fifth time, as a rebellious rose-branch scored a thin red line across her bare back.

"Your own fault," said Will unfeelingly. "You should have more clothes on."

"It's a sunsuit. For the sunshine, duckie."

"Nekkidness," said her younger brother solemnly, "be a shameful condition for a yooman bein'. Tain't roight. 'Tes a disgrace to the neighbour'ood, so 'tes."

Barabara looked at him. "There you stand, wearing even *less—*" she began indignantly; then stopped.

"Slow," said Stephen. "Very slow."

"Oh, you," Barbara said.

A car passed on the road; slowed suddenly; stopped; then began backing gradually until it was level with them. The driver switched off his engine, hauled himself across the seat and stuck a heavy-jowled red face out of the window.

"Might the biggest of you be Stephen Stanton?" he said with clumsy joviality.

"That's right," said Stephen from the top of the wall. He gave one last blow to a stake. "What can I do for you?"

"Name's Moore," the man said. "You had a little run-in with one of my boys the other day, I gather."

"Richie," said Will.

"Ah," said Stephen. He jumped down from the wall to stand next to the car. "How do you do, Mr. Moore. I dropped your son into some water, I believe."

"Green water," said the man. "Ruined his shirt."

"I should be happy to buy him a new one," Stephen said easily. "What size is he?"

"Don't talk rubbish," the man said, expressionless. "I just wanted to get the rights and wrongs of it, that's all. Wondered why a young man like you should be playing those sort of games with kids."

Stephen said, "It wasn't a game, Mr. Moore. I simply felt very strongly that your son deserved to be dropped into the water."

Mr. Moore ran one hand over his large glistening forehead. "Maybe. Maybe. He's a wild kid, that one. They kick him around, he kicks back. What did he do to you?"

"Didn't he tell you?" Will said.

Mr. Moore looked across the low wall at Will as though he were something small and irrelevant, like a beetle. "What Richie told me, it wasn't something that gets people dropped in streams. So like as not it wasn't true. That's what I want to get straight."

"He was tormenting a younger boy," Stephen said. "There's not much point in going into detail."

"Having a bit of fun, he said."

"Not much fun for the other one."

"Richie said he didn't lay a finger on him," Mr. Moore said.

"He just threw his music-case full of music into the stream, that's all," Will said shortly.

"We—ell," Mr. Moore said. He paused, tapping the edge of the car window absently. "It was that Indian kid from the Common, I gather."

The three Stantons stood looking at him in silence. He stared back, blankly. At length Barbara said, in a small polite voice, "Does that make a difference?"

Before the man could answer, Mr. Stanton said amiably from behind them, "Good afternoon."

"Afternoon," said Mr. Moore, turning his head, with a tinge of relief in his tone. "I'm Jim Moore. We were just—"

"Yes, I heard some of it," Mr. Stanton said. He propped himself against the edge of the wheelbarrow he had just set down, and took out his pipe and matches. "I must say I thought Steve might have over-reached himself a bit that day. Still—"

"The thing is, you can't always believe these people, you see," said the man in the car, smiling, confident of agreement.

There was a silence. Mr. Stanton lit his pipe. He said, puffing, blowing out the match, "I don't quite follow, I'm afraid."

Stephen said coldly, "It wasn't a case of believing anyone, just of what I happened to see for myself."

Mr. Moore was looking at Mr. Stanton with a kind of anxious adult *bonhomie*. "Made a lot of fuss about nothing, that kid, I dare say. You know how they are, always on about something."

"True, true," said Roger Stanton, his round face placid. "Mine usually are."

"Oh no, no," said Mr. Moore heartily, "I'm sure your bunch are very nice. I meant coloureds, not kids."

He went on, ploughing unawares through the silence that came again, "I see a lot of them at work. I'm in personnel, you know—Thames Manufacturing. Not much I don't know about Indians and Pakkies, after all these years. Of course I've got nothing against them personally. Very intelligent, well-educated, some of them. Got myself an op from an Indian doctor at the Memorial Hospital last year—clever little chap, he was."

Barbara said, in the same small polite voice, "I expect even some of your best friends are Indians and Pakistanis."

Her father gave her a sharp warning glance, but the words went flickering quite over Mr. Moore's stubbly head. He chuckled at Barbara, very much the jovial appreciative male indulging a pretty seventeen-year-old. "Well no, I wouldn't go that far! I'll be honest with you, I don't think they should be here, them or the West Indians. Got no right, have they? Taking jobs that should go to Englishmen, with the country in the state it is. . . ."

Stephen said quietly, "We do have unions, Mr. Moore, and they aren't exactly helpless. Most of those famous jobs are the ones Englishmen don't want to do—or that the immigrants do better."

The man looked at Stephen with resentment and dislike, his thick jaw hardening. "One of those, are you? A bleeding-heart. Don't try and teach me, young man. I've seen too much of the real thing. One Pakkie family rents a two-bedroom house and the next thing you know, they've got sixteen of their friends and relations living there. Like rabbits. And half of them having babies free on the National Health Service, at the British taxpayer's expense."

"Remember your Indian doctor?" Stephen said, still softly. "If it weren't for the immigrant doctors and nurses, the National Health Service would fall apart tomorrow."

Mr. Moore made a contemptuous noise. "Just don't try and tell me about coloured people," he said. "I *know*."

Stephen leaned back against the wall, twisting a piece of raffia between his fingers. "Do you know Calcutta, Mr. Moore?" he said. "Have you ever had beggars grabbing at your feet, calling out to you, children half the size of Will here with an arm missing, or an eye, and ribs like xylophones and their legs stinking with sores? If I lived in a place with that kind of despair round me, I think I just might decide to bring up my kids in a country where they'd have a better chance. Specially a country that had exploited my own for about two hundred years. Wouldn't you? Or Jamaica, now. Do you know how many children get to a secondary school there? D'you know the unemployment rate? D'you know what the slums are like in Kingston? *Do you know—*"

"Stephen," said his father gently.

Stephen stopped. The raffia string in his hands snapped.

"So what about it? All that stuff?" The man's face had darkened. He leaned belligerently out of the window; his breath came more quickly. "Let them solve their own problems, not come whining over here! What's all that have to do with us? They don't belong here, none of 'em; they should all be thrown out. And if you think they're so bloody marvellous you'd better go and live in their lousy countries with them!" He caught Mr. Stanton's calm eye suddenly and tried visibly to control himself, jerking his head back from the window and sliding across into the driver's seat.

Mr. Stanton came close to the wall, where the car stood, and took his pipe from his mouth. "If your son shares your views, Mr. Moore," he said clearly, "as I am glad to find my son shares mine, then the stream episode isn't hard to explain, is it? We only have to decide what reparation you'd like." The pipe went back between his teeth, abruptly.

"Reparation hell!" The man started his engine with a deliberate roar. He leaned over the seat, shouting above the noise. "You just see what happens to anyone laying a finger on my boy again, for the sake of some snivelling little wog, that's all. Just see!"

He lurched back at the wheel and drove off, gears snarling. They stood looking after the car.

Stephen opened his mouth.

"Don't say it," said his father, "don't say it! You know how many there are. You can't convince them and you can't kill 'em. You can only do your best in the opposite direction—which you did." He looked around, embracing Will and Barbara in a rueful smile. "Come on. Let's go and have tea."

Will came last, trailing despondently. From the moment when he had heard the man in the car begin to shout, and seen the look in his eyes, he had been no Stanton at all but wholly an Old One, dreadfully and suddenly aware of danger. The mindless ferocity of this man, and all those like him, their real loathing born of nothing more solid than insecurity and fear . . . it was a channel. Will knew that he had been gazing into the channel down which the powers of the Dark, if they gained their freedom, could ride in an instant to complete control of the earth. He was filled with a terrible anxiety, a sense of urgency for the Light, and knew that it would remain with him, silently shouting at him, far more vividly than the fading memory of a single bigot like Mr. Moore.

"Come on, Tarzan," said Paul, thumping his bare shoulder as he came past out of the house. So Will came back, slowly, into the other part of his mind.

They all gathered for tea as though the disturbing Mr. Moore had never been. By one of those unspoken censorships that come sometimes in close families, those who had seen him made no mention of him to those who had not. Tea was laid out on the orange wicker table, glass-topped, that stood outdoors with its matching chairs in high summer. Will's spirits began to rise. For an Old One with the tastes and appetite of a small boy, it was hard to despair for long over the eternal fallibility of mankind when confronted with home-made bread, farm butter, sardine-and-tomato paste, raspberry jam, scones, and Mrs. Stanton's delicious, delicate, unmatchable sponge-cake.

He sat on the grass. His senses were crammed with summer: the persistent zooming of a wasp lured by the jam; the grass-smell of James's partly cut lawn mingling with the scent of a nearby buddleia bush; the dappled light all around him

54

as sunshine filtered through the apple tree overhead, lush in full green leaf now, with small green apples beginning to swell. Many of the apples were fallen already, victims of over-population, never to grow. Will picked up one of the little thick-stemmed oval objects and gazed at it pensively.

"Put it down," Barbara said. "This'll taste better." She was holding out a plate with two scones spread thickly with butter and jam.

"Hey," said Will. "Thanks." It was a small warm kindliness; in a family as big as the Stantons', self-service was the general rule. Barbara smiled at him briefly, and Will could sense her formless maternal concern that her youngest brother had been upset by the violence of the man in the car. His spirits lifted. The Old One within him thought: *The other side. Don't forget. There's always the other side of people too.*

"Three and a half more weeks of school," James said, in a tone that was half delight, half grumble. He looked up at the sky. "I hope the holiday's all like this."

"The long-range forecast says it will begin pouring with rain the day you break up," said Paul seriously, folding a piece of bread-and-butter. He went on, through a mouthful, "It's due to go on for three weeks without stopping. Except once, for August week-end."

"Oh no!" said James, in unguarded horror.

Paul looked at him owlishly over his horn-rimmed glasses. "There may very well be hail. And on the last day of July they're expecting a blizzard."

James's face relaxed into a grin, as relief twined with shame-faced rage. "Paul, you swine. I'll—"

"Don't kill him," Stephen said. "Too fatiguing. Bad for digestions. Tell me what you're going to do for the holidays, instead."

"Scout camp, some of the time," James said happily. "Two weeks in Devon."

"Very nice too."

"I'm doing summer courses at the Academy—and playing in a jazz club at night," Paul said with a crooked grin.

"Good Lord!"

"Ah, the worm turns. Not exactly your kind of jazz, though."

"Better nor nowt. What are you going to do, Will?"

"Loaf about, like me," said Barbara comfortably, from an armchair.

"Well as a matter of fact," Mrs. Stanton said, "Will has an invitation he hasn't heard about yet. Quite a surprise." She leaned forward with the teapot and began filling cups. "Your Aunt Jen telephoned this afternoon from London—she and David are up for a day or two, with some group from Wales. And she wanted to know, Will, if you'd like to spend part of the holidays at the farm—as soon as school ends, if you like."

Will said slowly, "That's good."

"Wow!" said James. "Don't tell Mary, she'll be livid—she thought she was going to get invited back to Wales this year."

"Jen said something about Will getting along very well last year with a rather lonely boy who lived there," Mrs. Stanton said.

"Yes," Will said. "Yes, I did. His name was Bran."

"You'll have to make sure it's a working holiday, you know," said his father. "Make yourself useful to your uncle. I know that part of Wales is almost all sheep, but it's a busy time of the year on any farm."

"Oh yes," Will said. He picked up another of the small immature apples and twirled it round and round, fast, by its stem. "Yes. There'll be a lot of work to do."

PART TWO
THE SINGING MOUNTAINS

CHAPTER FIVE

FIVE

"HAVE WE BEEN HERE before?" Barney said. "I keep feeling—"

"No," Simon said.

"Not even when you were little, and I was a baby? You might have forgotten."

"Forgotten this?"

Simon swung one arm rather theatrically to embrace the panorama that lay spread around them, where they sat on the wiry grass halfway up the mountain, among spiny bushes of brilliant yellow gorse. Over all the right-hand half of their view was the blue sea of Cardigan Bay, with its long beaches stretching far into the haze of distance. Directly below them lay the green undulations of Aberdyfi golf course, behind its uneven dunes. To the left, the beaches ran into the broad estuary of the River Dyfi, full and blue now with water at high tide. And beyond, over the flat stretch of marsh on the other side of the river-mouth, the mountain mass of Mid-Wales rolled along the skyline, purple and brown and dull green, its colours shifting and patching constantly as clouds sailed over the summer sky past the sun.

"No," Jane said. "We've never been to Wales before, Barney. But Dad's grandmother was born here. Right in Aberdyfi. Perhaps memories can float about in your blood or something."

"In your blood!" Simon said scornfully. He had recently announced that instead of going to sea, he proposed to become a doctor, like their father, and the side-effects of this weighty decision were beginning to try Jane and Barney's patience.

Jane sighed. "I didn't mean it like that." She groped in her shirt pocket. "Here. Halfway snack time. Have some chocolate before it melts."

"Good!" said Barney promptly.

"And don't tell me it's bad for our teeth, Simon, because I know it is."

"Course it is," said her elder brother with a disarming grin. "Utter disaster. Where's mine?"

They sat munching fruit-and-nut chocolate for a contented space, gazing out over the estuary.

"I just know I've been here before," Barney said.

"Don't keep on," Jane said. "You've seen pictures."

"I mean it."

"If you've been here before," Simon said, long-suffering, "you can tell us what we'll see when we get to the top of the ridge."

Barney turned, flipping his blonde forelock out of his eyes, and stared up the mountain, over the bracken and the green slope. He said nothing.

"Another ridge," Jane said cheerfully. "And from that one you'll see another."

"What'll we see, Barney?" Simon persisted. "Cader Idris? Snowdon? Ireland?"

Barney looked at him for a long blank moment, his eyes empty. He said at last, "Someone."

"Someone? Who?"

"I don't know." He jumped up suddenly. "If we sit here all day we'll never find out, will we? Race you!"

He leapt up off the slope, and in an instant Simon was bounding confidently after him. Jane watched them, grinning. In the last year or so, though her younger brother had remained fairly neat and small, Simon seemed to have sprouted legs far too long for his body, like a giraffe. There were very few family races now that he failed to win.

Both boys had disappeared above her. The sun was hot on the back of her neck, as she climbed slowly after them. She stumbled on an outcrop of rock, and paused. Somewhere far away on the mountain a tractor's engine purred; a pipit shrilled overhead. The rocky outcrops led to the top of the ridge here in an erratic progression, through bracken and gorse and billowing piles of heather; hare-bells starred the low sheep-cropped grass, and little creeping white flowers she did not recognise. Far, far below, the road wound like a thread past the dune-fringed golf course, and the first grey roofs of Aberdyfi village. Jane shivered suddenly, with a sense of being very much alone.

"Simon!" she called. "Barney!"

There was no answer. The birds sang. The sun beat down out of a lightly-hazed blue sky; nothing moved anywhere. Then very faintly Jane heard a strange long musical note. High and clear, it was like the call of a hunting horn, and yet not so harsh or demanding. It came again, closer. Jane found that she smiled as she listened; it was a lovely beckoning sound, and suddenly she was filled with an urgent desire to find out where it came from, what instrument could play so beautiful a note. She went on more swiftly up the hillside, until all at once she was over a last rocky edge and could see before her the first few yards of the ridge of the hill. The long sweet note came again, and on the highest grey granite outcropping that met the sky, she saw a boy, lowering from his lips the small curved horn with which he had just blown a call over the mountains, out into nowhere. His face was turned away from Jane, and she could see little except that he had longish straight hair. Then as he moved one hand in an automatic swift gesture to push back the hair from his forehead, she knew suddenly and positively that she had seen that gesture before, and knew who this boy was.

She went forward up the last slope to the rock, and he saw her and stood waiting.

Jane said, "Will Stanton!"

"Hello, Jane Drew," he said.

"*Oh!*" Jane said happily. Then she paused, surveying him. "I can't think why I'm not more surprised," she said. "The

61

last time I saw you was when we left you on Platform Four at Paddington Station. A year ago. More. What are you doing on the top of a mountain in Wales, for goodness' sake?"

"Calling," Will said.

Jane looked at him for a long moment full of remembering, thinking back to a dark adventure in a beleaguered Cornish village, where her Great-Uncle Merriman had brought her and Simon and Barney together with an unremarkable round-faced, straight-haired Buckinghamshire boy—who had seemed to her in the end as alarming and yet as reassuring as Merriman himself.

"Different, I said you were then," she said.

Will said gently, "You three are not altogether ordinary, as you very well know."

"Sometimes," said Jane. She grinned at him suddenly, reaching back to hitch up the ribbon on her pony-tail. "Mostly we are. Well. I said I hoped we should see you again someday. Didn't I?"

Will grinned back, and Jane remembered the way his smile had always transformed his rather solemn face. "And I said I was pretty sure you would." He came a few paces down the rock, then paused and raised the horn to his lips again. Tilting it to the sky, he blew a string of short staccato notes and then one long one. The sound curved out into the summer air, then down, like an arrow dropping.

"That'll bring them," he said. "They used to call it the *avaunt*."

The note of the horn was still echoing round Jane's head. "It's a lovely, lovely sound, not a bit like the ones they use for fox-hunts. Not that I've ever heard those except on television. That one—it's just—it's *music*—" She broke off, flapping one hand wordlessly.

Will held up the small curved horn, looking at it with his head on one side. Though it seemed old and battered, it gleamed like gold in the sunlight. "Ah," he said softly. "Two occasions there will be, for its using. That much I know. The second is hidden to me. But the first time is now, for the gathering of the Six."

"The Six?" Jane said blankly.

"We are two," Will said. She stared at him.

"Jane? Jane!" It was Simon's voice, loud and peremptory, from over the ridge. She turned her head.

"Jane—? Oh there you are!" Barney clambered over the rock a few yards away, turning over his shoulder to call, "Over here!"

Will said in the same tranquil voice, "And then there were four."

Both boys' heads swung round in the same instant.

"Will!" Barney's voice was a yelp.

Jane heard the sharp inward gasp of Simon's breath; then he let it out in a long slow hiss. "Well . . . I'll . . . be. . . ."

"Someone," Barney said. "Didn't I tell you? Someone. Was that you blowing the horn, Will? Let's see, do let me see!" He was hopping about, reaching, fascinated.

Will handed it over.

Simon said slowly, "You can't tell me this is a coincidence."

"No," Will said.

Barney was standing still now on the rock, holding the small battered horn, watching the sun glint on its golden rim. He looked over it, at Will. "Something's happening, isn't it?" he said quietly.

"Yes," said Will.

"Can you tell us?" Jane said.

"Not yet. In a little while. It's the hardest thing of all, and the last thing. And . . . it needs you."

"I should have known." Simon looked at Jane with a small wry smile. "This morning. You weren't there. Dad happened to mention who it was that suggested we stay at this particular golfing hotel."

"Well?"

"Great-Uncle Merry," Simon said.

Will said, "He will be here before long."

"It really is serious," Barney said.

"Of course. I told you. The hardest, and the last."

"It really had better be the last," Simon said rather pompously. "I start boarding school after these holidays."

Will looked at him. The corner of his mouth twitched.

Simon seemed to hear in his mind the echo of his own words; he looked down, scuffing at the grass with one foot. "Well I mean," he said. "I mean my holidays will be even more different from the other's, so we may not be going to . . . to the same places all the time. Right, Jane?" He turned in appeal to his sister: then paused. "Jane?"

Jane was gazing past him, eyes wide and fixed. She was see-ing, now, nothing but a figure on the mountain, a figure standing looking at them, outlined by the blazing light of the high-summer sun. It stood slim and straight. Its hair was like a silver flame. She had a sudden extraordinary sense of great rank, of high natural degree, almost as if she were in the presence of a king. For a moment she resisted a strong irrational impulse to curtsey.

"Will?" she said softly, without turning her head. "Then there were five, Will?"

Will's voice came strong and casual and eminently normal, snapping the tension. "Hey Bran! Over here! Bran!" He pro-nounced the name with a long vowel, Jane noticed, like the sound inside farm, or barn. She had never heard a name like it before. She had never seen anyone like this before.

The boy on the skyline came slowly down towards them. Jane stared at him, hardly breathing. She could see him clearly now. He wore a white sweater and black jeans, with dark glasses over his eyes, and there was no colour in him anywhere. His skin had a strange pale translucence. His hair was quite white; so were his eyebrows. He was not merely blonde, as her brother Barney was blonde, with his mop of yellowish hair falling over a sun-browned face. This boy seemed almost crippled by his lack of colour; its absence hit the eye as hard as if an arm or a leg had been missing. And then he pulled off his glasses as he drew level with them, and she saw that after all the lack was not total; she saw his eyes, and they too were like nothing she had seen before. They were yellow, tawny, flecked with gold, like the eyes of an owl; they blazed at her, bright as new coins. She felt a sense of challenge—and then she was conscious of her staring, and

64

though she would never normally have shaken hands with anyone her own age, in a kind of apology she thrust out her hand towards him.

"Hallo," she said.

Will said at once, beside her, matter-of-fact, "That's Bran Davies. Bran, this is Jane Drew. And Simon, he's the big one, and Barney."

The white-haired boy took Jane's hand briefly, awkwardly, and nodded at Barney and Simon. "Pleased to meet you." He sounded very Welsh.

"Bran lives in one of the houses on my uncle's farm," Will said.

"You have an uncle down here?" Barney's voice was high with astonishment.

"Well, actually he isn't my real uncle," Will said cheerfully. "Adopted. He married my mum's best friend. Comes to the same thing. Like you and Merriman. Or is he your real great-uncle?"

"I've never really known," Simon said.

"He probably isn't," Jane said. "Considering."

Barney said pertly, "Considering what?"

"You know perfectly well." She was uneasily conscious of Bran silently listening.

"Yes," Barney said. He handed the small gleaming horn back to Will. Instantly Bran's cold golden eyes were on it; then up glaring at Barney, fierce, accusing.

"Was that you blowing the horn?"

Will said quickly, "No, of course not, it was me. Calling, like I said. Calling you, and them."

Something in Jane's mind flickered at the note in his voice: a small strange difference, so slight that she could not be sure she was not imagining it. It seemed a kind of respect, that Will did not show even when he spoke to Merriman. Or not respect, but an . . . awareness of . . . of *something*. . . . She glanced quickly, nervously at the white-haired boy and then away again.

Simon said, "Have you known Will for long?" His tone was carefully neutral.

Bran said calmly, "*Calan Gaeaf* last year, I got to know Will. Last *Samain*. If you can work that out, you'll know how long. You staying at the Trefeddian then, you three?" He pronounced it *Trevethian*, natural and Welsh; not as they had themselves when they first arrived, Jane painfully remembered.

"Yes," she said. "Daddy's playing golf. Mother paints."

"Is she good?" Bran said.

"Yes," Barney said. "Very." Jane could hear the same wariness in his voice as there had been in Simon's, but without hostility. "I mean she's a real painter, not just hobby stuff. She has a studio, shows in galleries, all that."

"You're lucky," Bran said quietly.

Will was looking at Simon. "Is it hard to get away?"

"From the A.P.s? Oh no. Mother takes off in the car with her easel, Father's on the golf course all day." Glancing at Bran, Simon added, "Sorry—A.P.s—Aged Parents."

"Believe it or not," Bran said, "they teach Dickens in Welsh schools too."

"Sorry," Simon said stiffly. "I didn't mean—"

"That's all right." Bran smiled suddenly, for the first time. "We are going to be doing things together, Simon Drew. I think we had better get along. Don't worry. I am not one of those Welshmen with a chip. No fixations about the snotty English, or being a subject race, and all that. No point, is there, when the Welsh are so clearly superior?"

"Bah, humbug," Will said cheerfully.

Barney said rather hesitantly, looking at Bran, "You said, *We're going to be doing things together*. . . . Are you one of—are you like Great-Uncle Merry and Will?"

"In a way I suppose I am," Bran said slowly. "I can't explain. You'll see. But I am not one of the Old Ones, not a part of the Circle of the Light as they are. . . ." He grinned at Will. "Not a *dewin*, a wizard, like that one there, with all his tricks."

Will shook his round head with only half a smile. "We need more than tricks, this last time. There is something we have to find, all of us, and I don't even know what it is. All we have is the last line of an old verse, that you three heard, once upon a time, when first we deciphered it. It was in Welsh, which I can't possibly remember, but in English it meant, *The mountains are singing, and the Lady comes.*"

"*Yr mynyddoedd yn canu,*" Bran said, "*ac y mae'r arglwyddoes yn dod.*"

"Wow," Barney said.

"The Lady?" Jane said. "Who is the Lady?"

"The Lady is . . . the Lady. One of the great figures of the Light." Unconsciously Will's voice seemed to deepen, taking on an eerie resonance, and Jane felt a prickling along her spine. "She is the greatest of all, the one essential. But when a little while ago we called the Circle together, all the Old Ones of the earth out of all time, for the beginning of the end of this long battle, the Lady did not come. Something is wrong. Something holds her. And without her we can go no further. So the first thing that I—all of us—must do now is find her. With only four words to help us, that do not mean very much to me. *The mountains are singing.*"

He stopped abruptly, and looked around at them all.

"We need Great-Uncle Merry," Barney said gloomily.

"Well, we haven't got him. Yet." Jane sat down on the nearest rock, playing with a stem of the heather that grew round it in springy mounds of purple and green. Beside her, poking through a clump of dead brown gorse, grew a cluster of the little nodding harebells of the Welsh uplands: delicate pale-blue caps quivering in the slightest breeze. Jane touched one of them gently with her little finger. "Isn't there any Welsh place name that helps?" she said. "Nothing that means the Singing Mountain, or anything like that?"

Bran was' pacing to and fro, hands in pockets, the dark glasses back again over his pale eyes. "No, no," he said impatiently. "I have thought and thought, and there is nothing at all like that. Nothing."

"Well," said Simon, "how about any very old places—I mean old old, like Stonehenge? Ruins, or something?"

"I have thought of that too and still there is nothing," Bran said. "Like, there is a stone in St. Cadfan's Church in

Tywyn that has on it the oldest piece of Welsh ever written down—but all that tells is where St. Cadfan is buried. Or there is Castell y Bere, a ruined castle, very romantic, right near Cader. But that wasn't built till the thirteenth century, when Prince Llewellyn wanted to make himself a head-quarters to rule all of Wales that the English hadn't grabbed."

"No chip?" Barney said mischievously.

The dark glasses glared at him; then Bran grinned. "History I am telling you, boy, not comment. Old Llewellyn had the chip . . . and a fine one too, like Owain Glyndwr later. . . ." The grin faded. "But none of that takes us anywhere either."

"Isn't there anything to do with King Arthur?" Barney said.

And he and Jane and even Simon could feel the sudden weight of silence around them like a blanket. Neither Will nor Bran moved; they simply stood looking at Barney. And the emptiness of the mountain, up there on top of the world, was all at once so oppressive that every smallest sound seemed to take on immense significance. The rustle of heather as Barney shifted his feet; the deep distant call of a sheep; the persistent tuneless chirruping of some small unseen bird. Jane and Simon and Barney stood very still; surprised, uncertain.

Will said at last, lightly, "Why?"

"Barney has a fixation about King Arthur, that's all," Simon said.

For an instant Will paused still; then he smiled, and the strange oppressiveness fell away as if it had never been there. "Well," he said, "there's the biggest mountain of all, next to Snowdon—Cader Idris. Over there. It means in English 'the seat of Arthur.'"

"Any good?" said Barney hopefully.

"No," Will said, glancing at Bran. He offered no explanation for the total finality in his voice. Jane found herself resenting the feeling of exclusion that was growing in her.

Bran said slowly, "Or there's one other. I hadn't thought about it. Carn March Arthur."

"What's that mean?"

"It means, the hoof of Arthur's horse. It is not much to look at—just a mark on a stone, up behind Aberdyfi, on the mountain above Cwm Maethlon. Arthur is supposed to have pulled an *afanc*, a monster, out of a lake up there, and this is the footprint his horse made when he was leaping away." Bran wrinkled his nose. "Of course it is all rubbish, so I never gave it a thought. But—the name is there."

They looked at Will. He spread his hands. "We have to start somewhere. Why not?"

Barney said hopefully, "Today?"

Will shook his head. "Tomorrow. It's a long way home from here, for us."

"Carn March Arthur will be a longish walk," Bran said. "The quickest way from this side is up past the vicarage on a path over the mountain. Not so nice in summer, because of visitors' cars. Still. If you can get to the Square in the morning, perhaps we can too. Depends if we get a lift again, eh, Will?"

Will looked at his watch. "Twenty minutes before we meet him. Let's go and ask."

Jane never could remember, afterwards, the precise manner of the asking, though over and over again she tried. As they slithered and leapt over the grass and heather of the mountain ridge, there was little time for talking, and she felt obscurely that however much breath Will had he would not have explained much more about John Rowlands.

"He's shepherd on my uncle's farm. Among other things. He's . . . special. And this week he goes to a big annual market in Machynlleth, up the Dyfi valley. You must have come through it, on the way down."

"Slate roofs and grey rock," Jane said. "Grey, everything grey."

"That's the one. For the three days of the market now John is driving there every day, through Tywyn and Aberdyfi. That's how we got here today. He dropped us off this morning and he's picking us up now. So perhaps we can persuade him to do the same tomorrow."

Will slowed on a gentler, grassy slope as they came to a stile, and stood diffidently aside to let Jane climb over first.

"D'you think he will?" she said. "What's he like?"

"You'll see," said Will.

But all that Jane saw, when they trotted breathless down the last side road and out on to the main road by the village station, was a waiting Land-Rover with a frowning face in the window. It was a brown, lean face, much lined; dark-eyed, given now a mask of severity by the joined brows and straight unsmiling mouth.

Bran said something penitent-sounding, in Welsh.

"It is not good enough," John Rowlands said. "Ten minutes we have been sitting here. I told you five o'clock, and Will has a watch."

"I'm sorry," Will said. "It was my fault. We met some old friends of mine on the mountain. Visiting from London. This is Jane Drew, and Simon, and Barnabas."

"How d'you do?" John Rowlands said gruffly. The dark eyes flickered over them.

Jane said, before her brothers could speak, "How d'you do, Mr. Rowlands, I'm sorry they're late. We slowed them down, you see, not being so good at running down mountains." She gave him a small hopeful smile.

John Rowlands looked at her more carefully. "Hmm," he said.

Bran cleared his throat. "It is not the best time to ask, but we wondered if you would bring us in with you again tomorrow. If Mr. Evans would let us go."

"I am not at all sure about that," John Rowlands said.

"Oh come along now, John." Unexpectedly a soft, musical voice came from inside the car. "Of course David Evans will let them go. They have worked hard these last few days—and there is nothing much doing on the farm, except waiting for what comes from market."

"Hmm," John Rowlands said again. "Where will you be going?"

"Up over Cwm Maethlon," Bran said. "To show these three Panorama Walk, and all that."

"Go on, John," said the soft voice coaxingly.

"Pick up afterwards on time, is it?" The lines on the strong dark face were relaxing gradually, as if it had been an effort for them to make a frown in the first place.

"Honest," Will said. "Truly."

"I shall go without you if you're not here. Then you would have to make your own way back."

"All right."

"Very well then. I will drop you here at nine, and pick you up at four. If your uncle agrees."

Will stood on tiptoe to see past him into the car. "Thank you, Mrs. Rowlands!"

Amusement creased John Rowlands' eyes, and his wife leaned past him, laughing at them. Jane liked her instantly; it was a face like the voice, gentle and warm and beautiful all at once, with a glow of kindliness.

"Enjoying your stay?" Mrs. Rowlands said.

"Very much, thank you."

"Happy Valley and the Bearded Lake tomorrow, then, is it?"

Jane looked at Will. There was barely a fraction of a second's hesitation, and then he said heartily, "Yes, that's right. Real tourist stuff. But I've never seen them either."

"Lovely up there," Mrs. Rowlands said warmly. "John had better drop you in the Square, you can all meet by the chapel." She smiled at Jane. "It's a long walk, you know. Take your lunch. And good strong shoes, and jackets in case of rain."

"Oh, it won't rain," Simon said confidently, looking up at the hazy blue sky.

"You're in Snowdonia now, boy," Bran said. "Mean annual rainfall a hundred and fifty inches, high up. Only place that didn't die of the drought, back in nineteen seventy-six. Bring a raincoat. See you tomorrow."

He and Will climbed into the back of the car, and the Land-Rover roared away.

"A hundred and fifty inches?" Simon said. "That's impossible."

Barney hopped happily round in a circle, kicking a stone. "Things are happening!" he said. Then he paused. "I wonder if Will should have said where we were going?"

"That's all right," Jane said. "He said John Rowlands was special."

"Sounds a touristy kind of place anyway," Simon said. "I don't suppose it'll be any help at all."

CHAPTER SIX

THE BEARDED LAKE

THERE WAS NO RAIN at first, though clouds swirled over the blue sky like billowing smoke. Silent for want of breath, they toiled up the long winding lane that led from the village of Aberdyfi into the hills. The road rose very steeply, climbing out of the broad valley of the Dyfi estuary, so that whenever they paused to look back they could see, spread beneath them, a widening sweep of the coast and hills and the broad sea, with the silver ribbon of the Dyfi River snaking through gleaming acres of brown-gold sand left by the falling tide. Then another bend in the lane cut away all this southern view, and they were left climbing towards the mountains of the north, not yet visible.

High grassy banks enclosed them in the lane, banks as high as their heads, starred with yellow ragwort and hawkweed, white flat heads of yarrow, and a few late foxgloves. Higher yet above the banks, hedges of hazel and bramble and hawthorn reached to the sky, heavy with half-ripe berries and nuts, and fragrant with invading honeysuckle.

"Keep in," Will called from the rear. "Car!"

They pressed themselves against the grass wall of the lane, dodging the prickly embrace of bramble shoots, while a bright red mini whipped past in a tenor snarl of low gear.

"*Visitors!*" Bran said.

"That's the sixth."

"We're visitors too," Jane said.

"Ah, but such a superior brand," said Barney solemnly.

"At least you are walking on your legs," Bran said. He re-settled the peaked Swedish-type cap he wore over his white hair, and gave it a resigned tug. "All these cars, they are like flies on a sunny day, this time of year. And because of them, up in the wild places you find not just the sheep and the wind and the emptiness now, but little wooden chalets for people from Birmingham."

"No way out of it, is there?" Simon said. "I mean there don't seem to be many ways left of making a living, round here, except tourism."

"Farming, too," said Will.

"Not for many."

"True enough," Bran said. "The ones who go away to college after leaving school, they never come back. Nothing for them here."

Jane said curiously, "Will you go away?"

"*Duw,*" Bran said. "Have a heart. That's years away, anything could happen. Power stations in the estuary. Holiday camps on Snowdon."

"Watch out!" Simon said suddenly. "Another one!"

This time the car was pale blue, chugging and coughing past them like a small tank. Two small children could be seen fighting in the back seat. It disappeared round the next bend.

"Cars, cars," said Will. "D'you know there's even something on the Machynlleth road called a chaltel? A *chaltel!* Presumably a cross between a motel and—" He broke off, staring at the road ahead.

"Look at that! Golly!" Barney grabbed Jane's arm, pointing. "Whatever are they?"

Paused halfway across the lane a few yards ahead of them were two strange sinuous animals, as big as cats but slender-bodied. Their fur was reddish-ginger, like the coat of a red fox; they had cat-like tails, held just above the ground. Their heads were turned, bright-eyed. They stared at the children. Then first one and then the other, deliberately, without haste, turned back and made off in a slinking, undulating motion across the road, apparently disappearing into the bank.

"Stoats!" Simon said.

Barney looked doubtful. "Weren't they too big?"

"Much too big," said Bran. "And these had white only on the muzzle. A stoat has a white belly and chest."

"What were they, then?"

"*Yr ffwlbartau*. Polecats. But I've never seen one bright red before." Bran went forward and peered cautiously at the bank, raising a warning hand as Simon joined him. "Careful. They are not nice creatures. . . . There's a rabbit hole. They must have taken it over."

"Funny the cars don't seem to bother them," Barney said. "Or people, for that matter."

"They are not nice," Bran said again, looking thoughtfully at the hole. "Vicious. Not afraid. They even kill for fun."

"Like the mink," Will said. His voice was husky. Impatiently, he cleared his throat. Jane noticed with surprise that he seemed to have turned very pale; sweat glistened on his forehead, and one of his hands was tight-clenched.

"Mink?" Bran said. "Don't have those in Wales."

"They look like those. Only black. Or brown, I think. They . . . enjoy killing, too." Will's voice still seemed strained. Jane watched him out of the corner of her eye, trying not to appear curious.

"There's a farm just round the corner, that might be why they're about the place in daytime." Bran seemed to have lost interest in the polecats; he strode off up the lane. "Come on —it's a long way yet."

Jane paused to pull up a sock and let the boys pass her; then followed, alone and thoughtful. Above the farm the lane widened a little; the grass banks dropped to a mere foot or so, topped sometimes by wire fencing. The way led more gently upward now, through rock-studded grassland where Welsh Black cattle grazed here and there, or stood contemplatively in the middle of the road. Jane warily skirted a large bullock, and tried to collect the elusive feelings that were running like quicksilver in and out of her mind. What was happening? Why was Will anxious, and why did Bran on the contrary seem to feel nothing, and anyway who *was* this Bran? She felt a vague formless resentment of the way his presence somehow complicated their relationship with Will: *it's not just us any more,* she thought, *the way it was last time.* . . . And over everything she was beginning to feel a great unease about whatever lay ahead, as if some sense at the back of her mind were trying to tell her something she did not consciously know.

Then walking blindly on she bumped into Barney, and found all the others standing still in sudden silence, and looked up and saw why.

They were on the rim of a magnificent valley. At their feet the hillside dropped away in a sweep of waving green bracken, where a few sheep precariously grazed on scattered patches of grass. Far, far below, among the green and golden fields of the valley floor, a road ran like a wavering thread, past a toy church and a tiny farm. And across the valley, beyond its further side patched blue with cloud-shadows and dark with close-planted fir, there rolled in line after line the massing ancient hills of Wales.

"Oh!" Jane said softly.

"Cwm Maethlon," Bran said.

"Happy Valley," said Will.

"Now you see why they call this path Panorama Walk," Bran said. "This is what brings the cars. And walkers too, fair play."

"Wake up, Jane," Will said lightly.

Jane was standing quite still, staring out over the valley, her eyes wide. She turned her head slowly and looked at Will, but did not smile. "It's . . . it's . . . I can't explain. Beautiful. Lovely. But—frightening, somehow."

"Vertigo," Simon said confidently. "You'll feel better in a minute. Don't look over the edge."

"Come on," Will said, expressionless, suddenly reminding her of Merriman. He turned and continued up the path along the edge of Happy Valley. Simon followed.

"Vertigo, my foot," Jane said.

Bran said curtly, "Frightening, my foot, too. If you start listening to silly feelings, up here, you will never stop. Will has enough to worry about without that."

Astonished, Jane stared, but he had turned and was plodding up the road again with Simon and Will.

She looked crossly after him. "Who does he think he is? My feelings are in my head, not his."

Barney stuck his fingers into the knapsack straps over his shoulders. "Now perhaps you'll understand what I meant yesterday."

Jane raised her eyebrows.

"Up on the hill over the sea," Barney said. "That was sort of frightening too. When I was sure I'd been there before, and you both said rubbish. Only, I've been thinking—it's really more like living inside something that's happened before. Without its really having happened at all."

They went on in silence after the others.

The rain began soon afterwards: a gentle persistent rain, from the low grey clouds that had been growing steadily larger and had begun to merge now into a covering over all the broad sky. They pulled anoraks and raincoats from the rucksacks and went doggedly on along the high moorland road, between open grassy slopes with no shelter anywhere.

One by one, cars came back down the road past them. Round one last bend, the paved road ended at an iron gate, and a footworn earthen track went on instead, past a lone white farmhouse and away over the mountain. Five cars were parked tipsily on the grass before the gate; back down the mountain came a straggle of damp holiday-makers with drooping headscarves and complaining children.

"There's one thing to be said for rain," Barney said. "It does wash the people away."

Simon glanced back. "Gloomy-looking lot, aren't they?"

"Those two kids from the blue car are still thumping one another. I suppose anyone'd look gloomy with brats like that."

"You aren't long out of the brat stage yourself, chummy."

Barney opened and shut his mouth, hunting the right insult; but then glanced at Jane instead. She stood silent, unsmiling, gazing at nothing.

"You aren't still feeling odd, Jane?" Simon peered at her.

"Look at them," Jane said in a strange small, tight voice. She pointed ahead to Will and Bran, trudging one after the other up the track through the grass: two matching figures in oilskins rather too big for them, distinguishable only by Bran's cap and the sou'wester pulled low over Will's head. "Look at them!" Jane said again, miserably. "It's all mad! Who are they, where are they going, why are we doing what they want to do? How do we know what's going to happen?"

"We don't," Barney said. "But then we never have, have we?"

"We ought not to be here," Jane said. Impatiently she tugged the hood of her anorak closer over her head. "It's all too . . . vague. And it doesn't feel right. And"—the last words burst out defiantly—"I'm scared."

Barney blinked at her, out of the folds of an enveloping plastic mackintosh. "But Jane, it's all right, it must be. Anything to do with Great-Uncle Merry—"

"But Gumerry isn't *here.*"

"No, he's not," Simon said. "But Will's here, and that's just about the same."

Surprise sang through Jane's head. She stared at him. "But you never liked Will, not really. I mean I know you never said anything, but there was always. . . ." She stopped. Firm ground seemed to have become suddenly shaky; Simon was now so much bigger than she, as well as being almost a year older, that somehow she had imperceptibly begun to take him more seriously than before, paying attention to his opinions and prejudices even when she disagreed with them herself. It was unnerving to find one of those opinions turning itself upside down.

"Look," Simon said. "I don't pretend to understand anything that's ever happened to us with Great-Uncle Merry and Will. But there's not much point in trying, is there? I mean basically it's very simple, it's a matter of—well, there's a good side and a bad, and those two are absolutely without question the good side."

"Well, of course," Jane said pettishly.

"Well then. Where's the problem?"

"It's not a *problem*. It's that Bran. It's just—oh dear, you wouldn't understand." Jane poked dolefully at a tuft of grass.

"They're waiting for us," Barney said.

High up on the path beyond the farmhouse, beside another gate, the two small dark figures stood turned, looking back.

"Come on, Jane," said Simon. He patted her tentatively on the back.

Barney said, in a sudden rush of discovery, "You know, if you're really scared—it isn't like you—you ought to think whether you're being"—he flapped one hand vaguely—"being got at."

"Got at?" said Jane.

"The Dark," Barney said. "You remember—the way it makes something wriggle into your mind and say *I don't want you, go away.* . . . Makes you feel something terrible is going to happen."

"Yes," Jane said. "Oh yes. I do remember."

Barney hopped in front of her like some small fierce animal. "Well, if you fight it, it can't get hold. Push it off, run away from it—" He grabbed her sleeve. "Come on. Race you up the hill!"

Jane tried to smile. "All right!"

They rushed up the path to the waiting figures on the hill, raindrops scattering from their coats as they ran. Simon followed, more slowly. He had been listening with only half his attention. The rest had been caught, while Barney spoke, by two sinuous red animals slinking into the bracken from a thicket of gorse; and then out of the gorse, if he had not been imagining it, two bright pairs of eyes, watching them.

But it seemed a bad moment to mention that to Jane.

Bran said, as they watched Barney and Jane running towards them up the path. "What was that all about, d'you think?"

"They could just have been discussing whether it was time for lunch," Will said.

Bran pulled his glasses down his nose, and the tawny eyes

regarded Will steadily for a moment, between the dark lenses and cap. "Old One," Bran said softly. "You know better than that." Then he pushed his glasses back and grinned. "Anyway, it's too early."

But Will looked soberly down at the approaching figures. "The Light needs those three. It always has, in this whole long quest. So the Dark must be watching them very hard, now. We must stay close to them, Bran—specially Barney, perhaps."

Barney came panting up to them, his hood flapping on his shoulders and his yellow hair damp-dark with rain. "When's lunch?" he said.

Bran laughed. "Carn March Arthur is just over the next slope."

"What does it look like?" Without waiting for an answer Barney was gone, trotting up the path, mackintosh flapping.

Bran turned to go after him. But Jane was in his way. She stood there, breathing unevenly, looking coolly at them both in a way Will did not recognize. "It won't do, you know," she said. "We're all marching along as if everything was ordinary but we just can't go on pretending to one another."

Will looked at her, patience battling urgency in his mind; his head dropped for a moment on to his chest and he let out a short hiss of breath. "All right then. What do you want us to say?"

"Just something about what we might find, up there," Jane said, quavering, exasperated. "About what we're *doing* here."

Bran was on the words like a terrier at a bone, before Will could open his mouth. "Doing? Nothing, girl—you will probably have nothing to do but look at a valley and a lake and say, oh, how pretty. What's the fuss? If you don't like the rain, wrap yourself up and go home. Go on!"

"Bran!" Will said sharply.

Jane stood very still, eyes wide.

Bran said angrily, "The hell with it! If you have seen the raising of fear, and the killing of love, and the Dark creeping in over all things, you do not ask stupid questions. You do what you are intended to do, and no nonsense. And so that is what we should all be doing now, going on to where we might perhaps find out the next right move."

"And no nonsense!" said Jane tightly.

Simon came up behind her, silent, listening, but she paid no attention.

"Right!" Bran snapped.

Watching Jane, Will felt suddenly that he was seeing someone he had never met before. Her face was drawn into furious lines of emotion that seemed to belong to someone else.

"You!" Jane said to Bran, pushing her hands fiercely into her pockets. "You, you think you're so special, don't you, with the white hair and the difference, and the eyes behind those silly glasses. Super-different. You can tell us what we ought to do, you think you're even more special than Will. But who are you, anyway? We never met you at all until yesterday, in the middle of nowhere on a mountain, and why should we get into danger just because you—" Her voice quivered and dwindled, and she swung away from them, up the hill, towards Barney's small eager vanishing form.

Simon began to go after her and then paused, irresolute.

"Special, is it?" Bran said softly as if to himself. "Special. That's nice. After all the years of people sneering and muttering about the boy with no colour in his creepy skin. That's lovely. Special. And what is this about the eyes?"

"Yes," Will said shortly. "Special. You know it."

Bran hesitated; he pulled off his glasses and stuffed them in his pocket. "That is separate. She knows nothing of that. And that is not at all what she meant."

"No," Will said. "But you and I may not forget it for a moment. And you may not . . . let go, like that."

"I know," Bran said. "I'm sorry." He looked deliberately at Simon as he spoke, including him in the apology.

Simon said awkwardly, "I don't know what all this is about, but you shouldn't be bothered by Jane flying off the handle. It doesn't mean anything."

"Doesn't seem like her," Will said.

"Well . . . now and then she does it, these days. A sort

of flare-up . . . I think," Simon said confidingly, "she's going through a *stage*."

"Maybe," Will said. He was looking at Bran. "Or maybe it is Jane we should be specially watching?"

"Come on," Bran said. He brushed raindrops from the brim of his cap. "Carn March Arthur."

They climbed on, to the line where the green grassy slope met a grey sky. On the downward sweep of the path on the other side, Jane and Barney were crouched beside a small outcropping of rock, identical with every other rocky scar on the hill but singled out by a neat slate marker like a label. Will came slowly down the path, his senses open and alert as the ears of a hunting dog, but he felt nothing. Glancing across, he saw the same blankness on Bran's face.

"There's a sort of carved-out circle here that's supposed to be where the hoof of Arthur's horse trod—look, it's marked." Barney measured the hollow in the rock with his hand. "And another over there." He sniffed, unimpressed. "Pretty small horse."

"They are hoof-shaped, though," Jane said. Her head was down, her voice slightly husky. "I wonder what really made them?"

"Erosion," Simon said. "Water swirling round."

"With dirt rubbing," Bran said.

Jane said hesitantly, "And frost, cracking the rock."

"Or the hoof of a magic horse, coming down hard," Barney said. He looked up at Will. "Only it wasn't, was it?"

"No," Will said, smiling. "Hardly. If Arthur had ridden over every hollow called Arthur's Hoofprint, or sat on every rock called Arthur's Seat, or drunk from every spring called Arthur's Well, he'd have spent his whole life travelling round Britain without a stop."

"And so would the knights," Barney said cheerfully, "to sit round every hill called King Arthur's Round Table."

"Yes," Will said. He picked up a small white quartz pebble and rolled it round and round his palm. "Those too. Some of the names mean . . . other things."

Barney jumped up. "Where's the lake, the one he's supposed to have taken the monster from?"

"Llyn Barfog," Bran said. "The Bearded Lake. Over here."

He led them on, down the path into a hollow between hill-tops, curving round a slope; the rain, which had been gentle, began here to whip at their faces in uneven gusts, as the high wind eddied round the gullied land. The cloud was low over their heads.

"Such a funny name, the Bearded Lake," Jane said. The words were aimed at Bran, though she walked without look-ing at him; Will felt a pang of compassion for her groping unspoken apology. "Bearded. Not exactly romantic."

"I'll show you why in a minute," Bran said without ran-cour. "Watch where you tread, now, there's boggy patches." He strode ahead of them all, dodging tussocks of reedy grass that marked wet ground. And then Will looked up, and suddenly there ahead of him through the driving rain he could see the far side of the Happy Valley again, misted and grey. But this time, on this side, on their own steep edge overhanging the valley, there lay a lake.

It was a strange small reed-edged lake, little larger than a pond; its dark surface seemed curiously patched and pat-terned. Then Will saw that its open surface was rippled by the wind, but that only a small part of it was open, a triangle at the closest end of the lake. All the rest of its surface, from the end at the edge of the valley to a trailing V-shape in the centre, was covered with the leaves and stems and creamy white bloom of waterlilies. And from a singing in his ears like the sudden rise of waves on a loud sea, he knew too that somewhere up here, after all, was the place to which they were intended to come. Something waited for them here, somewhere up on this rolling rock-strewn mountaintop, be-tween the Happy Valley and the estuary of the Dyfi River.

Through a mist that was not the rain in the air but a blurring inside his mind, he saw with a vague distant sur-prise that this feeling did not seem to have come to Bran. The white-haired boy stood on the path with Simon and Jane, one hand raised over his eyes against the wind and rain, the other pointing.

"The Bearded Lake—see, it's the weed on the water that gives it the name. Some years when there is not much rain it gets much smaller, and the weed is left all around it like a beard. John Rowlands says perhaps the name is not from that, perhaps long ago there was much more water in the lake and it would spill out over the edge of the mountain and down into the valley in a waterfall. That could be, too. But a long time ago indeed, the way it looks now."

The little lake lay dark and silent under the shifting grey sky. They could hear the wind whining over the hills, and rustling through their clothes. Down in the valley, far away, a curlew gave its sad ghostly call. Then closer by, somewhere, they heard a muffled shout.

Barney turned his head. "What's that?"

Bran looked across the lake at the slope that seemed to be the highest part of the mountain on which they stood. He sighed. "Visitors. Shouting for the echo. Come and see."

Will lagged behind as they balanced their way one after the other along the muddy, rock-strewn path edging the lake.

He gazed out once more across the water, and its white-starred green carpet of weed, to the far shore where the land fell abruptly away into the valley. The rain blew back into his eyes, the mist whirled over the hills. But nothing came into his consciousness; nothing spoke to him. There was only the strong sense pulsing through his mind that they were in the presence of the High Magic, in some form he did not understand.

So then Will followed the others, along the path and round the next high slope. He found them standing on a bluff overlooking a flat hollow in the hills perhaps fifty yards square, a space much like the one occupied by the Bearded Lake, but here holding only the bright patches of coarse reedy grass that warned of marsh. A man and woman wearing startling orange anoraks stood lower down the slope, with three children of assorted sizes roaming about them shouting across the flat green hollow. A steep cliff-like rock on the opposite side threw an echo back.

"Hey! . . . *Hey*. . . ."

"Ooooo! . . . *Ooooo*. . . ."

"Baa baa black sheep! . . . *black sheep . . . sheep*. . . ."

"Hey fat face! . . . *face* . . . *face*. . . ."

Jane said, "If you listen carefully it's really a double echo, the second very faint."

"Fat face!" shouted the most raucous of the children again, delighted with himself.

Barney said in a clear precise voice, "Funny how people can never think of anything intelligent to shout to make an echo."

"It's like never knowing what to say to find out if a microphone's working," Will said. "Testing testing, one two three."

"The English master at school has a very rude rhyme he uses for that," Simon said.

"You can't shout rude rhymes for an echo," Barney said coldly. "Echoes are special. People ought to . . . to sing to them."

"Sing!" said Jane. The small children were still screeching at the mountain; she looked at them with distaste.

"Well, why not? Or do some Shakespeare. Simon was Prospero last term—why not a bit of that?"

"Were you really?" Bran looked at Simon with new interest.

"Only because I was the tallest," Simon said depreciatingly. "And had the right kind of voice."

"Fat face!" shouted all the awful children together.

"Oh really!" said Jane, losing patience. "What's the matter with their stupid parents?" She swung round irritably, and walked a little way back down the slope. The wind seemed less gusty here, and the rain had calmed to a fine mist. Underbrush scratched at her ankles; the slope was thick with heather and low-growing bilberry bushes, studded here and there with tiny blue-black berries among the leaves.

The others' voices receded as she wandered away. She thrust her hands deep into her pockets and hunched her shoulders as if to shake something from her back. *Black dog on my shoulder*, she thought wrily: it was the family term for a brief bad mood, generally her own these days. Yet somehow this time, Jane felt, there was more than a mood invading her mind; this was a strangeness she could not define, had never known before. A restlessness, a half-fearful anticipa-

85

tion of something part of her seemed to understand and part not. . . . Jane sighed. It was like being two people at once: living with someone without having the least idea what the other would do or feel next.

A flash of orange caught her eye through a gap in the hilly skyline; the noisy family was leaving, the mother dragging one rebellious child crossly by the arm. They disappeared behind the slope, heading for the path. But Jane did not go back to the others; she wandered aimlessly still on her own, through the heather and the wet grass, until suddenly the wind was cold on her face again and she found she was back at the Bearded Lake. From behind, she heard a faint laugh and a call from Barney, and then the same call again: a summons for the echo. She stood looking bleakly out over the dark weed-shrouded water, at the distant valley beyond. The wind sang in her ears. The cloud of the heavy grey sky was so low now that it blew ragged over the hilltop in white tails and tatters of mist, whirling down to the lake, curling, blowing away into the valley. The whole world seemed grey, as if all colour had drained from the summer grass.

In an eddy of the wind that brought a sudden stillness after it, Jane heard Simon's voice faintly behind her, a sudden snatch of sound. ". . . *thou earth, thou! Speak!* . . ." And very faintly indeed, perhaps only in imagining, she heard the echo: ". . . *speak . . . speak. . . .*"

Then some words came in another voice, clear and strange, and she knew that it was Bran calling in Welsh; and again the echo came faintly back, bringing the words to her again, familiar even while meaningless.

The wind flurried, the mist blew in a ragged shroud over the far side of the lake, hiding the Happy Valley. And on the echo of Bran's call, as if following a cue, a third voice came, singing, singing so high and sweet and unearthly that Jane stood without breathing, caught out of movement, feeling every stilled muscle and yet as totally transported as if she had no body at all. She knew it was Will; she could not remember if she had ever heard him sing before; she could not even think, or do anything but hear. The voice soared up on the wind, from behind the hill, distant but clear, in a strange lovely line of melody, and with it and behind it very faint in a following descant came the echo of the song, a ghostly second voice twining with the first.

It was as if the mountains were singing.

And as Jane gazed unseeing at the clouds blowing low over the lake, someone came.

Somewhere in the shifting greyness, a patch of colour began faintly to glow, red and pink and blue merging into one another too fast for the eye to follow. Glimmering soft and warm on the cold mountain, it held Jane's gaze as hypnotically as a flame; then gradually it began to focus itself, and Jane blinked in disbelief as she realized that a form was taking shape around it. Not definite clear shape, but a suggestion, a hint of what might be seen with the right eyes. . . .

The brightness grew more intense until suddenly it was all contained in a glowing rose-coloured stone set into a ring, and the ring on the finger of a slender figure standing before her, leaning a little as if resting on a stick. There was at first such brightness around the figure that Jane could not look directly at it; instead her eyes flickered down to the ground on which it stood, only to realize with a shock that no ground was there. The figure was floating before her, an isolate fragment of whatever world lay there behind the greyness. It was the delicate form of an old lady, she saw now, wearing a long light-coloured robe; the face was fine-boned, kindly yet arrogant, with clear blue eyes that shone strangely young in the old, old cobweb-lined face.

Jane had forgotten the others, forgotten the mountain and the rain, forgotten everything but the face that watched her and now, gently, smiled. But still the old lady did not speak.

Jane said huskily, "You are the Lady. Will's Lady."

The Lady inclined her head, a slow graceful nod. "And since you can see that much, I may speak to you, Jane Drew. It was intended, from the beginning, that you should carry the last message."

"Message?" Jane's voice came out in a whisper.

"Some things there are that may be communicated only between like and like," the sweet soft voice said from the mist. "It is the pattern of a child's game of dominoes. For you and I are much the same, Jane, Jana, Juno, Jane, in clear ways that separate us from all others concerned in this quest. And you and Will are alike in your youth and your vigour, neither of which I share."

The voice grew fainter, as if with a great weariness; then rallied, and the light glowed more brightly from the rose-coloured ring on the Lady's hand. She drew herself upright, and her robe shone clear white now, bright as a moon over the grey lake.

"Jane," she said.

"Madam?" Jane said at once, and without any self-consciousness she bowed her head and dipped one knee almost to kneeling, oblivious of her jeans and anorak, as if she were dropping a deep curtsey of respect, out of another age.

The Lady said clearly, "You must tell him that they must go to the Lost Land, in the moment when it shall show itself between the land and the sea. And a white bone will prevent them, and a flying may-tree will save them, and only the horn can stop the wheel. And in the glass tower among the seven trees, they will find the crystal sword of the Light."

Her voice wavered, ending in a gasp, as if clutching for some last strength.

Jane said, struggling to hold the words, struggling to hold her image of the Lady, "In the glass tower among the seven trees. And—a white bone will prevent them, and a flying may-tree save them. And only the—the horn will stop the wheel."

"Remember," the Lady said. Her white form was beginning to fade, and the glow dying in the rose of the ring. The voice grew softer, softer. "Remember, my daughter. And be brave, Jane. Be brave . . . brave. . . ."

The sound died, the wind whirled; Jane stared desperately out into the grey mist, searching to see the clear blue eyes in the old, lined face as if only they could fix the words in her memory. But she was alone among the dark hills and the lake with the low clouds blowing, and in her ears only the wind and the last imagined thread of a dying voice. And, now, as if it had never left her consciousness from the first instant, there came instead the clear high echo-twined melody of Will's voice, that had seemed to her like the mountains singing.

Suddenly the singing broke off. Will's voice flung through the air in a hoarse, urgent shout. "Jane! Jane!" The echo followed it ". . . *Jane!* . . . *Jane!* . . ." like a whispered warning. In quick instinct Jane swung round towards the voice, but saw only the green slope of the hill.

Then she looked back at the lake, and found that in the brief moment of her turning, such horror had arisen before her that panic engulfed her like ice-cold water. She tried to scream, and brought out only a strangled croak.

Out of the dark water an immense neck rose, swaying before her, dripping, tipped by a small pointed head, open-mouthed, black-toothed. Two horn-like antennae moved sluggishly to and fro on the head, like the horns of a snail; a fringe like a mane began between them and ran down the whole length of the neck, bent to one side by the water that hung from it, dripping slimily into the lake. The neck rose higher and higher, huge, endless. Gazing in motionless terror Jane saw that it was everywhere a dark green, shot with a strange dull iridescence, except on the underside that faced her, a dead silvery-white like the belly of a fish. High over her head the creature towered and swayed, menacing; the air was filled with a stench of weed and marsh-gas and decaying things.

Jane's arms and legs would not move. She stood, staring. The great serpent lunged to and fro towards her, nearer, nearer, blindly searching. Its mouth hung open. Slime dripped from the black jaws. It swung close to her, reeking, dreadful, and seemed to sense her; the head drew back to strike.

Jane screamed, and closed her eyes.

CHAPTER SEVEN

AFANC

IN THE HOLLOW beside the echo rock, all other sound had seemed to die away when Will began to sing. The loud wind dropped, and Simon, Bran and Barney stood motionless, astonished, listening. The music fell through the air like sunlight; a strange, haunting melody, like nothing they had ever heard before. Will sang, standing there unselfconscious and relaxed, with his hands in his pockets, his high clear choirboy's voice singing words of a tongue none of them could recognize. They knew that this was the music of the Old Ones, shot through with an enchantment that was more than melody. The clear voice soared through the mountains, entwining with its echoes, and listening they stood rapt, caught up out of time.

But then suddenly the song broke off in the middle of a note, and Will reeled back as if he had been struck in the face. They saw his face twisted by horror, and he threw back his head and yelled, in dreadful unboyish warning, "Jane! Jane!"

The echo threw the words back at them: *"Jane . . . Jane!"*

But before the first echo came, Bran had begun to move. He came rushing past Simon and Barney, as if flung forward by the same urgent impulse that had hold of Will. His cap tumbled off, his white hair blew like a flag as he went leaping over the grass and the rocks, away towards the Bearded Lake, away on a pursuit of something none of them could see.

* * *

The monstrous head swung past Jane's face, once, twice, three times; not quite close enough to touch, but each time fanning past her a wave of abominable decay. Jane opened slits of eyes, peering through the shaking hands she held over her face, convinced she was still alive only by feeling a powerful urge to be sick. It was impossible that anything so hideous could exist; yet the creature was there. Her mind clutched for support, wavering beneath an awful awareness of evil. It was *wrong*, this thing from the lake: malevolent, vicious, full of the festering resentment it had nursed through the centuries of some terrible nightmare sleep. She could feel its will groping for hers, just as the blind head groped through the air before her. And then breaking into her head like a howl, yet not with any sound to be heard with the ears, the voice came.

"*Tell!*"

Jane shut her eyes tight.

"*Tell me!*" The command beat at her mind. "*I am the afanc! Tell me the instruction that comes only through you! Tell!*"

"No!" Desperately Jane tried to shut off her mind and her memory.

"*Tell! Tell!*"

She tried to find images to hold as a defense against the hammer-blow demands; she thought of Will's pleasant round face, with the straight brown hair falling sideways; she thought of Merriman's fierce eyes beneath his bristling white brows; of a golden grail and the finding of it. Reaching closer, into the last few days in Wales, she thought of John Rowlands' lean brown face, and the gentle kindly smile of his wife.

But even as she began to find a steadiness, suddenly it shattered, and the high shrieking voice broke again into her mind and beat and beat at her, until she felt she would go mad. She whimpered, staggering, holding both hands to her head.

And all at once, mercifully muffling the high shriek, came another voice, gentle, reassuring: *It's all right, Jenny, it's all right,* and relief flooded warm through her mind, and after it came only darkness. . . .

They saw her crumple and fall in a heap on the wet grass, as they came stumbling up from the echo rock. Simon and Barney started forward, but Will seized each of them in an astonishing grip, and even tall Simon was held helpless by the hand clamped like a steel band round his arm. They gasped at the sight of the *afanc,* thrashing furiously now in the lake with its great neck bending to and fro. And then they saw Bran, upright and bare-headed, standing angry in challenge before it on a tall rock, with his white hair blowing in the wind.

The creature screamed in fury, stirring a foam in the lake, throwing it up to join the gusting ragged cloud and the blowing rain so that all the world seemed one whirling grey mist.

"Go back!" Bran shouted across the lake towards it. "Go back where you should be!"

From the horned head in the mist a high thin voice came, cold as death; they shuddered at the sound.

"I am the *afanc* of Llyn Barfog!" the high voice cried. "This place is mine!"

Bran stood unmoving. "My father cast you from it, away into Lyn Cau. What right had you to return?"

Up on the hillside, Will felt Barney's hand clutch convulsively at his sleeve. The younger boy was looking up at him, very pale. *"His father, Will?"*

Will met his gaze, but said nothing.

The water churned, the voice was angry and obstinate. "The Dark outlived that lord, the Dark brought me home. The Dark is my master. I must have what the girl will tell!"

"You are a stupid creature," Bran said, clear and contemptuous.

The *afanc* roared and screamed and thrashed; its noise was terrifying. But gradually now, they began to realize that it was no more than noise: that in spite of the creature's horrifying bulk, it seemed to have the power only to utter threats. It was a nightmare—but no more than that.

Bran's white hair gleamed like a beacon through the grey mist; his lilting Welsh voice rang out over the lake. "And your masters are stupid too, to think that the mere force of terror could overcome one of the Six. This girl, she has seen more dreadful sights than you, and stood the test." His voice hardened into a command, sounding suddenly deeper and more adult; he stood erect, pointing. "Go, *afanc*, back to the dark water where you belong! Go back to the Dark, and never come out again! *Ewch nôl! Ewch y llyn!*"

And suddenly there was total silence over the lake, but for the wind whistling and the patter of the rain on their clothes. The huge green neck bowed and coiled in submission, dripping slime and weed; and the horned snail-like head dipped into the water and slowly the creature disappeared. A few large sluggish bubbles broke on the dark surface of the lake, their ripples spreading to be lost in the water-lily leaves. And then there was nothing.

Will let out a yell of exuberant relief, and with Simon and Barney he went slithering and sliding down the grassy slope. Jane was sitting at the bottom of the slope, on the grass edging the reeds that fringed the lake; her face was pale.

Simon crouched beside her. "Are you all right?"

Jane said, illogically, "I was watching him."

"But you didn't hurt yourself? When you fell?"

"Fell?" Jane said.

Will said gently, "She'll be all right now."

"Will?" Jane said. She was looking out across the lake, to where Bran still stood motionless on his rock. Her voice shook. "Will . . . Who—what—is Bran?"

Simon helped her to her feet, and the four of them stood looking at Bran. The white-haired boy turned slowly away from the lake, pulling his coat closer at the collar, shaking his head dog-fashion to get rid of the rain.

"He is the Pendragon," Will said simply. "The son of Arthur. Heir to the same responsibility, in a different age. . . . When he was born, his mother Guinevere brought him forward in Time, with Merriman's help, because once before she had deceived her lord and she was afraid Arthur would not now believe that Bran was truly his son. And she left him here, so that he grew up in our time in Wales, with a new father who adopted him. So he belongs to this age just as much as we do, yet at the same time he does not. . . . And sometimes I think he is exactly aware of all this all the time, and other times I think one side of his life is for him no more than a dream. . . ." His voice quickened, became more matter-of-fact. "I can't tell you any more now. Come on."

They went, each one hesitant, to meet Bran, through the rain that was growing heavier again now. He grinned cheerfully at them, totally without strain, and wrinkled his nose. *"Daro!"* he said. "What a nasty!"

"Thank you, Bran," Jane said.

"O'r gore," said Bran. "You're welcome."

"Will it really never come back *ever?*" Barney said, looking fascinated at the lake.

"Never," Bran said.

Simon took a deep breath and let it out again. "I shan't laugh at stories of the Loch Ness Monster from now on."

"But this one was a creature of the Dark," Will said. "Made out of the stuff of nightmare, in order to break Jane. Because they wanted something that she had." He looked at her. "What happened?"

"It was when you sang," Jane said. "And the echo sang with you. It sounded . . . it sounded. . . ."

"The mountains are singing," Bran said slowly. *"And the Lady comes."*

Jane said, "And she did come."

There was silence.

Will said nothing. He stood staring at Jane with a strange medley of emotions crossing his face: blank astonishment, chased by envy, followed by the dawning of an understanding that relaxed into his usual amiable look. He said softly, "I didn't know."

"This . . . Lady—" Simon said. He stopped.

"Well?" said Jane.

"Well . . . where did she come from? Where is she now?"

"I don't know. Either of those things. She just . . . appeared. And she said—" Jane paused, a warmth running through her as she remembered those things the Lady had said for her, Jane, alone. Then she put them aside. "She said, tell him, that they must go to the Lost Land, when it shows itself between the shore and the sea. She said, a white bone will prevent them, and a—a flying may-tree will save them. And—" She shut her eyes, trying desperately to remember the right words. "And only the horn will stop the wheel, she said. And they will find the crystal sword of the Light in the glass tower among the seven trees."

She let out a quick breath, and opened her eyes. "That's not perfect, but it's what she said. And then she . . . went away. She seemed awfully tired, she just sort of faded out."

"She is very tired indeed," Will said soberly. He touched Jane's shoulder briefly. "You did marvelously. The moment the Dark sensed she had told you, they must have come rushing, sending the *afanc* to shock you into giving up what she had said. That was their only possible way—they couldn't have heard it for themselves. There is a protection sometimes round the Six, through which the Dark cannot see or hear."

"But there's only five of us," Barney said.

Bran chuckled. "That one is so sharp he will cut himself."

Barney said hastily, "I'm sorry—I know. Of course things work just the same whether it's five or six. But where *is* Great-Uncle Merry?" For a moment his voice dropped unwittingly into the unselfconscious plaint of a small child.

"I don't know," Will said. "He'll come, Barney. When he can."

Simon suddenly gave a gigantic sneeze, ducking his head. Rainwater ran off the edge of his hood in a thin stream. No mist blew over the lake now, and the clouds seemed higher, broken, racing across the sky in a wind they hardly felt, there below. But the rain fell steadily.

"Where is the Lost Land?" said Barney.

"We shall find it," Will said. "When the time comes. No question. Come on, let's go down before we all get pneumonia."

They went single file back over the path edging the lake,

hopping over puddles, skirting patches of mud; then trooped through the long wet grass towards the little grey outcrop of Carn March Arthur, and the path back over the ridge. Jane turned for one last look at the lake, but it was hidden by the slope.

"Will," she said. "Tell me something. Just about a second before I saw that—that thing, I heard you shout *Jane!* Like a warning."

Barney said promptly, "Yes, he did. He looked awful—as if he could already see it." He realized what he had said, and looked thoughtfully at Will.

"Could you?" Jane said.

Will brushed his hand over the top of the slate marking Carn March Arthur, which Bran, ahead of them, had passed without a glance. He walked on in silence. Then he said, "When the Dark comes, anywhere, we can feel it. It's like, I dunno, like an animal smelling man. So I knew—and I knew you were in danger, so I had to yell." He glanced back at Jane over his shoulder with a shy half-grin. *"Halloo your name to the reverberate hills,"* he said.

"Huh?" said Simon, beside her.

"You aren't the only one who knows a few bits of Shakespeare," Will said.

"What's that one?"

"Oh—just some speech we had to learn last term."

"The reverberate hills," said Jane. She looked back at the hill that rose behind them now, masking the echo rock. Then she frowned. "Will—if you could sense the Dark, why couldn't you sense the Light?"

"The Lady?" Will shook his head. "I don't know. That was her doing. For her own reasons. I think—I think perhaps there will be a test for each of us, before all this is done. Each time different and each time unexpected. And maybe the Bearded Lake was yours, Jane, yours on your own."

"I hope mine isn't like that," Barney said cheerfully. He pointed. "Look—the clouds are breaking up."

Hints of blue were emerging in the sky to the west, among the racing ragged clouds; the rain had dwindled to a fine sprinkle, and was dying altogether now. They went on down the hill, past the small white farm built sturdy as a fort against winter gales; through other gates, over the clanking metal pipes of a cattle grid set to keep the wandering Welsh Black bullocks within bounds. The Happy Valley unfolded far below them again, the last low shreds of mist blowing away past the mountains of its further side. Sunshine flickered now and then through the clouds, and the air grew warmer; jackets were opened, and raincoats shaken free of water. As if to give final proof that the rain was over, a small car came humming up the hill past them, bringing the first of the next flow of visitors to wander the hillside among the sheep-droppings and rabbit holes; to collect feathers, and the tufts of greyish wool that barbed-wire fences grab from sheep, and small rough pebbles of white quartz. Will found himself trying hard to remember that he had no right whatsoever to resent these people wandering through the bracken and the heather, the gorse and the harebells, dropping their cigarette ends on the short, springy grass.

Seagulls keened in the distance. As the track swung round a hill, suddenly there ahead they saw the sea, and the broad estuary of the Dyfi, with the silver thread of the river wandering through glistening stretches of golden low-tide sand.

They all stopped to stand and gaze. Sunshine shafting out from between the clouds sparkled on the river, glimmered on the sandy bar that lay across its entrance to the sea.

"I'm hungry," Barney said.

"Now that's a good idea," said Simon. "Lunch?"

Bran said, "Rocks to sit on, though—try up here."

They clambered up the slope edging the track, to the unfenced land where the cattle grazed. Several large black bullocks lumbered reproachfully out of their way. In a few moments they were over the crest of a small ridge, with the track out of sight behind them and the sea and the estuary lying spread below. They perched on humps of slatey rock and fell upon their sandwiches. The wet grass smelt clean, and somewhere a skylark bubbled its long ecstatic song. High overhead a small hawk hung in the air.

Jane said, looking out over the estuary as she munched, "What an enormous lot of flat land there is on the other side of the river. Miles of it, miles and miles, before the mountains start again."

"*Cors Fochno*," Bran said, his strange white hair drying fluffy in the sun. "Bog, most of it—see the drainage channels, all so straight? Some very interesting plants there are, over in that part, if you are a botanist. Which I am not. . . . And old things have been found there, a golden girdle with spikes on it, once, and a gold necklace, and thirty-two gold coins that are in the National Museum now. And there are stumps of drowned trees out there on the sands, near the dunes. Some on this side of the river too, on the sands between Aberdyfi and Tywyn."

"Drowned trees?" Simon said.

"Sure," Bran said. He chuckled. "From the Drowned Hundred, no doubt."

Barney said blankly, "Whatever's that?"

"Haven't you heard that old story yet? About where the Bells of Aberdyfi ring, all ghostly out at sea on a summer night, over there?" Masked by the dark glasses that covered his pale eyes once more, Bran got to his feet and pointed out at the mouth of the estuary, all of it sunlit now beneath wider patches of blue. "That was supposed to be *Cantr'er Gwaelod*, the Lowland Hundred, the lovely fertile land of the King Gwyddno Garanhir, centuries ago. The only trouble was, it was so flat that the seawater had to be kept out by dykes, and one night there was a terrible storm and the sea-wall broke, and all the water came in. And the land was drowned."

Will stood up and came quietly forward to stand beside him, looking down at the estuary. He tried to keep the excitement from his voice. "Drowned," he said. "Lost. . . ."

The mountain was very quiet. The skylark had finished its song. Very far away once more they heard gulls faintly crying, out over the sea.

Bran stood very still, without turning. "Dear God," he said.

98

The others scrambled to their feet. Simon said, *"The Lost Land?"*

"I have known that old story always, as well as I know my own name," Bran said slowly, "and yet I never thought. . . ."

"Could that really be it?" Simon said. "But—"

Barney burst out, "It has to be! It couldn't be anything else! Isn't that right, Will?"

"I think so," Will said. He was trying to stop his face from breaking into a broad stupid smile. Confidence was running through him like the warmth of the sun. He could feel again, rapidly growing as strong as before, the sense of the High Magic all around. It was a kind of intoxication, a wonderful expectancy of marvellous things: the feeling of Christmas Eve, or the new-green mist of trees in early spring, or the first summer-holiday sight of the sea. Impulsively he stretched both arms upward, as if to catch a cloud.

"Something—" he said, talking out of his feelings, without any thought of what he said. "There's something—" He whirled about, staring round him on the mountain; delight was singing all through him, he scarcely knew that the others were there. Except one of them.

"Bran?" he said. "Bran? Do you feel it—do you—" He flapped one hand impatiently as he found he had no words; but then looked and knew that he needed none, from the rapt astonishment on Bran's pale face. The Welsh boy too turned, looking out over the mountains, out at the sky, as if hunting for something, trying to hear a voice calling. Will laughed aloud, to see the reflection of the same indefinable joy that flooded his own mind.

Jane, behind them, watching, sensed the intensity of their feeling and was afraid of it. Unconsciously she drew closer to Simon, and reached an arm to keep Barney beside her; and chilled by the same instinct Barney did not resist, but stepped slowly backward, away from Will and Bran. The Drews stood there, three together, watching.

And out over the hill, a mile beyond in the blue and gold patterning of the estuary, a flickering of the air came, like the quiver of heat that is over a paved road in high sum-

mer. At the same time a whispering music drifted to their
ears, very distant and faint, but so sweet that they strained
to hear it better, yet could never catch more than a hint of
the delicate elusive melody. The quivering air grew bright,
brighter, glowing as if it were lit from within by the sun;
their eyes dazzled, but through the brightness they seemed
to see a changing out in the estuary, a movement of the water.

Although the tide was already low, there seemed to be
more sand shining golden now beyond the furthest low-tide
mark. The waves had stilled, the water had begun to go back.
Further and further the white rim of the blue sea withdrew,
and the shore rose out of it; first sand, then the glimmering
green of weed. But it was not weed, Jane saw incredulously,
it was grass; for after it, as the sea fell back and back, there
rose trees, and flowers, and walls and buildings of grey stone,
blue slate and glimmering gold. A whole city lay there, growing gradually out of the retreating sea: a live city, with here
and there thin strands of smoke rising from unseen fires
through the unmoving summer air. Towers and glittering
pinnacles reached up like guardians, over the flat fertile land
patched green and gold, stretching beside the mountains.
And far away at the distant edge of the new land, where the
blue of the vanished sea at last began again, they glimpsed
a pencil of light standing, a faraway tower gleaming like
white fire.

Up on the highest ridge of the slope, looking out over the
lost land and the city that seemed to govern it, Will and Bran
stood together, outlined against the blue sky. They seemed to
Jane to be poised there, expectant, like musicians waiting for
the first sweep of a conductor's baton. She saw Will raise his
head suddenly and look out to sea. And then the brightness
that filled the air began to grow again, dazzling, blinding, so
that only the faintest outline of the strange land could be
seen through it, and it seemed to Jane as she flinched back,
shielding her eyes, that the luminous air drew itself into a
shining broad ribbon like a road, stretching from their feet
far, far out into the air and over the valley, down beyond the
mouth of the Dyfi River.

She heard the sound of the music again, lovely and elusive, and she saw Will and Bran step together on to the bright road of light and move away, over the river, through the air, into the haze and towards the Lost Land.

Her arm tightened across Barney's shoulder, and at her other side she felt Simon's hand touch her own. They stood together in silence.

Then the music dwindled into the sound of gulls crying, far away, and the shining road of light faded, and with it the figures that had been walking upon it. And as brightness fell from the air they saw, looking out over the estuary, no towering city, no new green fields, no thin smoke rising, but only the sea and the river and the low-tide shore just as they had been in the beginning.

Simon and Jane and Barney turned, in silence, and gathered coats and the remnants of picnic lunches into the rucksacks, and walked back to the road.

CHAPTER EIGHT

THREE FROM
THE TRACK

THEY WALKED in single file, back along the path over the hills. The wet grass glittered in the sunshine now; raindrops hung sparkling on bracken, heather, the patches of yellow-starred gorse.

Barney said, "What are we going to say?"

"I don't know," Jane said.

"We'll have to meet John Rowlands in the Square, where they were going to," Simon said. "And say—and say—"

"Better if we don't," Jane said suddenly. "Then he'll just think they're late, and go without them. He warned them he would, remember?"

"That won't solve anything for long."

"Maybe they won't need long."

They went on in silence. At the turn where the path curved back down towards Aberdyfi, Jane paused and stood gazing ahead over the fields, over to the next ridge of high moorland where they had first encountered Will and Bran.

She pointed. "Can't we go on over the hills, and down to the hotel from the ridge?"

Simon said doubtfully. "There isn't any footpath."

"Be a lot quicker than going down to the village," Barney said. "And we shouldn't see Mr. Rowlands either."

"There's bound to be a sheep trail at least, after this field," Jane said.

Simon shrugged. "I don't care. Go on then." He seemed detached, indifferent, as though his mind were still half-paralyzed. Jane swung open the gate to the first field that would lead them away from the little road, and he followed listlessly.

Barney trotted behind, taking the gate from Jane; but before he could swing it shut again, suddenly ahead of him Jane screamed, a dreadful high muffled sound. She seemed to leap into the air, cannoning sideways into Simon; Simon too yelled, and then he and Jane were flinging themselves at Barney, pushing him back through the gate. And behind them in a horrible hasty flash Barney saw, coming at them from all parts of the field, the red rippling bodies of dozens of polecats like the two they had seen on the road before, on their way up the mountain.

Desperately Simon slammed the gate shut, in a hopeless instinctive clutch at defense. But instantly the animals were after them as before, pouring through the open rails that would have kept out nothing smaller than a sheep. The children kicked out at them; the lithe red creatures slipped aside and were at their heels again in a moment, white teeth glinting, black eyes shining; never biting, always nagging, hovering, chivvying. Driving . . . *driving*, Barney thought suddenly; driving us, as if we were sheep and they were sheepdogs. He glanced up, and saw that the small hard bodies darting sideways against his ankles were pushing toward the open gate of the farm they had passed earlier that day. Deliberately he turned away, and at once the animals were at his heels, hissing, snapping, making dreadful small yipping sounds, turning him; until in spite of himself Barney turned back to Simon and Jane, and all three of them flung themselves for refuge towards the yard of the farm.

"Slowly, now!" The voice was warm, relaxed, amused; as Jane skidded desperately into the farmyard she glimpsed the figure of a woman ahead, holding out an arm to catch her. The smiling face seemed somehow familiar . . . Jane thought no further, but collapsed in exhausted relief against the comforting outstretched arm. Behind her, Barney glanced apprehensively over his shoulder—and saw that every single polecat had disappeared.

"Goodness me now!" The woman's voice was gentle. "Break your necks you will, tearing in here like that as if the devil were at your heels. What is the trouble, what's wrong?" Then she looked more closely at Jane. "Why, I know you—you're the children who were with Bran and Will Stanton, yesterday."

Barney said suddenly, "You're Mrs. Rowlands!"

"Yes indeed." Blodwen Rowlands' voice sharpened."What is wrong, has something happened to the boys?"

They stared at her, unable for a moment to gather enough wit for an answer.

"No no," Jane said then, stumbling. "No . . . they're all right, they . . . went down. They said they were going to meet you in the Square."

"That is right." Mrs. Rowlands' round face cleared. "Came up here just for John to see Llew Owen, we did, we were just on our way down now. We did wonder whether we might meet the boys on the way." She looked at Jane in concern. "Your hair is all wet, *cariad*, that rain must have caught you. . . . Now why were you three in such a fright?"

"Not a fright really," Simon said gruffly. Now that every trace of the polecats had gone, he was beginning to feel shame at his panic. "It was just—"

"There were these animals," Jane said, too exhausted to pretend. "Polecats, Bran said they were. We'd seen two this morning, near here. And then just now on the path, lots of them just jumped at us out of nowhere—and—and—they were horrible. Their teeth—" She gulped.

"Oh dear me," Mrs. Rowlands said comfortingly, cossetingly, as if to a small child. "Never you mind now, there's nothing now, they've gone. . . ." She put her arm round Jane's shoulders and led her towards the farm. Simon made a face at Barney that said: *She doesn't believe it.* Barney shrugged, and they followed.

Before they reached the farmhouse John Rowlands came out of its door; they could see his Land-Rover parked close by. He knew them at once; surprise creased his lean brown face.

"Well well," he said. "Three out of five—and where are my two?"

"They went on down," Barney said, all blithe self-possession now, keeping instinctively as close to the literal truth as Jane had done. "We thought we'd go across the top and then down to the Trefeddian that way. But there didn't seem to be a path."

"Hard to find it nowadays," John Rowlands said, "since all those new houses down the hill have covered up the path. Gone, it is, the old way we went when I was a boy." He had cast one sharp look at Jane's pale face, but seemed disinclined to question them further; there was a preoccupied look behind his eyes.

"Come with us," Mrs. Rowlands said. "Give you a lift, now." She waved farewell to the farmer's wife emerging enquiringly from the farmhouse, and opened the Land-Rover's back door.

"Yes, of course," John Rowlands said.

"Thank you very much." They climbed in. Jane peered closely at hedgerow and field as the car turned out into the lane, and saw Barney gazing too, but there was no sign of anything except white fool's parsley, and rose-bay willow-herb tall in the grass, and the sweep of the tall green hedges above.

Simon, sitting beside her, saw the strain in her face and brushed a fist gently against her arm. He said, very low, "But they *were* there."

The Land-Rover crept down the last elbow turn of the steep little road and into Chapel Square, there to wait in line while a miniature traffic jam of cars fidgeted in the single tiny one-way street leading to the main road.

"Goodness gracious," Blodwen Rowlands said. "Look at them all. I want to call in at Royal House, John, but how you will find a parking place I cannot think."

"We shall just have to be visitors, and go in the car park,"

John Rowlands said, swinging to the right and edging through sweaters and parkas, push-chairs and buckets and spades, their owners all vaguely wandering or gazing out at the sea.

The Land-Rover was left in the park, its square roof looming over its smaller neighbors like a landmark. They threaded their way back along the crowded streets; Mrs. Rowlands paused beside a shop-window filled with jerseys and swim-suits and shorts.

"Wyt ti'n dwad i mewn hefyd, cariad?"

"No, I won't come," John Rowlands said, pulling his pipe from his pocket and peering into its bowl. "We will be over on the wharf, I dare say. The best place to look out for Bran and Will. No hurry, Blod, take your time."

He led the children across the road, between a huge black shed labelled Outward Bound Sea School and a cluster of masts, their rigging gently singing in the breeze, where the boats of the Aberdyfi Yacht Club lay in lines on the beach. Sand spilled out over the pavement.

They walked across the wharf and out on to the short dog-leg jetty. John Rowlands paused, filling his pipe from an old black leather pouch. "A different jetty we had here when I was a boy," he said absently. "All of wood, great beams of black creosoted timber. . . . We used to climb all over them at low tide, and fall off where the green weed was slippery, and fish for crabs."

"Did you live here?" Barney said.

"See over there?" Following John Rowlands' pointing finger, they looked back at the long terrace of stately, narrow, three-storey Victorian houses that stood facing out over the road, over the beach, to the mouth of the Dyfi River and the sea.

"That one in the middle, with the green paint," John Rowlands said, "that's where I was born. And my father before me. He was a sailor, and so was *his* father. My grandfather Captain Evan Rowlands of the schooner *Ellen Davies*—he built that house. All built by the old captains, they were, the houses along that road, in the days when Aberdyfi was still a real shipping port."

Jane said curiously, "Didn't you want to be a sailor too?"

John Rowlands smiled at her through puffs of blue smoke as he lighted his pipe, dark eyes narrowed by the lines of his brown face. "Once I did, I dare say. But my da was drowned when I was six, you see, and my mother took my brothers and me away from Aberdyfi then, back to her parents' farm near Abergynolwyn. Back in the hills near Cader Idris—behind the valley where you were today. So what with one thing and another, it was sheep for me, not the sea."

"What a shame," Simon said.

"Oh, not really. The shipping days have been gone a long time now, and even the fishing too. They were dying already in my father's time."

Barney said, "Fancy him drowning. A sailor."

"A lot of sailors can't swim," Simon said. "Even Nelson couldn't. He used to get seasick, too."

John Rowlands puffed reflectively. "For a lot of them there was never time to learn, I fancy. The men in those sailing ships—no playing in the sea for them. The sea was their mistress, their mother, their living, their life. But everything serious. Nothing for fun." He turned slowly back towards the street, his eyes carefully searching—just as, Jane suddenly realized, they had been already searching the wharf and the beach. "I don't see any sign at all of Bran and Will. How long before you left, was it, that they came down?"

Jane hesitated, and saw Simon open his mouth and shut it again, confused. Barney simply shrugged.

She said, "About—about half an hour, I suppose."

"Perhaps they caught a bus?" Barney said helpfully.

John Rowlands stood for a moment, pipe between teeth, his face without expression. He said, "Have you known Will Stanton for long?"

"We were all on holiday together once," Jane said. "About two years ago. In Cornwall."

"Did anything . . . unusual . . . happen on that holiday?" The Welshman's voice was casual still, but suddenly he was looking very closely and specifically at Simon, the dark eyes bright and intent.

Simon blinked, taken by surprise. "Well—yes, I suppose."
"What sort of thing?"

"Just . . . well, just things." Simon's face was flushed; he
floundered, caught between honesty and bewilderment.

Jane saw Barney's face crease in a resentful frown. She
said, surprised at the cool self-possession in her voice, "What
do you mean exactly, Mr. Rowlands?"

"How much do you three know about Will?" John Rowlands said. His face was unreadable, his voice curt.

"Quite a lot," said Jane, and her mouth shut sharply like
a closing door. She stood looking at him. On either side of her
she could feel Simon and Barney rigid and challenging as
herself; the three of them arrayed against questions that, they
instinctively knew, nobody outside the pattern of their deal-
ings with Merriman and Will should be bothering to ask.

Rowlands was looking at her now: a strange searching uncertain look. "You are not like him," he said. "You three, you
are no more than I am, you are not . . . of that kind."

"No," Jane said.

Something seemed to collapse behind John Rowlands' eyes;
his face twisted into a kind of taut despair, and Jane was all
at once rocked by distress as she saw him gazing at her in
open appeal. "*Diawl*," he said, tight and unhappy, "will you
stop mistrusting me, for the love of God? You cannot have
seen more of the nature of those two than I have seen, this
past year. Those two—for Bran is someone you may know
nothing about at all. And there is fear shouting all through
me now, about what may be happening to them, about who
may have taken hold of them, at a time when they may be
in worse danger than they have ever been before."

Behind Jane's shoulder Barney said suddenly, "He means
it, Jane. And Will did trust him."

"That's true," Simon said.

"What did you mean, Mr. Rowlands," Jane said slowly,
"about what you had seen, this past year?"

"Not a year all spread out," John Rowlands said. "Last
summer it was, when Will came visiting his uncle. As soon as
he came to the valley, things . . . things began to happen.

Forces woke that had been sleeping, and people grew and changed, and the Grey King of Cader Idris rose in his power, and fell again . . . it was all a confronting between the Light and the Dark, and I did not understand what it was all about and I did not want to." He looked at them, grave and intent, his pipe forgotten in his hand. "I have told Will that, all along," he said. "I know he is part of the power called the Light, and Bran Davies perhaps even deeper into the pattern. But that is enough for me. I will help Will Stanton when he needs me, and Bran, too, because I feel for him as if he were my own—only, I do not want to know what it is that they are doing."

Barney said curiously, "Why not?"

"Because I am not of their kind," John Rowlands said sharply. "And nor are you either, and it is not proper." For a moment he sounded stern, censorious—and very sure of himself.

Simon said unexpectedly, "I know just what you mean. I've always felt the same. And anyway we don't really know either." He looked at Jane. "Do we?"

She had opened her mouth to protest, but now she paused instead. "Well . . . no. Great-Uncle Merry never said anything much. Only that the Dark is rising, or trying to, and must be stopped. Everything we did seemed to be a step on the way to somewhere else. Something else. And we never really have known what."

"Safer for you that it should be so," John Rowlands said.

"And for them too, right?" said Simon.

John Rowlands gave his head a small wry shake that was like a shrug; smiled, and began re-lighting his pipe.

Jane said, "I don't think we shall be seeing Will and Bran here, Mr. Rowlands. They went away, somewhere. Safe. But . . . a long way away." She looked out at the estuary, where a few white sails tacked to and fro over the blue water. "I don't know for how long. An hour, a day. . . . They . . . they just went."

"Well," John Rowlands said, "we shall just have to wait and see. And I must dream up something to tell to Blodwen, because to this day I do not know whether she has any idea at all of what is in those two boys. I think not, really. She has a warm heart and a wise head, bless her, and she is content to be fond of them for what they seem to be."

A motor-boat whizzed past on the river behind them, almost drowning his voice. Somewhere the beat of rock music thumped insistently through the warm air; it rose and then retreated, as a group of people carrying a portable radio passed on the wharf. Looking over at the road, Jane saw Blodwen Rowlands emerge from the draper's shop and pause on the crowded pavement; then she was cut out of view, as a large motor-coach crept with difficulty down the village street.

John Rowlands sighed. "Look at it all," he said. "How it has changed, *Aberdyfi fach*. Of course that had to come, but I remember . . . I remember . . . in the old days, all the old fishermen used to be in a line over there, leaning on that rail in front of the Dovey Hotel, over the water. And when I was a lad about Barney's age one of my favourite things was to hang around and listen to them, when I was allowed. Lovely it was. They remembered so far back—a hundred years and more, it would be now. Back to the days when nearly all Aberdyfi men were sailors, my *taid*'s time, when the masts bristled thick as a forest along the wharf by here, loading up slate from the quarries. And there were seven yards building ships in the river, seven, building dozens of ships—schooners and brigs, and small boats too. . . ."

His deep Welsh voice made a threnody, recalling and mourning the lost days that even he had not seen, except through others' eyes. They listened in silence, fascinated, until the present sounds and sights of the crowded summer resort seemed to retreat, and they could almost imagine that they saw the tall ships coming into the river round the bar, and stacks of cut slate piled around them on a different wharf, built of black wood instead of concrete.

A seagull rose slowly into the air from the end of the jetty, crying out, slow and harsh and sorrowful, and Jane turned her head to follow the flap and sweep of its black-tipped wings. The breeze seemed to feel stronger than before against her cheek. The gull swung sideways past them, close, still crying. . . .

. . . and when Jane brought her gaze down again from watching it, she saw the wooden beams of the jetty black beneath her feet, stacked with rows of grey-blue slate, and beyond, on the river, a tall ship coming in close towards land, flapping and creaking as men hauled down her sails.

Jane stood motionless, staring. She heard laughter, and shrill voices, and milling round her on the jetty came a gaggle of small boys, pushing and hopping and thrusting one another aside in perilous clamour along the edge. "Firsties . . . firsties . . . get off my foot, Freddie Evans! . . . look out! . . . don't shove! . . ." They were a mixture, clean and grubby, barefoot and booted, and one of them, yellow-haired, bumping and laughing among the rest, was her brother Barney.

Jane could only think, ridiculously, *"But in those days they'd have been speaking Welsh. . . ."*

Further along the jetty she could see Simon talking earnestly in a group of two or three boys his own age. They turned to watch the ship draw gradually closer. With a snapping rush of canvas her mainsail came down in a heap, to be seized and furled; she was a brigantine, square-rigged on the foremast and fore-and-aft rigged on the main, and only two foresails now hung billowing to draw her inshore. Her figurehead glinted beneath the jutting bowsprit: a lifesize girl, with streaming golden hair. On the bow Jane could read the name now: *Frances Amelia.*

"Carrying timber," John Rowlands' deep voice said beside her. "See some of it stowed there on the deck? Mostly for John Jones the builder, that will be—he has been expecting it. A cargo of yellow pine, from Labrador."

Jane glanced at him; his face was tranquil, the pipe still clenched between his teeth. But on the hand that reached up to the pipe now there was tattooed between the knuckles a small blue star that she had not seen before, and at his throat he wore the wing collar and high-necked jacket of the nineteenth century. He had become someone else, belonging to this other time, and yet somehow was still himself as well. Jane shivered and closed her eyes for a moment, and did not look down to see how she herself was dressed.

Then there was a flurry and a sudden shriek from the edge of the jetty, where more and more people had gathered. Peering vainly past the heads, Jane could see only that the brigantine had begun to dock, lines flying down from bow and stern to be caught and made fast by darting figures ashore. From the end of the jetty where the small boys had gone running, there came out of a group of women a noisy scolding eruption, and all at once Barney and another boy, both very white in the face, were being dragged back towards Jane by a bustling distressed woman in bonnet and shawl. It was recognizably Blodwen Rowlands, yet a Blodwen Rowlands who did not seem to know Jane as Jane. She spoke to the world at large, scolding, yet in warm concern, "Always the same it is, this silly game to be the first to touch the ship that comes in, and all of them in the way there hindering the men. . . . One day one of them is going to get killed, and it was as near as a whistle for these two today, did you see them? Right on the edge, losing their balance, the side of the boat like to crush them against the jetty if there had been no one there to grab them out of it. . . . aah!" She gave each boy a little exasperated shake. "Have you forgotten last week, when Ellis Williams fell in?"

"And Freddie Evans the week before," said the boy with Barney, in a pert, lilting voice. "And much worse, that, because Evans the Barber was waiting for him with a strap when he got out, and beat him all the way home."

"*Mr.* Evans to you, young monkey," said Mrs. Rowlands, trying to suppress a smile. She gave Jane a little humorous shrug, released the boys with one finger wagging at them as she turned, and went back to the group of women greeting sailors on the ship.

"I like her," Barney said cheerfully. "She probably saved my life, you know that?" And he grinned at Jane and ran off with the other boy, disappearing along the road, behind the great stacks of slate.

Jane turned to call, but no sound came. Beside her, John Rowlands was shouting to one of the men aboard the *Frances Amelia.* "Iestyn! Iestyn Davies!"

"Evan boy!" the man called back, white teeth flashing. And even while the name puzzled her, Jane thought again of the strangeness that there was no Welsh to be heard, and then suddenly knew that of course all the speaking that she could hear was indeed in Welsh, her own included, with no word of English used anywhere at all.

"After all," she said shakily, knowing with no reason that Simon was now at her side, and turning to him, "it's no more odd to understand a language that you don't know, than to be switched into a time before you were born."

"No," Simon said, in a voice so reassuringly his own that Jane felt dissolved in relief. "No, not really odd at all."

John Rowlands called, beside them, "What news of the *Sarah Ellen?*"

The man stared. "You haven't heard?"

"A letter sent from Dublin was the last. It came yesterday."

The man on the *Frances Amelia* paused, put down the line he was coiling, called a few words to someone else on board, and leapt over the gunwale and down to the jetty. He came up to John Rowlands, his face lined with concern. "Bad news, Evan Rowlands, very bad. I am sorry. The *Sarah Ellen* foundered off Skye two days ago, with all hands. We heard yesterday."

"Oh my God," John Rowlands said. He put out a hand, gropingly, and clutched the man's arm for an instant; then turned and moved away, stumbling, as if he were suddenly old. His face was grey and hurt. Jane longed to go after him, but she could not move. How was it possible to comfort grief that was naked on a living face, and yet had been gone and forgotten for a hundred years? Which was more real: her own bewilderment, or Evan Rowlands' pain looking out of his grandson's eyes?

The man called Iestyn said, looking after John Rowlands,

"And his brother aboard." He looked round, at the two or three other men who had been standing near, and his face was grave. "Something is not good. That was the fourth boat built by John Jones Aberdyfi to go down in three months, and all of them new boats too. And it was not a great storm that took the *Sarah Ellen*, they say, but only a heavy following sea."

"They are all the same," one of the men said. "They dip the stern under. Every one of his vessels does it now, and then there is strain and the leaks come, and down she goes."

"Not every one," another man said.

"No, not every one, that is true. John Jones has built some very good boats indeed. But the bad ones. . . ."

"I have heard it suggested," said the man called Iestyn, "that it is not in the design but in the building. That it is not John Jones' fault at all, but one of his sawyers. And any work that he handles—"

He broke off, conscious suddenly of Jane's anxious stare, and switched on to his face a broad deliberate smile. "Waiting as usual, is it, like all the young ones, but too polite to ask?" He reached into one capacious jacket pocket and brought out a square package. "Here—put some in my pocket for the first of you who would come smiling and begging, I did. And for not asking at all you shall inherit it, little one."

"Thank you," said Jane, and for the second time that day startled herself by dropping a little bobbing curtsey. Folded in paper in her hands he had put four enormous wood-hard ship's biscuits.

"Off with you," said the man amiably. "Into the oven in a dish, covered with milk, isn't it, and a knob of butter on top, lovely. Lord knows it is good someone enjoys the hard biscuit the way you all do. Not so good halfway across the Atlantic, I can tell you. By then you would swap the lot for a good warm slice of *bara brith*."

The others laughed, and suddenly it was as if the last two words had turned a key back again to relock a door. For now they were speaking unintelligibly in Welsh together, and Jane knew that the difference was not in the language they used but in her own hearing of it. She had been able to understand it for a short enchanted while; now she could not. She clutched at Simon's unfamiliar stiff sleeve, and drew him away.

"What's happening?"

"I only wish I knew. There's no logic to it. Everything all mixed up."

"Where are we? And when? And why?"

"The why is the biggest."

"Let's go and find Barney."

"I know. All right." As they walked over the broad-spaced timbers to the street, Jane glanced sideways at her tall brother; somehow in the rough old-fashioned suit he seemed taller than ever, and more controlled. Had he changed too? *No*, she thought: *it's just that I wouldn't normally bother to think what he's like at all. . . .*

They were walking up the road, past little cottages gay with roses and snapdragon and sweet-smelling stock; past terraced houses far grander and newer looking than they had seemed in the days that were yet to come; past a resplendent coaching inn with its board hanging newly painted: *The Penhelig Arms.* Two men walking ahead of them greeted a stumpy sun-tanned figure standing in the doorway of the inn. "Good day, Captain Edwards."

Jane thought: *We are back in Welsh again. . . .*

"Good day."

"Did you hear about the *Sarah Ellen,* then?"

"I did," said Captain Edwards. "And I remembered what we spoke of, and I was thinking of paying a call upon John Jones." He paused. "And on one of his men, maybe."

"Perhaps we might go with you," one of the two men said, and as he turned Jane saw with a shock that it was John Rowlands again. She had not recognized him; not only the clothes were different, but the walk as well.

A sound of hammering came from somewhere below the road, down by the sea, and a high rhythmic screeching that Jane could not identify. At a cautious distance she and Simon followed the three men, to the edge of the road where it overlooked a flat yard just above the high-tide mark.

The shipyard was surprisingly simple: a couple of sheds,

with next to them a curious box-like structure, leaking threads of steam. It was perhaps two feet high and wide but very very long, dozens of feet long, and attached to it by a pipe was a big metal boiler. Nearby, the rough skeleton of a boat lay in a wooden cradle: a long keel branched by the bare oaken ribs to which only a few planks had as yet been set. Huge baulks of timber, the yellowish-white colour of pine, lay piled on the ground and beside them gaped a long deep pit, deeper than the height of a man, where sawyers cut the wood into planks. Jane stared, fascinated. A piece of timber lay lengthwise over each pit, supported on small logs set across; one man stood below it and another above, and between them they worked up and down a long saw, set in a frame, which produced the rhythmic shrieking she had heard from a distance. Two other sawyers worked in a similar pit close by. Others were shifting the timber, stacking planks, tending the steaming boiler, beneath which a fire burned so hot as to be almost invisible in the warm summer air.

A boy looked up and saw the three sailors, and gave a kind of salute; he ran to the sawyer working on top of one of the pits, shouting to be heard over the rasp of the saw.

"Captain Humphrey Edwards and Captain Ieuan Morgan, it is, and Captain Evan Rowlands, up aloft there."

The sawyer signalled to his partner, stilling the long blade before it came down again for the next cut. He stared up. Jane, peeping over the side of the rough rock-edged road, saw a pudgy face topped by astonishingly bright red hair; the man was scowling, with no sign of friendship or welcome.

"John Jones has gone to the wharf," the red-haired man called. "To see to a shipment of pine just come in." He bent down again, dismissively.

"Caradog Lewis," said the stumpy captain from the inn. He did not raise his voice, but even at normal pitch it was the kind of voice accustomed to being heard above a gale at sea.

The red-haired man jerked up petulantly, hands on hips. "There is work to do here, Humphrey Edwards, if you please."

"Aye," John Rowlands said. "It is your work we should like to talk to you about." He stepped over the low rocky wall and went down a flight of rough steps to the sawpits; the others followed him. So, a little later when no one was paying attention, did Simon and Jane.

"What boat is this you are working on, Caradog Lewis?" said Captain Edwards, looking thoughtfully at the graceful curving frame, all ribs and keel, standing skeletal on the stocks.

Lewis looked at him sourly, as if about to snarl, but seemed to change his mind. "She is the schooner *Courage,* for Elias Lewis. I should have thought you would have known that. Seventy-five feet, and a month overdue already. And over there—" he nodded at a half-rigged hull already launched, floating in the dock, "that is the *Jane Kate* for Captain Farr. They will be floating her spars over from Ynyslas tomorrow, and high time too."

"And you had a hand in both of them," John Rowlands said.

"Well of course, man," said Lewis irritably. "I am top sawyer for John Jones, isn't it."

"And no doubt responsible for much," said Captain Edwards, stroking his side-whiskers. "John Jones being a busy man, with a great many keels laid down on one another's tails these last few years."

"Well?"

"The *Integrity* was your work too?" John Rowlands said. "And the *Mary Rees?* And the *Eliza Davies?*" Each time Lewis nodded his red head impatiently. Rowlands went on, biting off his words like a child biting a biscuit. "And the *Charity?* And the *Sarah Ellen?*"

Lewis scowled. "You choose the ships of unfortunate men."

"Yes. I do indeed."

The sawyer and the other shipyard workers had put down their tools and came drifting close to listen; they stood in a group, restless, eyeing the captains resentfully.

"I have just heard about the *Sarah Ellen.*" Lewis shrugged, with shallow regret. "It is a pity, about your brother. But no new thing in this village."

"No new thing among the ships that you work on," Humphrey Edwards said.

Caradog Lewis's pale face flushed with anger, and Jane saw his hands tighten into fists. "Now look here—" he began.

"You look here to us, Caradog Lewis," said the third man, who had not spoken since they entered the yard. He was a small olive-skinned man with a fringe of grey beard. "Two of those boats I have watched at sea, keeping company on the Labrador run, and both had the same failing, and that none of John Jones' designing if I know him. Careless he is and a little greedy for work, so that he has not the time to supervise as those builders do who will not work on more than one keel at a time. But it is not his doing, for a boat to dig in her stern and founder in a following sea. That is the work of a man every time giving more length at the stern than there should be, and more than a few times letting planks go by that were steamed too quick and had cracks beginning."

A rumble of anger came from the listening workers.

The red-haired man was wet at the mouth with rage; he could scarcely speak. "Prove it, Ieuan Morgan!" he hissed. "Prove one small part of that! You think you can prove I have deliberately sent men to their deaths?"

"There must be some way to prove it," John Rowlands said, his voice grim and deep, "for true it is without a doubt. There is more in you than you show. We have been wondering a long time, we three, and now this loss of the *Sarah Ellen* is too much. And we are sure."

"Sure of what?"

"That you are . . . different, Caradog Lewis. With loyalties that are not like those of other men. Serving in some dreadful way a cause that is not that of men at all."

The words had such cold conviction in them that the men near Caradog Lewis shrank unconsciously away from him a little; and Lewis sensed it, and yelled at them in sudden fury so that they dived back at the nearest piece of work. But there was no fury in the way Caradog Lewis looked then at John Rowlands; there was instead an icy arrogant hatred that made Jane shiver, because she had seen it before, once, in a man dedicated to working the will of the Dark. Lewis, with his pasty face and his raw red hair, did not seem to be totally a creature of the Dark, but he was the more frightening as a result; such malice living without apparent reason in an ordinary man was something Jane could hardly bear to contemplate. She could sense anger rising in him like steam in a near-boiling kettle.

Lewis came slowly towards the three men, clear of his sawpit. He said tightly, "I am a man as you are, Evan Rowlands, and I will show you that I am." And all at once he seemed to erupt, flinging himself on John Rowlands, his face twisted horribly by snarling rage. Caught off-balance, Rowlands was thrown backwards in a rattling shower of grey slate, and Lewis was after him like a dog, arms flailing, smashing. The two other captains rushed to part them, but now the men from the shipyard had dropped their tools and come deliberately in the way, and there was suddenly a great melée on the ground. Stocky Captain Edwards knocked a man down, with a horrible click of teeth as his knuckles met the man's head; then he disappeared beneath a trio of others, and beside him, shouting and fighting, Ieuan Morgan hauled them away. Caradog Lewis, struggling with Rowlands, stumbled to his feet, gasping with malice, and reached for balance to kick with his hard-booted foot. Jane shrieked, and then Simon was past her in a flurry of arms and legs, clutching at Lewis, crying out as the toe of one heavy boot met his own shin.

Simon was never quite sure precisely what happened then. Fighting to drag Caradog Lewis away from John Rowlands' inert form, he found himself suddenly thrust down towards the sea in Lewis' grip, quite unable to resist. They splashed into the water together, still upright, still struggling, and suddenly Simon felt himself jerking outward, falling, falling, and the water closing cold over his head and no bottom to be felt with his feet beneath the sea. One brief touch of the sand he had with one foot, and then the water was swinging him round, a current catching him, pulling him deeper, deeper, alone. He reached up for air, kicking desperately; caught one breath; was swung around again by an eddy, reached out in frantic efforts to swim, his arms and legs heavy with the weight of the old-fashioned suit. There was a roaring in his ears, a blurring in his eyes; the water whirled him round and around.

Simon fought to keep back panic. He had a secret and terrible fear of deep water, even though he could swim well; three years earlier in a dinghy race on the Thames he had fallen from a capsizing boat and come up underneath the floating mainsail, kept down from the air like a cork in sealed jar. He had panicked then, splashing wildly, only by pure chance reaching the edge of the sail, and then in a desperate gurgling flurry the shore. Now he could feel the same panic rising again in his throat and mind; rising like the waves that whirled him about with only an occasional snatch of breath; rising to blur his brain, to swamp out all thought—

He thrust it away. He fought and fought; fought to keep in his mind the feel of each arm, each leg; to move as he chose to move, to seek the rhythm of swimming instead of the mindless flurrying of horror and despair. So by great effort, he kept from panic.

But still the water was there all around, less violent now, cradling him, and again he was going down. Water pressed in on him, it was in his ears and his eyes and his nose. Now it seemed not frightening but lulling, mothering, as if it were not after all alien, but his own element. It welcomed him, gently, as if he quite naturally breathed water, like a fish. Gentle, gentle, all-enveloping, relaxing, like the feeling of the moment before falling gradually asleep. . . .

Something, someone, seized Simon from behind in a fierce grip, two strong hands on his shoulders, pushing him upward, upward and out into bright air. Light cut into his eyes. Water bit the back of his throat. He gasped, retching, choking. The water swished in his lungs with each gurgling snatch at breath. Simon heard terrible frantic bubbling gasps and realized appalled that he was making them himself.

Then there was solid sand beneath his feet. The swimmer released him. Simon stumbled forward on to his hands and knees, and strong hands laid him on the beach, turned his head sideways and pressed down on his back. Water poured from his nose and mouth; he coughed, retching. The hands gently helped him to sit up. Simon sat with his head on his knees, breathing at last without the dreadful gurgling, without gasping, more slowly. He brushed his wet hair from his eyes, sniffing, and looked up.

First he saw Jane, wide-eyed, white-faced, crouching. Beside her a man was bent on one knee, his great height apparent even while stooped. His dark clothes dripped water. The face frowning in concern into Simon's was angular and craggy, dark eyes shadowed in deep sockets, bristling white eyebrows dripping water down the sides of the beak-like nose. The thick white hair, grey with wetness, lay in a tangle of loops and horns all over his head.

Simon said, in a high weak husky voice that was not his own, "Oh Gumerry."

He stopped, feeling a prickling in his eyes. He had not used that pet name for a long time.

"That was brave," Merriman said.

He pressed one hand on Simon's shoulder, and glanced up at Jane, beckoning her closer. Then he stood up. Jane put a diffident arm round Simon's shoulder, to help as he turned to watch.

John Rowlands was standing close by on the beach, dripping from head and clothes. Jane said in Simon's ear, "He jumped in the sea after you, trying to reach you, when—" her voice seemed to dry into nothing; she swallowed—"when Great-Uncle Merry just . . . just came *up*, out of nowhere."

Merriman loomed before them, angular in his wetness, tall as a tree. Before him on the beach, the men of the shipyard stood motionless in a group, with the two grey-whiskered captains angry and silent nearby. Caradog Lewis stood in the midst of the shipwrights, red hair gleaming. He was staring at Merriman transfixed, like some small animal caught in mid-stride by an angry badger or a fox.

And the anger in Merriman's eyes as he looked at the red-haired man was of such depth that both Simon and Jane, watching, shrank from it. Caradog Lewis moved slowly back, cringing, seeking escape. Then Merriman reached out one arm with the first finger stiff, pointing, and the man froze, pinned into stillness once more.

"Go," Merriman said softly, in his deep voice like black velvet. "Go, you who have sold yourself to the Dark, back from this bright Aberdyfi of the river to Dinas Mawddwy where you came from. Go back to where the Dark lurks in the hills round Cader Idris in the realm of the Grey King, where others wait in black hope like yourself. But remember that since you have failed in this attempt here, your masters now will have no time for you. So beware after this, in years to come, that you keep your sons and your daughters, and the sons of your daughters, away from any trifling with the Dark. For the Dark in its vengefulness will surely destroy any one of them that it can take into its power."

Without a word Caradog Lewis turned and walked away over the crackling grey slate, up the rough steps and away along the road, until they could no longer see him. Merriman looked at Simon and Jane; then he turned towards the sea, past the silent men and the shipyard huts and the half-built ship, and in a strange gentle gesture he opened his arms wide, like a man stretched on waking, looking up at the sky.

And out of nowhere a seagull came swooping past, low over the water, harshly crying. Their eyes followed it . . . followed. . . .

. . . and when it rose again out of sight suddenly they found that they were dressed once more in the jeans and shirts of their own time, standing on a narrow slatey beach a few feet below the level of the iron-railed pavement, alone with John Rowlands and Merriman. In Simon's right hand was a piece of flat slate; his first finger was curled round it as if for throwing. He looked down at it, shrugged, bent, and skimmed it over the surface of the water. It bounced impressively in a long skipping trail.

"Eight!" Simon said.

"You always win," said Jane.

Their clothes were dry; only Jane's hair was damp still, from the rains of the morning. There was nothing to show that Simon, Merriman and John Rowlands had ever been in the sea. Jane peeped at John Rowlands as he stood there blinking in perplexity, and she knew that he did not remember anything. He looked about, dazed; then he caught sight of Merriman and became very still. He stared at him for a long moment.

"*Daro,*" he said at last, huskily. "What is this? You. You! I have never forgotten you, from when I was a boy. Do you remember? *Is* it you?"

Jane and Simon stood listening, puzzled.

"You were Will's age then," said Merriman, looking at him with half a smile. "Up on your mountain. And you saw me . . . riding."

John Rowlands said slowly, "Riding on the wind."

"Riding on the wind. I wondered, after that, if you would remember. There was no harm in it, if you did—who would have believed you? But I put it into your mind that you had dreamed it, to leave you at rest."

"And indeed I did think that I had dreamed it, until this moment that I see the same face again, unchanged after so long. And wonder why it is here." John Rowlands turned his head and looked at Simon and Jane. "This is Will's master, is it not? And known to you as well."

Simon said automatically, "Great-Uncle Merry."

John Rowlands' voice rose, incredulous. "*Your great-uncle?*"

"A name," Merriman said. His eyes clouded; he looked away over the estuary at the sea. "I must go. Will needs me. As the Dark knew, Simon, when it caught you in peril in a time from which only I could ransom you, by leaving the place where I was."

"Are they all right?" Simon said.

"They will be, if all goes well."

Jane said anxiously, "What can we do?"

"Be on the beach at sunrise. Your beach," Merriman said. He looked at her with an odd strained smile, and pointed up the road. "And take your small brother home to tea."

Turning, they saw Barney's yellow-haired figure prancing towards them down the road, with Blodwen Rowlands in his wake; and when they turned back again to the beach and the sea, Merriman was not there.

PART THREE
THE LOST LAND

CHAPTER NINE

THE CITY

DOWN THROUGH the bright haze the strange road brought them, arching like a rainbow. Will and Bran found that they made no move of their own. Once they had stepped on to its surface, the road took them up, took them through space and through time with a motion they could not afterwards describe. Then out of that brightness they were down in the Lost Land, and the road was gone, and all else vanished from their minds as they looked up at the place where they were.

They stood high up, on a golden roof, behind a low lattice of wrought gold. Behind them, and at either side, stretched the roofs of a great city, gleaming, spires and towers and turrets crowding the skyline, some golden as the place where they stood, some dark as black flint. The city was very quiet. This seemed to be early morning, cool and silent. Before them, as far as they could see, a luminous white mist lapped round the broad-topped trees of a park. Dew glistened on the trees. Somewhere, beyond the park, the sun was rising into a haze of cloud.

Will gazed out at the trees. They were not packed close together in the random clusters of the wild, but well-spaced, each broad and proud and full; they rose out of the mist like glimmering green islands in a grey-white sea. He saw oak and beech and chestnut and elm; the shapes were as familiar as the buildings around him were strange.

Bran said softly, at his side, "Look!"

He was pointing past Will's back. Turning, Will saw among the peaks and ridges of the roofs a great golden dome, topped with a gold arrow pointing westward to the blue horizon-line of the sea. The sides of the dome caught the early sun, glittering; he realized that they were banded, up and down, with panels of crystal running between strips of gold.

Bran peered, cupping his hands around his smoky glasses. "Is it a church?"

"Could be. Looks a bit like St. Paul's."

"Or one of those Arab whatsits. Mosques."

They spoke in whispers, by instinct. The place was so quiet. Nothing anywhere broke the silence of the city, except once, for a few seconds, somewhere far off among the tops of the trees, a seagull's plaintive cry.

Will looked down at his feet. The roof on which they stood seemed to enclose them, its latticework of wrought gold stretching all round like a fence. He reached out. The top bar would not move. It was perhaps half his height; he thought of climbing over, but changed his mind at the sight of the sheer drop, twenty feet down to the next roof, on the other side.

Bran too reached out and took hold of the lattice in front of him; then suddenly he gasped. Beneath his touch, the whole criss-cross panel moved; swung free, balanced on a lower bar, then dropped down from his hands over the edge of the roof, lengthening in hinged sections as it fell, like a folded ladder opening.

"Clang! . . . clang! . . . clang! . . . clang! . . ." The metallic sounds rang out over the roofs, cracking the silence, ending in a resonant crash as the final section of the ladder-like golden framework hit the roof below. All over the silent city the echoes rose like birds.

Will and Bran stared about them, watching for movement, for the waking of someone, somewhere, that such a clattering must surely bring. But there was nothing.

"Dozy place, isn't it?" said Bran, a small shake in his voice beneath the bravado; and with Will following close after, he swung himself over the edge and clambered down the ladder of gold.

They stood now on a broad lower roof, slanting more gently downward, crossed with raised strips of some darker metal that served as ridges down which they could walk. At the bottom edge of this roof, expecting to find themselves over a perpendicular wall, they found instead a great sweeping stairway of grey stone, with the glitter of granite, stretching down, down from the very rim of the roof, far down into the mist and the trees.

Together they ran down the steps, keeping close, and as they ran, the mist below them faded into nothing, falling back so that the trees stood clear over a sweep of green grass. And they saw at the bottom of the stone steps, waiting, two horses standing saddled and bridled; untethered, with the reins laid loose over their necks. They were beautiful gleaming animals, lion-coloured, their long manes and tails yellow-white against the golden hide. The bits between their teeth, and their stirrups, were of silver, and the reins were red plaited silk. Will went up to the first and laid a wondering hand on its neck, and the horse blew softly through its nose and ducked its head as if inviting him to mount.

Bran said, gazing bemused at the horses, "Can you ride, Will?"

"Not really," Will said. "But I don't think that will matter." And he put one foot in the horse's stirrup and without sound or effort he was up on its back, smiling down, gathering up the reins. The second horse pawed the ground, and nudged gently at Bran's shoulder with its nose.

"Come on, Bran," Will said. "They've been waiting for us." He sat there, self-possessed as a huntsman, a small stocky figure in blue jeans and sweater on the tall golden horse, and Bran shook his head in wonder and reached for the saddle-bow. He was up, mounted, before he had a chance to think about it. The horse tossed its head and Bran caught the reins as they fell towards him.

"All right," said Will gently to his horse, stroking its white mane. "Take us where we should go. Please?" And the two horses moved off together, unhurried, confident, walking the stone-paved street at the base of the long sweep of rising stone steps.

The trees of the broad green park towered over them at one side, shading the road, lush and dew-flecked and cool. Sunlight lay on the grass between them in bright pools, but there was no sound. No birds sang. Only the clop-clop of the horses' hooves rang through the quiet city, changing to a hollower, deeper sound as the two golden horses turned abruptly away from the park and into a narrow side street. Great grey walls loomed up on either side, huge blank expanses of grey stone, without a window anywhere.

The street grew narrower, darker. Without altering their steady pace the horses went on between the towering walls, while Will and Bran sat loosely holding the reins and glancing nervously about.

They turned a corner. Still the high blank walls enclosed them, in a narrow alley, with the sky no more than a thin blue strip overhead. But this time they could see a small wooden door set into the wall at their right, and when they drew level with this door both animals stopped, and began tossing their heads and pawing at the ground. Will's horse shook its head from side to side, so that the silver harness musically rang and the long mane rippled and flowed like white-gold silk.

"All right," Will said. He dismounted; so did Bran. As soon as their riders were on the ground, the two horses turned without hurry in a brief confusion of clopping hooves and jingling harness, and together they trotted up the alley, back the way that they had come. Their bright loose tails swung like torches in the shadowy street.

"Beautiful!" Bran said softly, watching the golden shapes disappear.

Will was standing before the door, studying its plain wooden surface. It was dark and pitted as if by age. Absently he thrust his thumbs into his leather belt, and one of them met the curve of the small brass horn that he had blown on the mountain, in another life and another world. Unhooking the horn from his belt, he held it towards Bran.

"We've got to stay close together, whatever happens. You keep hold of one side of this and I'll take the other. That'll help."

Bran nodded his white head and slipped the fingers of his left hand through the single loop of the horn. Will looked again at the door. It had no handle, no bell, no lock or keyhole; no means at all of opening it that he could see.

He raised one hand and knocked, firmly.

The door swung outward. There was no one on the other side. Peering, they could see nothing within but darkness. Each gripping one side of the little hunting-horn as if it were a lifebelt, they went in, and behind them the door swung shut.

A glimmer of light from somewhere, untraceable, showed them they were in a narrow corridor, low-roofed, ending a few yards ahead where a ladder rose upwards out of sight.

Will said slowly, "I suppose we go up there."

"Is that safe?" Bran's voice was husky with uncertainty.

"Well, it's all we can do, isn't it? And somehow nothing seems to be telling me not to. You know?"

"That's true. It doesn't feel . . . bad. Mind you it doesn't feel too good either."

Will laughed softly. "That's going to be the same everywhere here. The Dark has no power in this land, I think—but nor does the Light."

"Then who has?"

"I suppose we shall find that out." Will took a firm grip on the horn. "Keep hold. Even if it'll be awkward climbing up there."

They went up the broad-runged ladder, one close after the other, still linked by their talisman, and emerged into an area so totally unexpected that for a few moments they both stood there motionless, looking.

They had come up through an open trapdoor, close to one end of a long gallery. The floor stretched before them in curious sections, one after the other, on differing levels, so that one might be higher than the one before, and the next lower than either. The place seemed to be a kind of library. Heavy square tables and chairs filled it, separated by low stacks of bookshelves, and the wall on their left was covered entirely with books. The ceiling was wood-panelled. The right-hand wall was not there.

Will stared, but could not understand. At his right, in this long room, a kind of carved wooden balustrade ran all the length of the floor. But no wall was beyond it, nor anything else visible: only blackness. Blank dark. There was no sense of an emptiness, or a perilous void. There was simply nothing.

Then he saw movement in the room. The first people they had seen in this land were appearing, through a door at the far end of the long gallery; drifting, singly, men and women of all ages, dressed in a variety of simple clothes that seemed to belong to no particular age. There were not many of them. One by one, each figure silently settled, collecting a pile of books from the shelves and sitting down with them at a table, or standing browsing over a single book. Not one of them paid the smallest attention to Will or Bran. One man came up close beside them and stood frowning at the shelves lining the wall at their backs.

Will said to him, greatly daring, "Can't you find it?" But the man made no sign of noticing. His face lightened suddenly; he reached out and took a book, and went back with it to sit down at a table nearby. Will peered at the title of the book as he went past, but it was written on the cover in a language he could not understand. And when the man opened the book, its pages were quite blank.

Bran said slowly, "They can't see us."

"No. Nor hear us. Come on."

They walked carefully together up the long gallery, skirting intent seated figures, cautious not to trip or nudge. Nobody gave any flicker of notice as they passed. And whenever they looked down at a book·that a man or woman was reading, they found that its pages seemed to bear no writing at all.

There was no real door at the far end of the gallery, but instead an opening in the panelled wall, from which a strange corridor led. This too was entirely panelled in wood; it was more like a square tunnel than a corridor, slanting down at a steep angle, turning corners in a zig-zag pattern, to and fro. Bran followed Will without question; he said only, once, with sudden helpless force, "This place doesn't *mean* anything."

"It will, when we arrive," Will said.

"Arrive at what?"

"Well—at the meaning! At the crystal sword. . . ."

"Look! What's that?"

Bran had stopped, head up, wary. Ahead of them as they turned a corner, the last section of the zig-zag slope was white and glaring, filled with strong light blazing in from whatever lay beyond. For an instant Will had a dreadful sense that they were descending into some great pit of fire. But this was a cold light, fierce without brilliance. He turned the last corner, stepping into the full light, and a strong resonant voice said ahead of him out of the brightness, "Welcome!"

A great empty expanse of floor stretched before them, its walls lost in shadow, its roof too high to be seen. In the middle of the space stood a single figure, dressed all in black. He was a smallish man, not much taller than themselves, with a strong-featured face creased by humour at the eyes and mouth, though with no sign of a smile now. The hair of his head was grey, tight-curled as a mat, and he had a neat, crisp curling grey beard with a curious dark line down the centre like a stripe. He spread both arms and turned a little, as if offering them the space around him. "Welcome," he said again. "Welcome to the City."

They stood together before him. Bran took a step forward, letting go the horn. He said, "Is there only the City, in the Lost Land?"

"No," the man said. "There is the City, and the Country, and the Castle. And you shall see all of them, but first you must tell us why you have come." His voice was warm and ringing, but there was still wariness in it, and still he did not smile. He was looking at Will. "Why have you come?" he said again. "Tell us."

As he spoke he made a small motion with one open hand toward 'he space before him. Will looked, and gasped. His head sang with shock; all at once he was very cold.

Out there, in a vast space that had been darkness a second before, stretched a huge crowd of blank upturned faces, row upon row, thousands of people. In tiers, in endless galleries they sat, staring at him. Their awareness pressed down on him like an unbearable weight, paralyzing his mind; it was like facing the whole world.

Will clenched his fists, and felt the cool metal of the hunting-horn still against his fingers. Taking a deep slow breath, he said in a loud clear voice, "We have come for the crystal sword."

And they laughed.

It was not tolerant, friendly laugher; it was horrible. A deep roar rose from the vast audience there, swelling like long thunder, mocking, jeering, breaking over him in a wave of contempt. He could see individuals, pointing, mouths wide with scornful mirth. The ocean of their loud mockery engulfed him so that he trembled, and knew himself to be small, insignificant, dwindling down. . . .

Bran's voice, beside him, shouted furiously into the uproar, *"We have come for Eirias!"*

All sound vanished, as totally as if someone had turned a switch. In an instant, all the jeering faces were gone.

Will drooped suddenly, hearing his tight-held breath go out in a small weak gasp.

Bran said again, wonderingly, to himself, "We have come for . . . Eirias." He seemed to be tasting the name.

The man with the grey beard said softly, "You have, indeed." He stepped forward, hands outspread. Taking each of them by the shoulder he turned them to face the black emptiness where the endless rows of faces had been.

He said, "There is nobody there. No one, nothing. Nothing but space. They were all . . . an appearance. But look up. Look up, behind you. And there you shall see—"

Automatically they turned; and stood, staring. Over their heads, like a balcony suspended in the air, was the bright-lit gallery through which they had walked among the unheeding reading people. Everything was there, the books, the shelves, the heavy tables. The readers still moved idly to and fro, or stood gazing at the shelves. And the space through which they were looking into the room was the fourth wall which had seemed not to be there.

Will said, "This place is a theatre come to life."

The man fingered the point of his beard, pushing it forward with one finger. "All life is theatre," he said. "We are all actors, you and I, in a play which nobody wrote and which nobody will see. We have no audience but ourselves. . . ." He laughed gently. "Some players would say that is the best kind of theatre there can be."

Bran smiled in response, a small rueful smile. But Will was still listening to a single word echoing inside his head. He said to Bran, "Eirias?"

"I didn't know," Bran said. "It just . . . came. It's a Welsh word. It means a big fire, a blaze."

"And the crystal sword blazes indeed," said the bearded man. "Or so they tell, for few living have ever seen it, within memory here."

"But we must find it," Will said.

"Yes," the man said. "I know why you are here. When you are asked questions in this land, it is not for our want of the answers. I know who you are, Will Stanton, Bran Davies. Perhaps even better"—he looked hard for an instant at Bran—"than you know yourselves. And as for me, you will know me soon. You may call me Gwion. And I shall show you the City."

"The Lost Land," Bran said, half to himself.

"Yes," said the man called Gwion. He was a lean, neat figure in his black clothes; his beard glinted in the bright light from overhead. "The Lost Land. And as I said to you, there lie within it the City, and the Country, and the Castle. And the Castle is where you must go, in the end, but you cannot get there except by way of the rest. So here you will begin, within the City, my City which I greatly love. You must take good note of it, for it is one of the wonders of the world that will not come again."

He smiled at them, a brilliant sudden smile that lit his face with warmth and affection, and lit their own spirits simply by looking.

"See!" he said, swinging round, opening his arms to the back of the space that was like a stage. And the bright-lit gallery overhead disappeared, and the light grew diffuse, glowing all around, and suddenly they found they were in a great open city square. It was edged by pillared grey-white buildings gleaming in the sunlight, filled with people and music and the calls of traders at bright-coloured stalls, and the sparkle and splash of water flung high by fountains.

The sun was warm on their faces. Will felt delight rushing through him as if the blood in his veins were dancing, and he looked at Bran and saw the same joy shining in his face.

Laughing at them, Gwion drew them across the square, through the crowd, among the people of the Lost Land.

CHAPTER TEN

THE ROSE-GARDEN

FACES FLASHED round them like a kaleidoscope's shaken images. A child swung a handful of bright streamers before their eyes, laughing, and was gone; a hopeful flurry of green-necked pigeons swooped by. They passed a group of people dancing, where a tall man decked with red ribbons played the flute, a gay, catchy little tune; they stumbled, almost, at a place on the smooth grey paving, over a fragile crumpled-looking old man who was drawing with chalks on the ground. Will had a sudden startled glimpse of the picture, a great green tree on a rounded hill, with a bright light shining out of its branches, before the flute-player led the dancers past him in a flurry of music, and he was whirled away.

Gwion's bearded face was still there in the crowd, moving beside him. "Stay close!" he called. But Will noticed now that no other eyes than Gwion's ever met their own in this crowd. The people all around seemed able to see him now, and glanced as they would glance at any other passerby, instead of turning a blind unwitting face to someone who was, for them, not there. Yet nobody properly looked at him, or at Bran; there was no recognition, no glimmer of the interest they showed in one another. He thought: we have come a little way along—we are *here* now, but only just. Perhaps they will really see us, later on, if we do well at whatever it is we are expected to do. . . .

Laughter swelled in the crowded square, from a circle of grinning faces watching a juggler. Marvelous smells wafted past from stalls selling food. A fine spray caressed Will's face, and he saw the glittering drops of a fountain, tossed in a diamond stream up to the sun and down again. He saw Bran in front of him, pale face alight behind the dark lenses, laughing as he shouted something to Gwion. Then there was a stir in the crowd, heads turning; bodies pressed back against Will. He heard the hooves of horses, the jingling of harness, a creaking and a rumbling of wheels; through the heads of the crowd he could glimpse riders bobbing by, bareheaded, dressed in blue. The rumbling grew; he could see a coach now, its roof dark blue and splendidly curlicued in gold, and blue plumes tossing before it from the foreheads of tall midnight-black horses.

Hoofbeats slowed, wheels squeaked on the stone street; the coach stopped, rocking gently to and fro. Gwion was close again, drawing Will and Bran forward. The crowd parted easily, respectfully, each one making way instantly at the sight of Gwion's erect grey head. Then the coach was before them, suddenly enormous, like a shining blue ship swaying there on strong leather straps hung from a high-wheeled curved frame. A crest was engraved in gold on the glossy door, higher than Will's head. The black horses stamped and blew. There was no coachman to be seen.

Gwion opened the coach door and, reaching inside, swung down a step for mounting.

"Come, Will," he said.

Will looked up, uncertain. Shadows hid the inside of the coach.

"No harm," Gwion said. "Trust your instinct, Old One."

Will looked sharply, curiously, at the smile-creased eyes in the strong face. He said, "Do you come too?"

"Not yet," Gwion said. "You and Bran, at first."

He helped them up, and shut the door. Will sat looking out. Around Gwion the crowd eddied and chattered once more, beginning to resume its own affairs, patchwork-bright in the sunshine. The coach, inside, was cool and dim-lit, with deep padded benches, leather-smelling. A horse whinnied; hooves clattered, and the coach began to move.

Will sat back, looking at Bran. The white-haired boy pulled off his glasses and grinned at him.

"First horses, then a coach-and-four. What'll they offer us next, then? Think they'll have a Rolls-Royce?" But he was not listening to himself; he blinked at the buildings moving past the windows, and propped the dark glasses back on his nose.

"A great bird," Will said softly. "Or a griffon, or a basilisk." He too looked out again at the brightness, moving with the jolting sway of the leather-slung coach. Few people were to be seen here. They were moving along a broad street lined by curving arcades of houses that seemed to him startlingly beautiful, with their clear lines and arched doors and wide-set, even windows, and walls of warm golden stone. It had never really occurred to him to think of buildings as beautiful before.

Bran said haltingly, speaking the same thought, "It's such a . . . well-made place."

"Everything the right shape," Will said.

"That's right. I mean, look at that!" Bran leaned forward, pointing. Set among the houses was the high curving entrance to a magnificent pillared courtyard. But the coach had passed before they could see what lay inside.

The world seemed to dim a little; Will saw that the sunlight was gone. They sat swaying in the coach, hoofbeats loud in their ears. Still the light seemed to die.

Will frowned. "Is it getting dark?"

"Must be clouds." Bran stood, braced between seats, and gazed out, clutching the door. "Yes, there are. Big grey clouds, up there. Looks like a real summer storm cooking up." Then his voice rose a little. "Will—there were riders dressed in blue in front of us, weren't there?"

"That's right. Like in a procession."

"No one there now. Nothing ahead. But something . . . following."

The tightness in his voice brought Will jerking to his feet, to peer out past the white head. Outside their rocking small space the broad street had grown so murky now that it was hard to see clearly; a dark group of figures seemed to be moving behind them, keeping the same speed, coming a little closer perhaps. He thought he could hear other hoofbeats behind the clatter of their own. Then instinct struck at him and his hand tightened on the window-frame: something was coming, something back there, of which he should be afraid.

"What's the matter?" Bran said; and gasped, as a sudden lurch sent him sprawling back onto the seat of the coach. Will staggered back, dropping beside him. The noise of the coach grew, jingling, thundering; they were flung to and fro, from side to side, as the coach pitched and tossed like a boat on an angry sea.

Bran yelled, "We're going too fast!"

"The horses are frightened!"

"What of?"

"Of . . . of . . . back there." Words would not come; Will's throat was dry. Bran's white face danced before him; the Welsh boy had pulled off the sheltering glasses again in the gloom, and there was fear in his strange tawny eyes. Then the eyes widened; Bran clutched Will's arm.

Outside, a flurry of dark figures came whirling past, on either side; horses furiously galloping, manes and tails flying on the wind, and dark cloaks streaming out behind the figures of hooded men riding. Here and there one figure was white-cloaked among the dark mass. They saw no faces inside the hoods. Nothing but shadow. There was no telling whether any faces were there to be seen.

But one figure, taller, came galloping past to the window of the flying coach, swaying out there in the grey half-light. The head turned towards them. Will heard Bran's stifled gasp.

The head tossed, flicking back the side of the flowing hood. And there was a face: a face which Will recognized with dread as it stared at him, filled with hatred and malevolence, bright blue eyes burning into his own.

Will heard a husky croak that was his own voice.
"Rider!"

White teeth flashed in the face, in a dreadful mirthless smile, and then the hood fell back. The cloaked figure leaned forward, urging on its horse, and vanished ahead of them into the dark mass of riding shadows. Hoofbeats thickened the air, beat at their hearing; then began to fade.

The world seemed to grow a little less dark, the frantic tossing of the coach to slow gradually down.

Bran was staring at Will, rigid. *"Who was that?"*

Will said emptily, "The Rider, the Black Rider, one of the great Lords of the Dark—" Suddenly he sat straight, fierce-eyed. "We mustn't let him go, now he's seen us, we must follow him!" His voice rose, shrill and demanding, calling as if to the whole coach, as if it were a live thing. "Follow! Follow him! Follow!"

The coach lurched faster again, the noise grew, the horses flung themselves frantically forward. Bran grabbed for support. "Will, you're mad! What are you doing? Follow . . . *that?"* His horror brought the word out in a half-shriek.

Will crouched in a swaying corner, his face set. "We must . . . we have to know. . . . Hold on. Hold on. *He* makes the terror, by his riding—if we chase, it grows less. Hold tight, wait and see. . . .

They were moving fast now, but without the wildness of panic. The horses kept up a steady strong gallop, swinging the coach like a child's toy on a string. The light grew and grew as if no cloud were anywhere near, and soon sunlight was shafting in again at them through the open windows. Arched stone buildings still edged one side of the broad street, but on the other side now they saw tall trees and smooth grass, stretching into a green distance; paths and gravelled walks criss-crossed the sweep of the grass, here and there.

"It must be . . . that park." Bran's voice swung in gulps between one bounce and the next. "The one we saw . . . at the beginning . . . from the roof."

"Perhaps it is. Look!"

Will pointed; ahead, two riders had turned from the road and were cantering, without apparent haste now, down one of the small roads across the park. A strange pair they made, two ritualistic figures like images from a chessboard: a rider in black hood and cloak on a coal-black horse, a rider in white hood and cloak on a horse white as snow.

"Follow!" Will called.

Bran peered back up the long empty sweep of the road as they turned from it. "But there were so many—like a big dark cloud. Where did they go?"

"Where the leaves go in autumn," Will said.

Bran looked at him and seemed suddenly to relax; he grinned. "There's poetic, now."

Will laughed. "It's true. Of course, the trouble with leaves is, they grow again. . . ."

But his attention was on the two tall riding figures starkly outlined ahead against the soft green of the park. In a few moments the White Rider, as he felt he must call him, dropped aside and trotted quietly away. The coach went on, following the black upright form of the other.

Bran said, "Why should some of the Riders of the Dark be dressed all in white and the rest all in black?"

"Without colour. . . ." Will said reflectively. "I don't know. Maybe because the Dark can only reach people at extremes—blinded by their own shining ideas, or locked up in the darkness of their own heads."

The wheels made a crunching sound on the path. They began to see formally patterned flowerbeds laid out at either side, with white stone seats set between them, and here and there people sitting on the seats, or strolling, or children playing. Not one of these gave more than a brief glance of mild interest at the Black Rider stalking ahead on his tall black horse, or the plumed stallions pulling the swaying blue coach with its gold-crested door.

Bran watched one old man glance up, look at the coach, and turn back at once to his book. "They can see us, now. But they seem . . . they don't *care*."

"Maybe they will, later," Will said. The coach stopped.

He opened the door, pushing the step down with his foot. They jumped down to the crunching gravel of the white path; then, as they saw what was all around them, both paused, held for a moment by delight.

The air was heavy with fragrance, and everywhere there were roses. Squares, triangles, circles of bright blossom patched the grass all around, red and yellow and white and all colours between. Before them was the entrance to an enclosed circular garden, a tall arch in a high hedge of tumbling red roses. They walked through, almost giddy with the scent. In the great circle of the garden inside, formal balustrades and seats of white marble were set round a glittering fountain where three white dolphins endlessly leapt, spouting a high triple spray of tasselled drops with a faint arching rainbow caught over all by the sun. And as if to offset the cool lines of the marble, mounds of roses billowed everywhere, enormous bushes growing rampant, tall as trees.

Before one of the largest shrubs, a spreading sweetbriar with small pink flowers and a fragrance wafting from it sweet as apples, there stood like a black brand the figure of the Rider on his tall dark horse.

Will and Bran drew level with the fountain and paused, facing the man and horse a little way off. The black horse side-stepped, stamping, restless; the Rider twitched sharply at his rein. He put back his hood a little way, and Will saw the fierce, handsome face that he had seen earlier in his life, and a glint of the red-brown hair.

"Well, Will Stanton," said the Rider softly. "It is a long road from the valley of the Thames to the Lost Land."

Will said, "And a long road from the ends of the earth, to which the Wild Hunt harried the Dark."

A grimace like pain flicked over the Rider's face; he turned his head a little so that it was shadowed by the hood, though not quickly enough to hide a dreadful scar across all his further cheek. But the turning was brief; in another instant he was erect again, his back a straight proud line.

"That was one victory for the Light, but one only," he said coldly. "There will be no other. We have reached our last rising, Old One; we are at the flood. You have no way of stopping us now."

"One way," Will said. "Just one."

The Rider turned his bright blue eyes from Will to Bran. He said formally, almost chanting, "The sword has not the power of the Pendragon until it is in his hand, nor does the Pendragon exist in his own right until his hand is on the sword." The blue eyes shifted back to Will, and the Rider smiled, but the eyes stayed cold as ice. "We are before you, Will Stanton. We have been here since first this land was lost, and you may try as you will to take Eirias the sword from the hand that holds it now, but you will not succeed. For that hand is ours."

Will could feel Bran turn to him in quick baffled concern, but he did not look at him; he was studying the Rider. The confidence in the man's face and bearing was immense, seeming a total arrogance, and yet something in Will's instincts told him that it was not altogether complete. Somewhere vulnerability lay; somewhere there was a crack, a tiny crack, in the Dark's certainty of triumph. And in that crack was the only hope the Light had left, now, to check the rising of the Dark.

He said nothing, but stared at the Rider for a long time, steadily, holding his gaze, until at last the blue eyes flickered briefly aside like the eyes of an animal. Then he knew that he was right.

The Rider said lightly, to cover the movement, "You would do well to forget the foolishness of pursuing impossible ends, while you are here, and instead enjoy the wonders of the Lost Land. There is none here to help the Dark, and equally there is none here to help you. But there is much to enjoy."

The black horse shifted restlessly, and he twitched at the rein, turning the horse a few steps towards a climbing rose brilliant with enormous buds and full, down-curved yellow flowers.

With an assured, almost affected gesture the Rider bent and broke off one yellow rose and sniffed it. "Such flowers, now. Roses of all the centuries. *Maréchal Niel*, here, never such a scent anywhere . . . or that strange tall rose beside you with the small red flowers, called *moyesii*, that goes its own way. Sometimes blooming more heavily than any other rose and then perhaps for years not blooming at all."

"Roses are hard to predict, my lord," a voice said easily, conversationally; then a small edge came into it. "And so are the people of the Lost Land."

And Gwion was there, suddenly, a neat dark figure standing beside the fountain. They could not see where he came from; it was as if he stepped out of the rainbow floating over the glittering drops.

The Rider's horse stepped uneasily once again; he had difficulty stilling it. He said coldly, "A hard fate will come to you, minstrel, if you give aid to the Light."

"My fate is my own," Gwion said.

The black stallion tossed its head; it seemed now, Will thought, to be straining to get away from the high-hedged garden. He glanced over his shoulder at the rose-bright arch through which they had come in, and saw, standing out there, dazzling in the sunlight, the still form of the white-cloaked rider on the white horse.

Gwion's gaze followed him. He said softly, "Oho."

"I am not alone in this land," the Rider said.

"No," Gwion said. "Indeed you are not. The word was about that the greatest Lords of the Dark were gathered in this Kingdom, and I see it is true. Indeed you have all your strength here—and you will have need of it." He spoke lightly, without stress, but the last few words were dragged deliberately slowly, and the Rider's face darkened. With an abrupt gesture he pulled his hood about his face, and only the voice, hissing, came from the shadow.

"Save yourself, Taliesin. Or be lost with the useless hopes of the Light! Lost!"

He wheeled his horse round, the black cloak swinging; his words flickered out like stones. "Lost!" He gave rein to the restless horse and it sprang towards the arch, the White Rider wheeling in greeting as it approached; a thunder grew suddenly, rapidly out of the distance, and the horsemen of the

Dark who had passed Will and Bran earlier came rushing through the park like a great cloud marring the bright day. They bore down on the waiting horses of the two Riders, the Lords of the Dark, and enveloped them and seemed to carry them off; the dark cloud disappeared along the road and the thundering died. And Will and Bran and Gwion stood alone among the roses, in the City, in the sweet-scented garden of the Lost Land.

CHAPTER ELEVEN

THE EMPTY PALACE

WILL SAID, "Taliesin?"

"A name," Gwion said. "Just another name." He put his hand out caressingly to a spray of white roses beside him. "Do you like what you see of my City, now?"

Will did not quite return his quick smile. Something had been nibbling at his mind. "Did you know we should see the Rider, when you sent us off in the coach?"

Gwion grew sober, fingering his beard. "No, Old One, I did not. The coach was simply to bring you here. But perhaps he knew that. There is little the Dark does not know in the Lost Land. Yet also there is little that they can do." He swung abruptly towards the fountain. "Come."

They followed him to a spot before the centre of the fountain, where the water flung up in a glittering spiral from the intertwined white dolphins. Nearby climbed the biggest of all the great sprawling rose bushes, a tall mound of delicate white dog-roses as broad as a house. A fine spray from the fountain spangled their hair and dampened their faces; Will could see the sparkling drops caught even in Gwion's grey beard.

"Look for the arch of the Light," Gwion said.

Will gazed at the dancing water, the gleaming dolphins, the four-petalled roses; everything blurred together. "You mean the rainbow?"

It was there again suddenly, a sun-born curve of hazy colour within the fountain, with the hint of another faint rainbow arching above.

Gwion said softly, behind them, "Look well. Look long."

Intent and obedient they stared at the rainbow, gazed and gazed until their eyes dazzled in the sunlight reflecting from the marble and the leaping water. Then suddenly Bran cried, "Look!"—and in the same instant Will started forward, clenching his fists. They could see, faintly outlined behind the rainbow, the figure of a man seeming to float in the air; a man in a white robe with a green surcoat, head drooping, every line of his body drawn down by melancholy—and in his hand a glowing sword.

Will strained to see more clearly, hardly daring to breathe. The figure half-raised its head, almost as if it sensed their gaze and were seeking to look back; but then lethargy seemed to overtake it again and the head drooped, and the hand. . . .

. . . and nothing was there but the rainbow, arching through the fountain's glittering spray.

Bran said, his voice tight, "*Eirias*. That was the sword. Who was the man?"

"So sad," Will said. "Such a sad man."

Gwion let out a long breath, breaking his own tension. "Did you see? You saw clearly?" There was anxious appeal in his voice.

Will looked at him curiously. "Didn't you?"

"This is the fountain of the Light," Gwion said. "The one small touch of the Light's hand that is allowed in the Lost Land. Only those who are of the Light may see what it has to offer. And I am . . . not quite of the Light." He was looking keenly at Will and Bran. "You will know that face again? The sorrowful face, and the sword?"

"Anywhere," said Will.

"Always," Bran said. "It was—" He stopped, perplexed, and looked at Will.

Will said, "I know. There's no way of describing. But, we shall know him. Who is he?"

Gwion sighed. "That is the king. Gwyddno, Lost King of the Lost Land."

"And he has the sword," Bran said. "Where is he?" A curious intentness seemed to take possession of him, Will saw, whenever there was any mention of the crystal sword.

"He has the sword, and perhaps he will give it to you if he hears you when you speak to him. He has not heard anybody for a long time—not because he cannot hear with his ears, but because he has shut himself up in his mind."

Bran said again, "Where is he?"

"In his tower," Gwion said. "His tower in *Caer Wydyr*." As he spoke the Welsh words, Will realized suddenly that the faint lilt to his speaking of English had all along been the accent of a Welshman, though less pronounced than Bran's.

"*Caer Wydyr*," Bran said. He looked at Will, his forehead wrinkling. "That means, the castle of glass."

"A glass tower," Will said. "Which you can see in a rainbow." He looked back at the spiralling jets of the fountain shooting up, breaking, falling in diamond rain over the shining backs of the dolphins. Then he paused, peering more closely. "Look down there, Bran. I hadn't noticed. There's something written on the fountain, right down low."

They both bent to look, hands shielding their faces from the spray. A line of lettering was incised in the marble, half hidden by grass; the letters were patched green with moss. "*I am the.* . . ." Will parted the grass with his hands. "*I am the womb of every holt.*"

"Bran frowned. "*The womb of every holt.* The womb is where you come from in the mother, so that must be—the beginning, right? But holt? What's a holt?"

"A refuge," Gwion said quietly.

Bran pushed his dark glasses down his nose and peered at the carved words. "The beginning of every refuge? What the heck does that mean?"

"That I cannot tell you," Gwion said. "But I think you should perhaps remember it." He pointed out through the arch, at the blue coach waiting. "Will you come?"

Will said, as they climbed up the folding step into the coach, "What is that golden crest on the door, with the leaping fish and the roses?"

"A Dyfi salmon, that fish," Gwion said. "The heralds will call it, later, *Azure, a Salmon naiant Or between three Roses Argent seeded and barbed.*" He swung himself up over their heads to sit as coachman, gathering up the reins, and the last words came down faintly. "That is the crest of Gwyddno the king."

Then he flicked the reins and the black horses tossed their plumed heads and they were away, swinging and rattling through the gardens of the broad green park and out into the City's stone streets. Here and there groups and pairs of people were walking; they lifted their heads, now, as the coach jingled by, and looked after it with surprise and sometimes curiosity. None offered any greeting, but none ignored their passing as before; this time, every head turned.

The coach slowed; they swayed round a bend. Looking out, Will and Bran saw that they were turning in at the arched entrance to a courtyard. High pillared walls rose on all sides, set with tall nine-paned windows; fantastic pointed towers rose above the balustraded line of the roof. Every window was blank; they saw no face anywhere.

The coach stopped; they climbed out. Before them a narrowing stone staircase rose to a square pillared doorway ornamented with carved stone scrolls and figures—and, dominating the rest, a replica of the crest of the leaping fish from the carriage door. Will and Bran glanced at one another, and then ahead. The door stood open. Nothing but darkness was visible within.

Gwion said, behind them, "It is the palace of Gwyddno Garanhir. The Empty Palace, it has been called, since the day when the king retreated to his castle by the sea and never afterward came out. Go inside, the two of you together. And I will meet you in there, if you find your way."

Will looked back. The splendid coach and the midnight-black horses were quite gone. The great courtyard was empty. Gwion stood at the bottom of the steps, a neat dark figure, his bearded face upturned and sudden lines of anxiety written unaccountably clear upon it. He was tense, waiting.

Will nodded. He turned back to the immense open doorway of the palace. Bran stood there gazing in at the murk. He had not moved since before Gwion spoke. Without turning his white head he said, "Come on, then."

They went in, side by side. With a long creak and a deepechoing crash the huge door slammed shut behind them. Instantly the darkness burst into a blaze of white light. Will had a second in which to see Bran recoil, shielding his eyes, before the impact of what lay before them hit him and he gasped aloud.

All around, in an endless fierce glitter, were countless repeated images of himself and Bran. He spun round, staring; the Will-images spun round too, a long chorus-line retreating into space. He shouted, instinctively expecting an infinitely repeated echo to go bouncing to and fro, just as the reflections before him echoed through his sight. But only the one sound rang dully around them, and then died.

It was the sound that somehow gave Will a sense of the shape of the place where they stood: long, narrow.

"Is it a corridor?" he said, bemused.

"Mirrors!" Bran was looking wildly to and fro, eyes screwed into slits even behind the dark glasses. "Mirrors everywhere. It's *made* of mirrors."

Will's head steadied out of its whirling bewilderment; he began to sort out what he could see. "Mirrors, yes. Except for the floor." He looked down at glimmering darkness. "And that's black glass. Look, up and down. It's a corridor, a long curving corridor all made out of mirrors."

"I can see too many of me," Bran said with an uneasy laugh. There was a flash of white at each face as all the endless lines of Bran-images instantaneously laughed—and then sobered, staring.

Will took a few uncertain steps, flinching as the rows of reflected figures moved with him. The curve of the corridor opened before him a little, reflecting nothing but its own brilliance, like a gleaming empty page in a huge book. He reached out and tugged at Bran's sleeve.

"Hey. Walk alongside me. If there's someone else to look at, even out of the corner of your eye, all those reflections don't make you so giddy."

Bran came with him. He said uncertainly, "You're right." But when they had gone forward a little way he stopped suddenly; his face looked pinched and ill. "This is *awful*," he said, his voice tight. "The glass, the brightness, all of it pressing in so close. Pressing, pressing, it's like being in some terrible kind of box."

"Come on," Will said, trying to sound confident. "Maybe it opens out round that bend. It can't go on forever."

But as they rounded the curve, peopling the glass walls with their endlessly reflected figures, they came only to a pair of sharply angled corners, breaking the reflections into even more wildly repeated lines, where another mirrored corridor crossed the first so that they had now a choice of three forward directions to take.

Bran said unhappily, "Which way?"

"Goodness knows." Will reached into his pocket and brought out a penny. "Heads we go right or centre, tails we go left." He spun the coin, caught it, and held out his arm.

"It's tails," Bran said. "Left, then."

"Whoops!" Will had dropped the penny; they heard it roll and spin. "Where is it? Ought to be easy enough to find here. . . . Funny how there don't seem to be any joints anywhere in the glass—it's like being inside a sort of square tube—" He caught sight of the strain on Bran's face, and was shaken. "Come on—let's get out of here."

They went on, up the left-hand turning. But the glass corridor, identical with the first, seemed endless; it stretched on and on, curved sharply to the left, then straightened again. Their footsteps rang out, dropping into immediate silence whenever they paused. At length they came to another crossroads of corridors.

Bran looked round despondently. "Looks just the same as the other one."

A glitter that was not glass drew Will's eye to the floor;

stooping, he found it was his penny. He straightened, swallowing hard to muffle the sudden hollow feeling in his throat, and held out his hand to Bran.

"It is the same. Look."

"*Duw.* We've come in a circle." Bran looked at him, frowning. "You know what? I think we're in a maze."

"A maze. . . ."

"A maze of mirrors. Now there's something to spend your life in."

"Gwion knew, didn't he?" Will thought back, to the greybearded face looking up at him tense with concern. "Gwion said, *I shall meet you, if you find your way.* . . ."

"You know anything about mazes?"

"I was in one at Hampton Court once. Hedges. You had to keep turning right on the way in, and left on the way out. But that one had a centre. This one—"

"Those curves." Bran looked less ill now that he had something to puzzle him. "Think. Think. We went to our right when we started off, and it curved. . . ."

"It curved to the left."

"And then we came to the crossing, and we took the furthest corridor on the left, and *it* curved to the left and brought us back to the crossing in a circle."

Will closed his eyes and tried to visualize the pattern. "So turning left must be wrong. Do we turn right then?"

"Yes, look," Bran said. His pale face was alight with an idea now. Opening his mouth wide, he breathed a long breath over the mirrored wall of the corridor, and drew with his finger in the patch of mist an upward spiral pattern of a series of loops, rising without touching one another. The curving tops of the loops faced the left. It looked like a drawing of a very loose spring standing on end.

"It has to look like this. See that first loop? That's the pattern we've walked so far. And mazes always repeat themselves, right?"

"So if it goes one loop after another, it's a spiral," Will said, watching the mist-drawing gradually fade. "And we wouldn't have to go round each whole loop, we could just go up that side on the right where each loop crosses itself."

"By turning right every time. Come on." Bran slid triumphantly towards the right-hand corridor.

"Wait a minute." Will breathed at the wall, and drew
the spiral again. "We're facing the wrong way. See? We've
been all the way round the first loop, so now we're facing
backwards, back the way we first came. And if we turn right
now, we shall really be turning left."

"And just loop the loop again. Sorry, yes. In too much of
a hurry, I am." Bran swung his arms sideways and did a neat
jump to turn himself in the other direction. He looked with
dislike at the endless reflections of himself that had echoed
the jump. "Come on, I *hate* these mirrors."

Will looked at him thoughtfully as they followed the curving right-hand corridor. "You really mean that, don't you? I
mean I don't like them either, they're creepy. But you—"

"It's the brightness." Bran looked round uneasily, and
quickened his step. "And more than that. All that reflecting,
it *does* something, it's like having your mind sucked out of
you. Aah!" He shook his head for want of words.

"Here's the next crossroads. That was a lot quicker."

"So it should be, if we've really got the answer. Turn right
again."

Four times they turned to the right, trooping along with
their long, long rows of reflected images keeping endless step.

And then suddenly, curving after the fourth turn, they
came face to face with themselves: startled figures staring
back out of a blank mirrored wall.

"No!" Will said fiercely, and heard his voice tremble as he
saw Bran's head and shoulders droop in despair.

Bran said quietly, "Dead end."

"But how could we have gone wrong?"

"Pity knows. But we did. I suppose we have to go back and
. . . start again." Bran let his knees crumple, and sat down
in a heap on the black glass floor.

Will looked at him in the mirror. "I don't believe it."

"But there it is."

"I mean, I don't believe we have to start again."

"Oh yes we do." Bran looked up bleakly at their reflected images: the blue sweater and jeans of the standing figure, the white head and dark glasses of the figure hunched on the floor. "Once this happened to us before, once a long time ago —finding a blank wall stopping us. But that was where your magic as an Old One could help. It can't here, can it?"

"No," Will said. "No, not in the Lost Land."

"Well then."

"No," Will said obstinately. He bit at a thumbnail, staring round at the blind mirrored walls that could give back nothing but what they were given to reflect, and that yet, somehow, seemed to hold within them a spacious world of their own. "No. There's something . . . there must be something we ought to be remembering. . . ." He looked down at Bran, his eyes not quite seeing him. "Think, What has Gwion said to us in all the time since we first saw him, that seemed to be anything like a message? What has he *told* us to do?"

"Gwion? He told us to get into the coach. . . ." Bran scrambled to his feet, his pale forehead furrowed, as he thought backwards. "He said he would meet us if we found our way—but that was the very last thing. Before that . . . there was something he said we should remember, you're right. What was it? Remember, he said, remember. . . ."

Will stiffened. "Remember. The face of the man in the rainbow, and after that another thing, the writing on the fountain. *I think you should perhaps remember. . . .*"

Remembering, he stood very straight, stretching out both his arms stiff in front of him, and pointing all ten fingers at the mirrored glass wall that barred their way.

"*I am the womb of every holt,*" he said, slowly and clearly, in the words that they had read through the muffling grass on the mossy stone of the fountain in the park.

And above their heads on the glass, faintly and gradually, another single line of words began to glow, growing brighter and brighter until their brilliance flashed out dulling any other light around them. They had just time to look at the words and comprehend them: *I am the blaze on every hill.*

And then the light grew for an instant intolerably strong so that they flinched away from it, and with a strange soft sound, like an explosion muffled by many miles' distance, all the glass walls enclosing them shattered and musically fell.

And they stood free, with the bright words hanging in the darkness before them, and the maze of mirrors gone as if it had never been there.

CHAPTER TWELVE

THE JOURNEY

THE BLAZING WORDS faded from the air above Will's head, leaving the imprint of their brightness so that for a few moments the letters still hung ghostly across his vision. Beside him he heard Bran let out a long slow breath of relief.

Gwion's voice said warmly, from the shadows, "And you did find your way."

Blinking, Will saw him standing before them, in a high vaulted hall whose white walls were hung with rich tapestries and brilliant paintings. He looked back. There, across the hall, was the great carved door which had slammed behind them when they had first found themselves in the maze. Of the maze itself there was no sign at all.

Bran said, with a quiver still in his voice, "Was it real?" Then he gave a small shaking laugh. "There's a silly question, now."

Gwion came forward to them, smiling. "*Real* is a hard word," he said. "Almost as hard as *true*, or *now*. . . . Come. Now that you have proved yourselves by breaking the barrier of the City, I may set you on the way to the Castle."

He pulled back a tapestry curtain on the wall, revealing the entrance to a narrow circular staircase. He beckoned, and in line they went up the stairs: Will followed Gwion's feet, quiet in their soft leather shoes; the stairs seemed to wind endlessly up and up, in curving sections. On and on they went, for so long a climb that his breath began to rasp and he felt they must be hundreds of feet into the sky.

Then Gwion said, "Hold a moment," and paused. He took something from his pocket. It was a heavy iron key. In the dim light from one of the narrow opaque windows set into the staircase wall, Will saw that the top of the key was wrought into a decorative pattern: a circle, quartered by a cross. Will stared, motionless. Then he looked up and saw Gwion's dark eyes glittering enigmatically down at him.

"Ah, Old One," Gwion said softly. "The Lost Land is full of signs from long ago, but few of its people now remember what the signs mean."

He opened the small door barring their way, and suddenly sunlight was pouring down on them, washing away the last oppressive memories of the mirrored maze.

Will and Bran came out with their faces up to the blue sky as if they were prisoners emerging from jail. They found themselves behind a balustrade of wrought gold, looking out over the gold and glittering roofs of the City and the mounded green sweep of the park, just as they had done in the very beginning—but from a greater height than before. In a moment or two they saw that the balcony on which they stood was the lower rim of a great curving white and golden roof—and they realized that it was this, the palace of King Gwyddno, the Empty Palace of the Lost Land, which was topped by the marvelous dome, banded in crystal and gold, that they had first seen glittering in the dawn. Craning his neck, Will thought he could just make out the very top where the golden arrow pointed to the western sea.

Gwion came and stood at their backs, pointing in the same direction. Will noticed a ring on his fourth finger, with a dark stone carved into the shape of a leaping fish.

Out along the line of his arm, they saw the roofs of the City end, giving way to a green-gold patchwork of fields stretching into a haze of heat. Far, far away in the distance through the haze Will thought he could see dark trees, with behind them the purple sweep of mountains and the long glimmer of the sea, but he could not be sure. Only one thing out there seemed distinct: a glowing pencil of light rising out of the hazy green blur where the Lost Land seemed to meet the sea.

"Look at that," Bran said. For a moment his hand hovered in the air beside Gwion's, its fingers looking milky-pale and very young beside the lean brown hand with its dark ring. "That, there—we saw it from the mountain, Will, remember? Above Cwm Maethlon." He glanced ruefully at Will. "Another world, isn't it? D'you know, I had completely forgotten them? D'you think they are all right?"

"I think so," Will said slowly. He was staring out still at the hazed horizon, but not seeing it: lost in a concern that had been flickering through his mind since first they came to the Lost Land. "I wish I knew. And I wish I knew where Merriman is. I can't . . . reach him, Bran. I can't reach him, I can't hear him. Even though I think he meant to be with us, here."

"So he did, Old One," Gwion said unexpectedly. "But the enchantment of the Lost Land keeps him away, if he has missed the only moment for breaking it."

Will turned sharply to him, a deep instinct stirring. "You know him, don't you? Some time a long way back, you have been close to Merriman."

"Very close," Gwion said, with an ache of affection deep in the words. "And one thing I am permitted to say to you, now that you have spoken of him to me. He should have been here to join you, in this palace. But I am beginning to fear that in some way the Dark has held him back, in that other world of yours. And if now he has lost the moment for entering the Lost Land, he cannot now come."

Will said, "Not at all?"

"No," Gwion said.

Will suddenly realised how much he had been hoping for Merriman's strong presence to be there, soon, soon, as a support. He swallowed down panic, and looked at Bran.

"Then we have nothing but what the Lady said. That we shall find the crystal sword in the glass tower, among the seven trees, where the—the horn will stop the wheel."

Bran said, "And a white bone will prevent us, and a flying may-tree will save us. Whatever that may mean."

"The glass tower," Will said again. His eyes went back to the gleaming pencil on the horizon.

Gwion said, "That is Caer Wydyr, out there where you are looking. The Castle of the Lost Land, with its glass tower. Where my master sits, wrapped in a deathly melancholy that none can take away." His voice was bleak and sad.

Will said hesitantly, "May we know more than that?"

"Oh yes," Gwion said sombrely. "There are things I must tell you, of the Land and of the sword, for Merlion's sake. As much as I can." He came to the edge of the golden balustrade and gripped its rim with both hands, looking out over the city. His beard jutted, and the strong nose was outlined against the sky; he looked like a profiled head from a coin.

He said, "The Land is neither of the Dark nor the Light, nor ever was. Its enchantment was of a separate kind, the magic of the mind and the hand and the eye, that owes no allegiance because it is neither good nor bad. It has no more to do with the behaviour of men, or the great absolutes of the Light and the Dark, than does the blossom of a rose or the curving leap of a fish. Yet our craftsmen, the greatest ever in Time or out of it, did not . . . care to work for the Dark. They did their most marvellous work for the Lords of the Light. They wove tapestries, carved thrones and chests, forged candlesticks of silver and gold. They wrought four of the six great Signs of the Light."

Will looked up quickly.

Gwion smiled at him. "Ah, Sign-seeker," he said gently. "Long long ago in the Lost Land, forgotten by all its people now, there was the beginning of that gold-linked chain of yours, iron and bronze and water and fire. . . . And at the last, a craftsman of this land made the great sword Eirias for the Light."

Bran said, tense, "Who made it?"

"It was made by one who was close to the Light," Gwion said, "but who was neither a Lord of the Light nor one of

the Old Ones—there are none such, bred in this land. . . .
He was the only one who had the skill to make so great a
wonder. Even here, where many are skilled. A great craftsman, unparalleled." He spoke with a slow reverence, shaking
his head in wonder, remembering. "But the Riders of the
Dark, they could roam freely through the land, since we had
neither desire nor reason to keep any creature out—and when
they heard that the Light had asked for the sword, they
demanded that it should not be made. They knew, of course,
that words already long written foretold the use of Eirias,
once it was forged, for the vanquishing of the Dark."

Will said, "What did he do, the craftsman?"

"He called together all the makers in the land," Gwion
said. He tilted his head a little higher. "All those who wrote,
or brought life to others' words or music, or who made beautiful things. And he said to them, I have this work in me, I
know it, that will be the peak of everything I can ever make
or do, and the Dark is trying to forbid me to do it. We may all
suffer, if I deny them their will, and I cannot therefore be
responsible alone for deciding. Tell me. Tell me what I
should do."

Bran was gazing at him. "What did they say?"

"They said, *You must make it.*" Gwion smiled, proudly.
"Without any exception. *Make the sword,* they said. So he
went away into a place of his own, and made Eirias, and in a
land of wonders it was the most wonderful and powerful
thing that had ever been made. And the fury of the Dark
was very great, but impotent, for the Dark Lords knew that
they could neither destroy a work created for the Light, nor
steal it, nor bring any . . . harm to its creator."

He fell silent, gazing out at the misted horizon.

"Go on," Bran said urgently. "Go on!"

Gwion sighed. "So the Dark did a simple thing," he said.
"They showed the maker of the sword his own uncertainty
and fear. Fear of having done the wrong thing—fear that
having done this one great thing, he would never again be
able to accomplish anything of great worth—fear of age, of
insufficiency, of unmet promise. All such endless fears, that

are the doom of people given the gift of making, and lie always somewhere in their minds. And gradually, he was put into despair. Fear grew in him, and he escaped from it into lethargy—and so hope died, and a terrible paralyzing melancholy took its place. He is held by it now, he is held captive by his own mind. He, and the sword Eirias that he made, with him. Despair holds him prisoner, despair, the most terrible creation of all. For in great men, the mind can produce giant spectres of great power. And King Gwyddno is a great man."

"The King!" Will said slowly. "The King of the Lost Land made the sword?"

"Yes," Gwion said. "Long, long ago the king went alone into his castle, into the glass tower of Caer Wydyr. And he made the sword Eirias, and there he and the sword have been, alone, ever since. Held in a trap made by the king himself. And only you, perhaps, may spring that trap." He seemed to be speaking to both of them, but he was looking at Bran.

Bran said, his pale face drawn by horror, "All alone? All alone since then? Hasn't anyone ever seen him?"

"I have seen him," Gwion said. But there was suddenly such pain in his voice that no one asked him anything more.

The sun was warm on their faces; heat grew in the gold and crystal banding of the dome, and the roofs of the City shimmered before them. Somewhere in the distance, out over the green fields of the Lost Land, Will heard a seagull cry.

He had a sudden illusion of Merriman's presence, and at once then a sense of great urgency. Merriman was not there, not even to be heard in the mind: he knew it, and yet the urgency lingered, as if it were an echo from something happening somewhere else, a long way away. Will looked at Gwion's face and could see the awareness of it there too. Their eyes met.

"Yes," Gwion said. "It is time. You must journey to the Castle, across the Country that lies between, and that I have made possible as far as I can. But I cannot tell you what you may encounter on the way, nor protect you against it. Remember, you are in the Lost Land, and it is the enchantment of the Land which is in command here." He looked anxiously out at the gleaming distant tower on the horizon. "Look well, now, at the place where you must go, and set your minds on reaching it. And then, come."

They looked once at the finger of light, far out in the haze, and then they followed Gwion back down the staircase, into the Empty Palace where no king now lived. But even though the king was gone, they saw now that the palace still held others beside Gwion—and they found that they had been there before.

When they were halfway down the curving staircase, Gwion opened a door in the wall that Will had not noticed before. He led them down a different stair, straight and shallower, in towards the centre of the palace. And all at once they heard a faint murmur of voices ahead, and found themselves in a long wood-panelled room filled with books and bookshelves and heavy tables.

It was the long gallery, the room like a library. Will's eyes went to the side wall and saw that there still was the darkness, empty space with no light or shadow visible: the great theatre in which all life might be played. Other things, though, were not the same as before. People crowded the room now, filling it with a warm buzz of conversation, and any who glanced up at the three of them standing in the doorway smiled, or raised a hand in greeting.

They walked through, up and down over the strangely differing levels of its floor; many people they passed spoke a word or two to Gwion, and the warmth was clear in every face that looked at Will and Bran. One woman touched Will gently on the shoulder as they went by, and said, "Safe journey to you." As he looked up, startled, he heard a man beside them say softly to Bran, "*Pob hwyl!*"

Bran said in his ear, "*Good luck,* he said. How do they all know?"

Will shook his head, wondering. They followed Gwion's neat dark-clad figure down the room, walking quickly, and then at the far end a man who had been standing bent over a large book on a table straightened and turned as they approached, putting out a hand to halt them. Will thought he remembered the face as that of the man to whom he had spoken when they had first been in the room: a man who had not then seemed to see or hear him, and who had been reading a book whose pages were blank.

"See, before you go," the man said, with the lilt of North Wales stronger in his voice than Will heard it from Gwion or even Bran. "There is a part of this book that you must see, and remember."

"Remember. . . ." said Gwion softly, looking at them, and the echo woke in both their minds. The book lay open before them on the heavy oak table; on one curving vellum page was a painting, and on the other a single line of words.

Will was staring at the picture. In a stylized green world of trees and lawns, among beds of roses bright as those where they had encountered the Rider, it showed the figure of a young woman, fair-haired, robed in blue, standing looking out at them. Her face was heart-shaped, fine-boned, delicately beautiful; she was serious, neither smiling nor sad.

"It is the Lady!" Will said.

Bran said in surprise, "But you said she was very old." He reflected for a moment. "Of course, that just depends, doesn't it?"

"It is the Lady," Will said again, slowly. "There's that big rose-coloured ring on her finger, too, I've never seen her without it. And look there—in the picture behind her, isn't that—"

"The fountain!" Bran peered closer, looking over his glasses. "It's the same fountain, the one we were at in the park—and so that must be the same rose garden. But how—"

Will had his finger on the line of thick black manuscript on the facing page. He read aloud, *"I am the queen of every hive."*

"Remember," the man said. He closed the book.

"Remember," Gwion said. "And then go." Facing them, he put one hand briefly on a shoulder of each and looked carefully into their eyes. "Do you know this place, the gallery we are in? Of course. So you will remember the way by which you came into it, that you must follow now. I stay here, for a while. There are men and women of some art in this place, and they will tell me what they can of Merriman. I will be with you again, but you must go on, now, at once."

Will looked down, and found the square open trapdoor in the floor, and the ladder leading down beneath. "That way?"

"That way," Gwion said. "And then, take what you will find, and the finding will start you on your way." The strong grey-bearded face broke into its warm, illumining smile. "Go well, my friends."

Down into the shadows Bran and Will clambered, more confident than when they had scrambled up the ladder in the early morning, linked by the little horn that hung forgotten again now from Will's belt. On level ground once more, they groped their way forward in the murk, and came to the small wooden door. Will felt its pitted surface with the flat of his hands.

"No handle or anything on this side, either."

"It opened outwards, didn't it? Perhaps you just push."

And at the first gentle pressure the door did swing outward, so that they stood blinking for a moment at the light of the street outside. Then they went out, the door swinging shut behind them with a crash that showed it would not open so easily again. And there in the narrow shady street, waiting for them, were the two white-maned golden horses they had ridden there so long and so short a time ago.

The horses tossed their heads as if in greeting; the silver harness rang like sleighbells. Without a word Will and Bran swung themselves up into the saddles, with the same unaccountable ease as before, and the horses trotted away up the narrow street, between the high grey walls with the thin bright strip of blue sky far above.

They came out into a broader place, filled with people who seemed at once to recognize them; who stood waving, calling out in greeting. The horses walked carefully through the crowd; the calling grew into a spasmodic cheering; children ran alongside them, laughing and halloo-ing. Bran and Will grinned at one another in pleased embarrassment. On they went, down the broad paved street, until they reached a towering wall, with a great gateway in it through which the road ran. Through the arch they could see a glimpse of green fields and distant trees.

The crowds stood thick before the arch, but the golden horses went stepping on, never pausing, nudging their way gently through.

"Good fortune to you!"

"Safe travelling!"

"A good journey!"

All around, the people of the City called and waved; children ran and danced and shouted; a group of girls beside the gate stood laughing and throwing flowers. Will put up his hand half in self-defence and caught a wide red rose; looking down, he saw the dark-haired girl who had thrown it blushing and smiling. He grinned at her, and stuck the flower into his top pocket.

Then all at once they were outside the great gate of the City, and all the crowd was gone. Before them lay broad green fields, and a rough sandy road stretching brown-gold into the distance with a wood beyond. The voices from the city died away. Somewhere a lark sang in the summer sky; a blue sky, patched here and there with puffy fair-weather clouds, the sun high amongst them now. The horses turned up the sandy road and went on without breaking step, at a steady walk.

Bran eyed the flower in Will's pocket. "Oooh!" he said in a mocking falsetto. "A red rose, is it?"

Will said amiably, "Get lost."

"Not so pretty as Jane, that one who threw it."

"As who?" Will said.

"Jane Drew. Don't you think she's pretty, then?"

"I suppose so, yes," Will said, surprised. "I never thought about it."

Bran said, "One good thing about you, you're uncomplicated."

But Will's mind had jumped backward. He wound the

loose rein thoughtfully round one finger as he swayed steadily to and fro on the tall horse. "I hope they're all right, back there."

Bran said, roughly, abruptly, "Better forget them, for now."

Will looked up sharply. "What d'you mean?"

Without speaking, Bran pointed out to one side, past him. In the distance across the flat green fields Will saw a patch of black and white, moving fast, in a direction parallel to the road along which they were travelling. He knew it could only be the Riders of the Dark, heading, like themselves, for the Castle of the Lost Land.

CHAPTER THIRTEEN

THE MARI LLWYD

THEY WATCHED the troop of Riders, miniature in the distance, moving fast across the fields. Will's horse tossed its head suddenly, snuffing the air, and began to quicken its pace.

Bran came up level with him. "They're going a good lick. Trying to get to the Castle before we do?"

"I suppose so."

"Shall we race?"

"I don't know." Will looked down at his restless mount. "The horses want to."

Bran was sitting poised in the saddle, his pale face alert; he smiled. "Think you can stay on?"

Will laughed, a sudden wild exhilaration seizing him. "Just watch!" He gave no more than a flick to the reins before the horse was off, leaping out, galloping eagerly along the hard sandy track. Bran was beside him, leaning forward, white hair flying, yelling with delight. On and on they went, past stretches of ripening oats and wheat, past fields where placid cattle grazed—some the familiar black, but many pure white. The horses ran smoothly, confidently. In the distance, the Riders of the Dark raced parallel: then, after a while, disappeared behind the far edge of the wood which lay in the centre of the Country, between the City and the Castle of the Lost Land.

Will had assumed that their own road too would skirt this wood, on the nearer side. But when he raised his head out of the whirl of riding, he found that they had not turned; instead the trees seemed to be reaching out around them, cutting off their view of the shining glass tower. He and Bran were galloping straight towards the wood, and the wood was growing, rising before them, far darker and more dense than it had seemed before.

The horses began to slow their pace.

"Come on!" Bran twitched his reins impatiently.

"They know best," Will said. "I don't like the looks of that wood."

Bran glanced up, flinching at the size of the dark mass looming ahead. "They aren't stopping, though. Why didn't they go around it?"

"I suppose they have to go where the track goes. And I didn't notice where it *was* going. Should have done."

"We both should have done. Oh well." The horses were walking again now. Bran pushed one arm across his forehead. "Lord, it's hot. The sun's still high."

The woodland was sparse and open at first, leafy with bracken and undergrowth, still bright through the dappling shade. The road, though narrowed to a track, wound through the trees clear and sandy, but gradually it became less distinct, with patches of grass growing in the sand and the arms of creeping plants reaching across, and now the air was cool as the wood grew deeper. The horses stepped warily, in single file. Few birds sang here. Will and Bran began to be conscious of the silence. The trees were larger and thicker; the wood went on and on.

Will tried for as long as he could to ignore the feeling drifting insidiously into his mind as the light grew dim and the trees more dominant, but he knew he was afraid.

There was nothing to be heard now but the soft rise and fall of the horses' feet. The path they trod was completely overgrown yet still visible; covered, as if to mark it from its surroundings, by a mat of some small creeping weed with dark green leaves. Somewhere among the trees edging the path ahead, a bird whirred abruptly away; the horses checked nervously.

"They're as scared as I am," Will said, trying to brighten his voice. A branch rustled nearby in the wood, and he jumped.

Bran looked round in the gloom. He said uneasily, "Should we go back?" But as if in answer the horses began walking steadily forward again. Will stroked the light mane on the neck before him; the horse's ears were laid back flat, but still he went doggedly on.

"Perhaps it's just a . . . barrier," he said suddenly. "Like the maze. Perhaps they know there's not really anything to be scared of."

Some unseen creature rose in the underbrush beside the path and went crashing off through the still trees and the green seas of fern all around; Will and Bran gasped, but this time the horses walked on unheeding. The trees interlaced overhead. Will rode with his teeth clenched, fighting off panic, comforted only by the steady swaying of his tall horse. The air was cool and damp; they crossed a small sluggish stream half-buried in fern. Then almost imperceptibly, the horses' pace began to quicken. Light began to filter through the branches overhead once more; sand appeared between the tight-woven green leaves of the matted path.

"We're coming out!" Bran said in a half-whisper high with relief. "You were right, the horses knew it was just spookiness. We're coming out!"

The horses began to trot, an easy swinging motion; they tossed their heads as if from a sense of release. Will felt the pounding of his heart slide back to normal; he sat up straighter, ashamed of his fear, and looked up at the thinning trees.

"Blue sky again, look. Ouf, what a difference!"

And so they were both relaxed in the saddle, holding loose reins, looking up unprepared, when suddenly one of the horses gave a high terrified whinny, and both shied, rearing, as something large and loud rushed at them out of the trees.

And before they knew it Will and Bran were jerking backward, clutching wildly for rein or saddlebow, tumbling helpless to the ground. The two golden horses bolted in panic across the rough sedgy pasture that stretched away from the wood.

Will had a quick glimpse of the thing that was chasing them. He cried out, in horror and disbelief, *"No!"*

Bran gave a croaking shout without words, and they stumbled up and fled unthinking over the fields. In the heat of the summer sunshine Will felt cold. His head sang. He wanted to be sick. He was too frightened even to think of fear.

It was the skeleton of a giant horse, staring with the blind eye-sockets of a skull, running and leaping and prancing on legs of bone driven by ghostly muscles long rotted away. It caught them almost at once. Faster than any living horse it galloped, and without any sound. Silently it overtook them, head turned, grinning, an impossible horror. The white bones of its great rib-cage glittered in the sun. It tossed its dreadful silent head, and red ribbons dangled and fluttered like long banners from the grinning lower jaw.

The creature was playing with them, driving them this way and that, as a kitten plays with a beetle. It leapt to and fro before them, then stopped in its tracks, hooves skidding in the sandy soil. Then with the leering skull thrust out, jaws open wide, it charged at them in terrible silence—and was suddenly past them, behind them, waiting again. Swinging round wildly, Bran stumbled and fell.

The skull tossed on the spine that was a neck; the teeth glittered, the red ribbons danced round a strange broken stump in the centre of the bony forehead. In the same soundless menace it stood watching them out of the blind skull, hoof and bone pawing at the ground. Will swallowed.

"You all right? Get up!"

Bran was sitting up, blinking wide tawny eyes; his glasses were gone. "The *Mari Llwyd!*" he whispered. "The *Mari Llwyd!*" He was staring at the thing as if bewitched.

"Get up, quick!" Will had glimpsed a refuge nearby. In panic he dragged Bran to his feet. The spectre began to circle them, slowly, silently.

"Over here! Come *on!*"

It was a building, he saw. The strangest of buildings: a small low house made of blocks of grey stone, with a once-thatched roof covered in turf and straggling grass and a great swathe of branches blossoming white. A hawthorn tree was growing there from the ancient roof, a low tree not much bigger than a bush.

Bran stood transfixed, his eyes on the skeleton. "The *Mari Llwyd!*" he whispered again.

"Close your eyes!" Will said fiercely. He thrust his hand in front of Bran's face to cut off the sight of the monstrous horse, and in the same moment the right words came to him. "Quick, think, what did the Lady say?"

"The Lady?" Bran said dully. But his head turned.

"What did the Lady say to Jane? Think!"

"To Jane." Bran's face began to clear. "To tell us . . . a white bone will prevent you . . . and a flying may-tree—"

"Will save you. Look at it. Look at it!" Will turned him to the stone house with the blossoming white tree growing from its roof. The thing stalking them wheeled closer, closer. With a sound like a sob Bran stumbled forward; Will pushed him in through the door and slammed it shut behind them. He stood leaning against it, gasping for breath. There was a prickling silence outside.

Bran looked down at his hands. He was still clutching the saddlebag from his vanished horse, as if it were a lifebelt. Dropping it on the floor he rubbed his stiff fingers and looked at Will. "Sorry."

But Will was not listening; he had crossed to the one small window that let in a dim shadowy light through the chunky stone wall. A broken shutter hung from the window-frame; there was no glass. Will's face was pale; Bran saw fear in it.

Will said huskily, "Can you look?"

"I'm all right now." Bran came to stand beside him. And when he looked through the window he clutched Will's arm without knowing it, so hard that the fingertips dug in deep and afterwards left a mark behind.

The great white skeleton of the horned horse, dead and yet alive, was wheeling to and fro in front of the cottage, to and fro, to and fro. Its four bony legs danced beneath the curving empty white strips of the rib-cage and the flattened arcs of the hip-blades. The long beribboned skull was jerking up and down in a dreadful dead frenzy, faster and faster; each time it faced the cottage it dropped its forehead like a charging bull and paused for an instant before turning restlessly away and wheeling to and fro once more.

Will whispered, "It's going to run at us. Charge at the door. What can we do?"

"Block the door? Would that stop it?"

"Not a hope."

"Isn't there *anything* you can do, make happen—?"

"We're in the Lost Land. . . ."

And the monstrous thing out there in the sunshine made one last great curving turn before it would charge at the door to burst in to their destruction. Wheeling deliberately close to the window of the house, out of its hollow-eyed skull the creature laughed dreadfully, soundlessly in at them for a second. It was the last second. As the thing passed so close, a long flurry like snow came down past the window from above, a fluttering flickering cloud of white flakes falling on the apparition, all the petals of the hawthorn tree falling, dropped in a long soft shower. And the horse that was the skeleton of a horse collapsed, as if the strings had been cut from a marionette, and fell apart. Every bone fell from every other bone, clattering down to the ground, rattling as clear now as all had been silent before. And nothing was left but a heap of white bones gleaming in the sun, bleached, long dead, with faded red ribbons drooping from the long grinning skull that lay askew on top of the pile.

Bran let out a long soft breath, his hands going up to cover his eyes; he swung aside and slumped gently down to the floor. So it was only Will, standing wide-eyed in wonder beside the window, who saw the flurry of white petals rise again, fluttering, alive, like a great crowd of feathery white plume moths he had seen before, somewhere, somewhere—and rise flickering into the sky and out of sight, far away.

Will turned unsteadily, uncertain whether to trust his knees. He stood gazing at the dim-lit room. It was a little while before he properly saw anything. But as his churning senses began to calm again, he found he was looking at the door: an ancient door of rotting, battered wood, which would have withstood no impact of any kind at all. He could see some words written over it, with the faint glimmer of gold in them. There was not enough light to read what they said. Will went shakily across and pushed open the door; brightness came in.

Bran said slowly, behind him, reading: *"I am the shield for every head."*

"And it's written inside, where we couldn't see it," Will said, stepping back to peer up at the words. "So we might never have dared to come in, if it hadn't been for what the Lady said."

Bran was sitting up, arms over his knees, white head drooping. *"Duw.* That . . . thing. . . ."

"Don't talk about it," Will said; a shiver went over him like a cold breeze. Then he remembered something. "But—Bran, what was the name you called it? When it had you . . . hypnotized . . . you called it something in Welsh."

"Ah," Bran said. "The original Nightmare, that thing. There is an old Christmas custom, in South Wales, of something called the *Mari Llwyd,* the Grey Mare—a procession goes through the streets, and a man dressed up in a white sheet carries the skull of a horse stuck up on a pole. He can make its jaws open and shut and pretend to bite people. And one Christmas when I was very small the Rowlands took us down there visiting, my Da and me, and I saw the *Mari Llwyd* and it frightened the lights out of me. Terrible. Screaming nightmares for weeks." He looked up at Will with a weak smile. "If anyone had really wanted to put me out of my head, they couldn't have chosen a better way."

Will came back into the room, leaving the door open and

sunlight shafting in. "Was it the Dark? Hard to tell. One way or another it must have been. Some ancient haunting of the Lost Land, woken by—"

"By the Riders, maybe," Bran said thoughtfully. "The Riders, passing." He reached for the saddlebag he had dropped on the rough slate floor, and looked inside. "Hey—food! You hungry?"

"A bit," Will said. Prowling round the cottage, he peered into the only other room, at the back, but decided from the smell and tatters of ancient hay that it had only ever been used for animals. In the main room, the walls were drystone, heavy chunks of rock and slate fitted together without mortar; there was no furniture of any kind, though a few rough shelves were attached to one wall. It was a far cry from the sophisticated elegance of the City. But as he ran his finger idly along a shelf Will came upon one unexpected object: a small miror, set in a heavy oak frame carved with a pattern of leaping fish. He rubbed the dirt from the glass with his sleeve, and propped the mirror up on its shelf.

Bran came up behind him. "Here, cup your hands, boy. Gwion's Health Food, we have here—two apples and a big bag of hazelnuts. Shelled, mind you. Have some, they taste wonderful." Cheerfully chewing, he looked up and saw Will staring at the mirror. He grimaced. *"Ach y fi!* Haven't you had enough mirrors for a while?"

Will scarcely heard. Looking at Bran's reflection in the mirror, he could see another familiar face behind him.

"Merriman!" he cried joyously, whirling round.

But behind him he found only Bran, mouth half-open as the cheerful enjoyment on his face changed to alarm. The room was empty, save for the two of them.

Will looked back at the mirror, and Merriman was still there. The shadowed eyes in the angular face stared at him, from behind Bran's puzzled reflected head.

"I am here," said Merriman to him out of the mirror. His face was drawn and anxious. "With you and yet not with you, and I must tell you that Bran can neither see nor hear me, since he is not yet grown to power. . . . I am not allowed to come to you, Will, or even speak in the ways of the Old Ones. As Gwion told you, I had only one moment in which to pass through the Law of the Lost Land, and just as that moment came, the craft of the Dark caught me back to another time. But we have this crack of an instant. You do well. Be confident. There is nothing you cannot do now, if you try."

"Oh dear," Will said. His voice sounded to him small and lost, and suddenly he felt small and lost indeed.

"What's the matter?" Bran said, perplexed.

Will did not hear him. "Merriman, are the others all right?"

"Yes," Merriman said sombrely. "In danger—but all right for now."

A panic of loneliness fluttered at the back of Will's mind, yet somehow the memory of the destruction of the nightmare horse helped to keep it at bay. "What must we do?" he said.

Bran was standing very still, staring at him in the mirror without a word.

"Remember the Lady's words, as you have done." There was trust in Merriman's reflected face. "Go on now, and take care to remember other things you have been told, there in the Lost Land. You can do no more than your best. And remember one thing from me, Will—you may trust Gwion with your lives. As once long ago I trusted him with mine." An affectionate warmth deepened his voice. He gave Will one last hard look. "The Light will carry you, once you return with the sword. Go well, Old One," he said.

Then he was gone.

Will turned aside from the mirror, letting out a long breath.

Bran said in a whisper, "Was he here? Has he gone?"

"Yes."

"Why couldn't I see him? Where was he?"

"In the mirror."

"In the *mirror!*" Bran looked at it fearfully. Glancing down, he found the bag of nuts forgotten in his hands, and thrust it at Will. "Here. Eat. What did Merriman say?"

Suddenly hungry, Will stuffed his mouth with hazelnuts.

"That it's certain he can't come to the Lost Land," he said, muffled. "That we have to go on alone. To remember things we've been told—like that, he must mean." He pointed to the writing over the cottage door. "And—that we can trust Gwion."

"We knew that already," Bran said.

"Yes." Will thought of the lean figure with the strong grey-bearded face and the brilliant smile. "I wonder who Gwion is? And what he is. . . ."

"He is a maker," Bran said unexpectedly."

Will paused in his chewing. "A what?"

"He is a bard, I would bet. He has the callouses from the harp on his fingertips. But mostly it was the way he spoke of the makers, of all kinds, when he was telling us the king's story. With love. . . ."

"And he and Merriman must have gone through great danger together, once. . . . Well, I suppose we shall find out sometime. Here—" Will handed over the bag of nuts. "You have the rest. They *are* good. Did you say there were apples?"

"One each." Bran passed one over, and began rolling up the saddlebag.

Will went to the doorway, biting into his apple; it was small, hard and yellow, but astonishingly sweet and juicy. The heap of white bones lay dead and bleached in the sunlight; he tried not to look at it, but raised his gaze out to the Country.

"Bran! See how close we are!"

The sun was high in a blue sky flecked with puffy white clouds. Out over the rough pastureland, perhaps a mile away, a glittering tower rose from a clump of tall trees; the sunlight struck from it so brightly that its brilliance dazzled them.

Bran came out. They stood looking at the Castle for a long moment. Beyond it, the Lost Land ended in the flat shimmering horizon of the blue sea. Will turned from it for a last look at the low, spreading hawthorn tree that grew from the roof of the little house. He stared. The tree that had been covered in milky white blossom, the enchanted snowstorm to destroy the *Mari Llwyd*, was thick now with bright red berries, clustering along the branches, brilliant as flame.

Bran shook his head in wonder. Both he and Will wordlessly touched the sturdy stone wall of the cottage, in an instinctive grateful farewell. Then they set out on foot across the tussocky grass of the pasture, towards the glittering pointing tower.

And when they looked back once more at the little shielding house with the tree growing from its roof, they saw no house there at all, but only a thicket of clustering hawthorn bushes, red-berried, growing in the open field.

CHAPTER FOURTEEN

CAER WYDYR

THOUGH THEY TRIED, they never found the road again. There was no sign anywhere of the golden horses; panic had taken them far away. So Will and Bran turned their faces towards the shining tower and tramped over the rough reedy grass of the pastureland, through clumps of gorse on the firm ground and soggy patches of marsh on lower land where the water still lay. All the Lost Land was low: a coastal plain, with the sweep of Cardigan Bay at their left hand and the mountains rising hazily purple-brown far inland, to the right. Somewhere ahead, Will realized, the River Dyfi must run, towards a mouth considerably further out to sea than the one he had known before. It was as though all the coast of their own time had been given an extra half-mile stretch on its seaward side.

"Or rather," he said aloud, "given back the land it lost."

Bran looked at him with a half-smile of understanding. "Except that it hasn't been lost yet, has it?" he said. "Because we've gone back in time."

Will said pensively, "Have we?"

"Well of course we have!" Bran stared at him.

"I suppose so. Back, forward, forward, back." Will's mind was drifting. He looked out to a sweep of yellow irises among the reeds of a boggy area they had been carefully skirting. "Pretty, aren't they? Just like on the farm, near the river."

"We must be getting near a river ourselves," Bran said, eying him a little uncertainly. "Very wet, it is. I'm parched."

"Listen!" Will said. "Can you hear running water?"

"Won't be any good to us even if it is—probably brackish," Bran said, but he cocked his head to listen. Then he nodded. "Yes. Up ahead. Past those trees."

They went on. The bright tower loomed higher now, though almost obscured by trees. They could see that it was topped by a banded dome of crystal and gold, exactly like the dome of the king's palace in the city. There was even an identical golden arrow at the very top, pointing out at the sea.

Then they were among a group of scrubby willow trees, with the sound of water growing, growing, and suddenly they came upon a reed-fringed stream, moving curiously fast for water on such flat land. Curving round to meet them, it seemed to flow from the direction of the City out to join the River Dyfi on its way to the sea. The water looked clear and cool.

"I'm *thirsty!*" Bran said. "Cross your fingers." He dipped one hand in the water and tasted; then made a horrible face.

Will groaned in disappointment. "Salt?"

"No," Bran said, expressionless. "It's perfectly good." He dodged Will's grinning lunge and they both stretched out on the grassy riverbank and drank thirstily, splashing their hot faces until their hair was wet and dripping. In a gentle patch of water on the lee side of a rock Will caught sight of Bran's reflection, and was held by it. Only the glint of the tawny eyes was properly like Bran, for the reflected face was darkened by shade and the wet hair seemed streaked dark and light. Yet somehow Will felt a strange flash of recognition of the whole changed image. He said sharply, "I've seen you look like that before, somewhere."

"Of course you've seen me before," Bran said lazily. He put down his head and blew bubbles into the water, breaking the reflection. The water rippled into a hundred different surfaces, glinting, whirling; there seemed all at once a great deal of white in the pattern. Some small warning note rang in Will's mind. He rolled over, and saw against the sky, standing over them, the hooded White Rider on his white horse.

Bran brought his head out of the water, spluttering, pulling a green strand of weed from his mouth. He rubbed the water from his eyes, looked up—and was suddenly very still.

The White Rider looked down at Will with bright eyes set in a dim white face shadowed by the hood. "Where is your master, Old One?" The voice was soft and sibilant and puzzlingly familiar, though they knew they had not heard it before.

Will said shortly, "He is not here. As you know."

The White Rider's smile glinted. "And he told you no doubt that something had prevented him from coming, and you were simple enough to believe him. The lord Merriman is more shrewd than you, Old One. He knows the danger that is here, and takes care not to be exposed to it."

Will lay back deliberately on his elbows. "And you are more than simple, if you think to afflict me with such talk. The Dark must be in a sad way, to use the tricks of idiots."

The White Rider's back straightened; he seemed indefinably more dangerous than before. "Go back," said the soft hissing voice coldly, "Go back, while you still can."

"You cannot make us go," Will said.

"No," said the White Rider. "But we can make you wish you had never come. Especially. . . ." his gleaming eyes flickered towards Bran . . . especially the white-haired boy."

Will said softly, "You know who he is, Rider. He has a right to a name."

"He is not yet in his power," the White Rider said, "and until then he is nothing. And therefore he will be nothing forever, no more than a child of your century, for without your master you have no hope of gaining the sword. Go back, Old One, go back!" The soft voice rose to a nasal, ringing demand, and the white horse shifted uneasily. "Go back," the Rider said, "and we will give you safe passage out of the Lost Land to your own time."

The horse shifted again. Exclaiming in irritation, the White Rider gave rein and wheeled it round in a wide circle to calm its restlessness.

"Look!" Bran whispered. He was staring at the ground.

Will looked down. Under the high fierce sun, his shadow and Bran's lay short and stumpy together on the uneven grass; but as the White Rider and his horse curved back towards them, the grass beneath the four hooves lay bright and unshaded.

"Ah yes," Will said softly. "The Dark casts no shadow."

The White Rider said, clear and confident, "You will go back."

Will stood up. "We will not go back, Rider. We have come for the sword."

"The sword is neither for us nor for you. We shall let you go, in safety, and the sword will stay with its maker."

"Its maker made it for the Light," Will said, "and when we come for it, he will give it to us. And we shall then indeed go away in safety, my lord, whether the Dark allows it or not."

The lord in the white cloak looked down at him, his womanish mouth relaxed into a strange, unnerving sneer of relief. "If that is what you expect from the Land," he said, "then you are such fools that we have nothing to fear from you."

And without another word, he turned his horse's head and trotted away beside the curving river, out of sight behind the trees.

There was a silence. The water murmured.

Bran scrambled to his feet, looking uneasily after the Rider. "What did he mean?"

"I don't know. But I didn't like it." Will shivered suddenly. "The Dark is all around us. Can you feel it?"

"A little," Bran said. "Not really, not the way you do. I feel just . . . this is a *sad* place."

"Home of a sad king." Will looked around. "Should we follow the river?"

"Looks like it." They could see the dome and the golden pointing arrow of the Castle reaching up out of the trees, past the curve round which the river disappeared.

The riverbank was grassy; there was no path, but no trees

or bushes grew out to impede their way. The river itself remained narrow, perhaps twenty feet across, but its bed between the coarse grass of the banks grew broader and broader, a shining expanse of sand. It was clear golden sand now, without the murkiness of mud.

"Tide's low," Bran said, seeing Will look at it. "Like the Dyfi. That sand'll be covered when the tide starts coming in, and the river will grow twice its size. It's beginning to, already. Look."

He pointed; Will saw the water eddying in the river, as the direction of its flow began to change. The main stream in the centre still flowed out to the sea, but at either side the tidal flow from the sea came creeping in.

"Couldn't drink from it now," Bran said. "Too salt."

The river broadened as they walked further, and the incoming tide grew more powerful; on the further bank the trees were smaller and more sparse. They had an occasional glimpse of the broad estuary beyond the scrub and pasture, and the mountains rising far back. Then all at once they saw a square brown sail, and foaming towards them on the tidal current came a boat. Its sail bellied out at right angles to the mast between two sturdy wooden yards; almost at once these clattered to the deck, and the sail came down.

The boat swung towards the bank beside them. Will peered in astonishment at the figure furling the sail.

"It's Gwion!"

Gwion, lean and black-clad, leapt up nimbly into the bow with a line, and jumped ashore as the boat nudged the bank. He glanced at Will and Bran, his familiar smile breaking above the neat grey beard; then called something in Welsh over his shoulder to the boat. A chunky man with black hair and a red-brown face stood there at the long tiller behind the single stubby mast; it was a broad-beamed boat, not unlike a ship's lifeboat. The man called back to Gwion. Will looked enquiringly at Bran.

"About mooring the boat," Bran said. "And catching the tide, though I—*tafla 'r rhaff yna i mi*," he said suddenly to Gwion, reaching for a second line thrown from the boat, and together they moored her fore and aft to a pair of trees, swaying in the river as the tide washed by.

"Well done to be here safe," Gwion said, a hand pressing each on the shoulder. "Now then, come on." He set off at once along the riverbank, at a smart pace.

Will followed; he felt as though a great knot of tension had been loosed between his shoulder blades.

"Explain, explain," said Bran, lengthening his stride to keep up. "How did you get here? Why the boat? How did you know where to find us, and when?"

Gwion smiled at him. "When you are in your full power, Bran Davies of Clwyd, you will be confident as Will here and not bother to ask such questions. I am simply here, because you will need me. And thus I break the law of the Lost Land, which is to have no dealing with either Light or Dark when they are in conflict. As I shall go on breaking that law, I have no doubt, until the tail-end of Time. Gently, now. . . ." His voice dropped and he slowed his pace, stretching both arms sideways to hold them back.

They had come to an end of the scattering of wind-curved oak and pine that fringed this edge of the river. Before them now was the Castle of the Lost Land, a shining tower rising over a circle of tall trees.

Gwion was suddenly sober; he dropped his arms, and stood for a moment as if he had forgotten Will, Bran, himself and everything except the sight of the lonely glittering tower there before him.

"*Caer Wydyr,*" he said softly, almost whispering. "As beautiful as it has always been. And my great grieving king shut away inside never seeing its beauty. With indeed no one at all, in all the Lost Land, able to see its beauty except the Lords of the Dark."

Will looked all around, restlessly. "And they are everywhere, and yet not to be seen."

"Everywhere," Gwion said. "Among the guardian trees. But they cannot harm the trees, just as they cannot touch the king or his castle."

The great trees grew round the tower in an irregular circle, lapping it with their leaves and branches; it rose from them like an island from a green sea.

"Seven trees, the Lady said." Bran turned to Will. "Seven trees. Just as the seven Sleepers woke over Llyn Mwyngil, once before our eyes, to ride away into tomorrow." The tawny eyes were glittering in his pale face; he stared all around, unafraid, as if in challenge, caught up for a moment in a feverish confidence Will had not seen before.

Will said slowly, "But there were six Sleepers."

"Seven there will be," Bran said, "seven at the end. And not then Sleepers by name, but Riders, like the Lords of the Dark."

"Here is the first tree," Gwion said. His voice was without expression, but Will felt he was deliberately turning the talk aside. Facing them, close to the river, was a crowded clump of slender trunks, green-barked, with broad round dancing leaves.

"*Y gwernen,*" Bran said. "Alder. Growing with its feet wet, the way it does in our valley too, with John Rowlands cursing it up and down for a weed."

Gwion broke three small twigs from an alder branch, taking each at the joint where it would not bend or fray. "A weed-wood sometimes perhaps, but a wood that will neither split nor decay. The tree of fire, is alder. There is in it the power of fire to free the earth from water. And that we may need. Here." He gave each of them a twig and went on, towards the broad sweeping canopy, slender-branched, long-leafed, of a willow tree. Again he broke off three sprays and held out two.

"Willow, the enchanter's tree," Will said, his mind flickering a long way back to a certain ancient book shown him by Merriman when he was learning how to use the gifts of an Old One. "*Strong as a young lion, pliant as a loving woman, and bitter to the taste, as all enchantment in the end must be.*" He smiled wrily at Gwion. "They taught me my trees once, a while ago."

Gwion said quietly, "So they did indeed. Tell me the next."

"Birch," said Will. A great knotted white tree rose before

them, hard catkins dancing from its long thin brown twigs. Beneath the fluttering green leaves it was an old, old tree, with white-spotted scarlet toadstools growing between its roots and the long self-healed split of an ancient wound bringing the first signs of decay to its trunk.

Bran said in unthinking surprise, "I never saw a birch tree out here before." Then he looked at Will and grinned, mocking himself. "No—nor a great glass tower either, nor a may-tree growing from a roof."

"You say nothing foolish," said Gwion mildly, giving them twigs from the birch tree. "In this my time it is warmer and drier here in Wales than in yours, and we have forests of alder and birch and pine trees, where you have only oaks and the foreign trees that will be brought in by new men. And those"—he paused for an instant—"not in quite the same place as these trees of my day."

A kind of terror caught at Will's mind for a moment as he realized what Gwion must mean; but the Welshman drew them swiftly on, past the big birch tree, and suddenly the glass tower, Caer Wydyr, was facing them, visible for the first time from bottom to top, and they saw that it rose not from the ground, from the golden sand and green bank of the estuary, but from a great jagged rock. The stone was unfamiliar; it was neither the spangled grey of granite nor the grey-blue of slate, but a deep blue-black, studded here and there with bright slabs of white quartz. And they saw now that the sides of the tower itself were built too of a glassy rocklike quartz, white, translucent, with a strange milky glow. Slits of windows were set into the circling walls, here and there, and the surface was totally smooth.

"Is there no door?" Bran said.

Gwion gave no answer, but led them over the long coarse grass towards two other full, massive trees. The first was not tall, but broad and spreading, with the blunt rounded leaves and budding feathery nuts of half the hedges of England and Wales.

"Hazel for healing," Gwion said, taking three twigs.

"And for feeding starving travellers," said Bran.

Gwion laughed. "Were they good, then?"

"Marvellous. And the apples too."

Will said, remembering, "Apple is another of the trees."

"But first, holly." Gwion turned to a forbidding dark mound of a tree with a smooth grey trunk, its glossy dark green leaves sharp-spined on the lower branches and mild ovals above. He picked only the twigs with prickled leaves, and again handed them one each.

"And from the apple," he said, smiling, "you may take fruit as well. But I must be the one to pluck the twigs, from every tree."

"Why?" Bran said, as they went on through the grass.

"Because otherwise," Gwion said simply, "the tree would cry out, and the law would come into force, by which neither Light nor Dark may make any move for their own ends within the Lost Land." He paused for a moment, looking at them intently, fingering the neat dappled grey beard. His voice was grave. "Make no mistake now, the Lost Land is not a gentle place. There is a hardness here, and an indifference to all emotions other than those belonging to the Land, that is another face of the beauty of the rose garden, and the skill of the craftsmen, the makers. Do not underestimate that."

Bran said, "But only the Dark really stands in our way."

Gwion tilted his chin in a curious arrogant motion, yet with lines of pain clear about the mouth. He said quietly, "Where do you think the *Mari Llwyd* was called from, to drive you out of your wits almost, Bran Davies? Who do you think devised the mirrored maze? What is it that faces you now in the untasted despair of the task that is almost impossible, the task of reaching the Lost King and his crystal sword? Do you think the Dark has much to do with all this? Oh no. Here the Dark is next to helpless, compared to the powers that belong to this place. It is the Lost Land that you pit yourself against here, with all to win or all to lose."

"And that is the Wild Magic," Will said slowly. "Or something very close."

"A form of it," Gwion said. "And more besides."

Bran was standing uncertain, blinking at him. "And you are part of it?"

"Ah," Gwion said reflectively. "I am a renegade part, going

my own way. And although I love my own land most deeply, no good will come to me here." He turned his broad smile on Bran suddenly like a beam of warmth, nodding ahead. "Look there—go on, help yourself."

An ancient, sprawling apple tree curved to the ground before them like a bent-backed ancient man; it was the only tree that grew low and spreading, and did not tower above their heads. Small yellow apples, and others smaller yet but bright green, studded its dark branches among the sparse leaves. Bran stared. "Last year's apples as well as this year's?" He pulled off a yellow apple and bit into its juicy hardness.

Gwion chuckled. "Two years they hang there sometimes. This is a pippin from a long time before your own, remember. There are many things in your own day that were not dreamed of, except by Old Ones, in this age when the Land was lost. But equally there were once other remarkable things that have vanished forever, lost with the Land."

Will said gently, "Forever?" He picked a yellow apple and held it up, his eyes smiling at Gwion.

Gwion looked back at him with a strange faraway look on his strong bearded face. "For ever and ever, we say when we are young, or in our prayers. Twice, we say it, Old One, do we not? For ever and ever . . . so that a thing may be for ever, a life or a love or a quest, and yet begin again, and be for ever just as before. And any ending that may seem to come is not truly an ending, but an illusion. For Time does not die, Time has neither beginning nor end, and so nothing can end or die that has once had a place in Time."

Bran stood turning his pale face from one to the other of them, chewing his apple, saying nothing.

Will said, "And here we stand in a time long gone, that has not yet come. *Here.*"

Bran said suddenly, unexpectedly, "I have been here before."

"Yes," Gwion said. "You were born here. Among many trees like this one."

Will glanced up quickly, but the white-haired boy said nothing more. Nor did Gwion, but moved forward and broke three blackish gnarled twigs from the old apple tree.

A voice came from behind their backs instead: a soft voice, with an unidentifiable accent to it. "And the boy who was born here may well find himself staying here—for ever and ever." A malicious mockery sharpened the tone, flicking like a whip. "And that is a very long time, my friends, however metaphysical we may become about its meaning."

Will turned slowly, deliberately, to face the tall dark-cloaked figure seated on the great black stallion. The Black Rider had put back his hood; the sunlight glinted on his thick chestnut hair, with its reddish glitter like the fur of a fox, and his bright eyes blazed like blue coals. Behind him, further away, other mounted figures stood silently waiting, riders all in black or all in white, one beside every tree and others scattered further back than Will could plainly see.

"There are no more warnings now, Old One," the Black Rider said. "Now it will be a matter of simple challenge, and threat. And of promise."

Gwion said, his voice strong and deep, "Dark promises have no force in this land, my Lord."

The Black Rider glanced down at him as he might have glanced at a dog, or a toddling child. He said contemptuously, "It is wiser to fear the word of a Lord of the Dark than to heed that of a minstrel to a lost king."

Premonition prickled like some fast-crawling creature all across Will's body; it sang in his mind: *Oh, oh, you will be sorry for that word.* . . . But Gwion showed no hint of reaction; he simply moved forward, as if the Black Rider had not been there, and strode past him to the enormous sturdy oak tree in whose shade the dark figure stood.

"No leaf-collecting here, little player," the Rider said mockingly. "The king of trees is out of your reach, I think."

The warning shudder ran through Will even more strongly. Gwion's face was impassive. Carefully and with dignity he reached up one lean brown arm to its full length; caught a jagged-leaved branch, snapped it, and broke it into three.

The Rider said sharply, "I promise you, minstrel, that if

you get into that tower, you will never come out again." They saw the dreadful scar on the side of his face as he turned his head.

"You can do nothing to prevent us, my lord," Will said. Drawing Bran with him, he went towards Gwion and the great oak.

The Black Rider relaxed suddenly, smiling. "Oh, I have no need," he said, and slowly he eased his marvellous night-black stallion to sidestep away so that there was a clear view of the rearing glass tower before Will and Bran.

Will stopped, with a groan of dismay that he could not hide. The Black Rider gave a high snickering laugh. It was all too plain now what he had meant.

The great door of Caer Wydyr was visible at last, high on the rocky base at the top of a steep rough-hewn flight of steps. But it was a door barred against entry by an enchantment Will could never have imagined. Before it, spinning so fast that it was like a bright disc, hung a gigantic wheel. There was no axle, nor any kind of support. The wheel hung there in the air, deadly, forbidding approach, flashing round and round with a speed that gave out a menacing hum.

Bran said in a whisper, *"No!"*

From the Lords of the Dark on their black and white horses, stirring among the trees, there came a rustling of mockery, of malice satisfied. The Black Rider laughed again, an unpleasant menacing sound.

Swinging round in hopeless confusion, Will caught Gwion's bright eyes gazing at him, holding him, gleaming over the strong face and the strange dark stripe of its grey beard. Saying: I must tell you but I cannot tell you—*think*—

And Will thought and suddenly knew.

"Come on!"

Seizing Bran by the arm, he broke into a run and rushed up the steps of the great rock on which the tower stood, away from the mocking Dark, until he was on the top step, so close to the whirling wheel that it seemed likely to cut him in half. The humming shriek of its spinning filled their minds. Gwion was behind them, white teeth flashing in eager delight. Will bent to Bran's baffled, anxious face and said in his ear: "And what last thing did the Lady say?"

He saw relief break like a wave, and heard the words choke out: *"Only the horn can stop the wheel—"*

And Will reached to his belt and took the little gleaming hunting-horn that hung there. He paused, drew in a deep breath, put back his head and blew a single long clear note, high and lovely, singing out like a harmonic over the terrible hum of the spinning sharp wheel. And the wheel spun down at once to a halt, as if an immense force were stopping it, while a long howling shriek of rage rose from the Riders of the Dark below. Will and Bran had an instant to see that the wheel had four spokes, quartering the circle, before Gwion was urging the two of them in turn through the nearest quarter, and slipping through after them.

Gwion pressed the bunch of seven twigs that he held into Will's hand, and without looking at him Will knew now what to do. Seizing the twigs from Bran's hand too, so that he held all three bunches together, he reached out urgently through the spokes of the wheel, where a surge of darkness and fury and menace was streaming towards them up the steps to the tower. With all the force he could manage, he flung the twigs out into the Dark. An immense force like a soundless explosion swept outwards from the tower, and the great wheel began to spin again.

Faster and faster it whirled. The hum rose, the entrance was barred by spinning enchantment with the frustrated Dark screaming in shock and rage below, and Will and Bran and Gwion stood in a soft translucent brightness inside the glass tower of the Lost King.

CHAPTER FIFTEEN

THE KING OF THE LOST LAND

THEY STOOD staring at one another. Outside the tower the fury of the Dark rose as if the whole world were roaring; Will hunched his shoulders instinctively, feeling the force of it like a blow.

And then suddenly, it was gone. The tumult dropped, vanished altogether; they could hear nothing at all but the faint hum of the wheel whirling outside. The abrupt change was more unnerving even than the noise had been.

"What are they doing?" Bran said. He was taut as a tight-wound spring; Will could see a muscle twitching at the side of his jaw.

"Nothing," Will said, with a confidence that was not real. "They can do nothing here. Forget them." He stared round the square room, filling the length and breadth of the tower, into which they had just come. "Look!"

Brightness was everywhere: a soft, greenish light filtered through the quartz-like walls of the room. It could be a cave of ice, Will thought. But this was a cluttered, busy place, as if someone had left it in a hurry while preoccupied with some great complex matter. Piles of curling manuscript lay on the tables and shelves, and on the thick rush mat that covered the floor; against one wall an enormous heavy table was littered with strips of shining metal and chunks of glass and rock, red and white and greenish-blue, all among an array of delicate gleaming tools which reminded Will of the workshop behind his father's jewellery shop at home. Then his eye was caught by something high on the wall: a plain round shield, made of gleaming gold.

Gwion leapt light-footed up on to a table and took the shield down from the wall. He held it out.

"Take this, Will. Three shields, once in the days of his greatness, King Gwyddno made for the Light. Two of them were taken by the Light to places where danger might come, and the third they left here. I have never known why—but perhaps this moment now is why, and has been all along. Here."

Will took the round gleaming thing and slid his arm through the holding-straps on the inner side. "It's beautiful," he said. "And—so are the other two that he made. I have seen them, I think. In . . . other places. They have never been used."

"Let us hope this one need not be used either," Gwion said.

Bran said impatiently, "Where is the king?" He was looking up at a curving wrought-iron staircase, wonderfully curlicued, which spiralled its way up to disappear through an opening in the high glassy ceiling of the room.

"Yes," Gwion said. "Up there. We shall go up, but you must let me lead. We shall come to certain rooms in which you will see no one, and at the last we shall come to the king."

He set one hand on the curving rail of the staircase, and looked hard at Will. "Where is the belt of Signs?"

"It is at the Battle of Mount Badon," Will said wistfully. "Where Merriman took it to the great king, for as much of the winning as can be achieved there. And it will be at the last encounter too, when the Lady comes and all the power of the Light is joined. But not until then. And then only if—" He stopped.

"Eirias," Bran said, his voice tight. "Eirias."

Gwion said swiftly, "Do not say the name yet! That must wait. Only in the sword's own presence may it be named by its name, inside this tower. Come."

They climbed the spiralling staircase, up and up through rooms that were scattered with the impedimenta of living, of eating and sleeping, and yet had, too, the strange deserted look of places left abandoned for a long time. And then Will, last in line, came up to find Bran and Gwion standing silent in a great room unlike any that had gone before. The light filtering through these walls was not cool and icy-green, but dimmer, more subdued, for they stood now inside a great hemisphere, banded in gold and translucent glass so that Will knew it must be the domed top of the tower, from whose peak a golden arrow pointed out at the sea.

The dome was warm, its floor striped with the sunlight that slanted in through the banded roof; and yet it was a strangely gloomy place, bringing a heaviness to the senses. The room held only one square table, set to one side, a carved wooden screen, and a scattering of big high-backed chairs, as sturdy as if they were carved from solid blocks of wood.

"Gwion?" a voice said.

Soft echoes whispered round the dome. It was a husk of a voice, low and without strength. It came from a tall chair facing away from them on the far side of the dome; they could see nothing but the chair's back.

"I am here, my lord," Gwion said. His eyes were warm, and there was love and patience in his voice, as if he spoke to a troubled child. "And . . . and two from the Light are with me."

There was a long pause, with no sound in it except the faint crying of a distant seagull outside the dome.

The voice said at last, cold and abrupt, "You betray me. Send them away."

Gwion crossed the room swiftly and dropped on one knee before the tall carved chair; in the hands of dim light through the roof they saw his lean brindle-bearded face upturned to the unseen king. He said, loving loyalty bright as a flame in his face, *"I betray you, my lord?"*

"No, no," the voice said wearily. "I know better. But you must send them away, minstrel. In that, *you* should know better."

Will said impulsively, coming forward, "But Majesty, the danger is too great." He paused just behind the chair; he could see one thin hand lying limp on the chair-arm, wearing on one finger a great dark-stoned ring like Gwion's ring. He said, in as level a voice as he could manage, "My lord, the Dark is rising, in its last great attempt to take control of the earth from men. And we of the Light cannot prevent that attempt unless we are armed with all the Things of Power made for our purpose. We have all of them but the last, the crystal sword. Which long ago you made for us, my lord the king—and which now you guard."

"I guard nothing," the voice said listlessly. "I exist merely."

Will said, "But the sword is here, as it has been always since its making." He eyes were roving round the room in search as he spoke. "We may not take it unless you give it to us. Give it to us now, Majesty, I beg you."

"Leave me alone," the voice said. "Leave me alone." It was full of an aching sadness that made Will long to give some comfort; but the urgency of his quest was louder yet in his mind.

"The sword is for the Light," he said persistently, "and to the Light it must go." He was looking at a wonderfully carved wooden screen that stood against the slanting wall of the dome, near where the king sat. Was it there simply as a lovely object to be looked at, or to hide something else from view?

The voice said with dull petulance, "You do not say 'must' to me, Old One. If Old One is what you are. I have forgotten all such names."

Behind Will, Bran said sharply, "But we must have Eirias!"

The thin hand on the chair tightened briefly into life; the fingers curled, then fell back again. "Gwion," said the empty voice, "I can do nothing for them. Send them away."

Gwion still knelt, looking up, his face lined with concern. "You are weary," he said unhappily, dropping all ceremony. "I wish you were not always alone."

"Weary of life, minstrel. Weary of the world." The voice was a winter leaf blown by the wind: withered, dry. "No purpose, no savour. Time tosses my mind where it will. And my useless life is the empty cawing of a crow, and any talent I once may have had is dead. Let the toys that it made die with it."

The slow words came from so deep a despair, like a black pit giving back no sound when a stone is dropped in, that the small hairs crawled on the back of Will's neck. It was like listening to a dead man speak.

Bran said clearly, coldly, "You speak like the *Mari Llwyd,* not like a king."

The fingers of the hand curled in again briefly, and then again lay limp. Into the voice crept the weary contempt of long, long experience faced with the blind ignorant vigour of hope. "Boy, callow boy, do not speak to me of life that you have not lived. What do you know of the weight that drags down a king who has failed his people, an artist who has failed his gift? This life is a long cheat, full of promises that can never be kept, errors that can never be righted, omissions that can never be filled. I have forgotten as much of my life as I can manage to forget. Go away, so that I may be free to forget the rest."

As Will stood, speechless, held by the dreadful deep self-loathing in the husky voice, Bran came up level with him. And all Will's senses shouted at him suddenly that a change had begun; that from this moment Bran would no longer be merely the strange albino boy with the tawny eyes, obscure in a North Wales valley where the villagers looked at him sideways and the children mocked his pale face and white hair.

"Gwyddno Garanhir," Bran said in a quiet command as cold and hard as ice, with the Welshness very strong in his voice, "I am the Pendragon, and the destiny of the Light is in my hands to be held or lost. I will not countenance despair. Eirias is my birthright, made by you at my father's bidding. Where is the crystal sword?"

Will stood trembling, his fingernails digging into his palms.

Very slowly, the figure in the chair leaned forward a little and turned towards them, and they saw the face of the king just as they had seen it in the rainbow over the fountain in the rose garden, a little and a long while before. It was unmistakable: a thin face with cheekbones high as wings and lines carved deep in the flesh by sadness. Great channels of despair slanted down from nose to jaw, and shadows lay round the eyes like dark mountain pools. The king glanced first at Will, and then he saw Bran. His face changed.

He sat there motionless, dark eyes staring. There was a long moment of silence, and then the king said, whispering, *"But it was a dream."*

Gwion said softly, "What was a dream, Majesty?"

The king turned his head to Gwion; there was a heartbreaking simplicity in him suddenly, like a small child telling a secret to a friend.

"I dream, endlessly, my minstrel," he said. "I live in my dreams—they are the only thing this emptiness has not touched. Oh sometimes they are black and dreadful, nightmares from the pit. . . . But most of them are wonderful, full of happiness and lost joy, and delight in making and being. Without my dreams, I should have gone mad long ago."

"Ah," Gwion said wrily, "that is true of many men in this world."

"And I dreamed," the king said, looking wonderingly again at Bran, "of a white-headed boy who would come and bring both an end and a beginning. The son of a great father, with all his father's strength in him and more besides. And it seemed to me that I had known the father once, long ago—though I cannot tell where or when, through the mist the emptiness has put in my mind. The white-haired boy . . . there was no colour in him anywhere, in my dream. He had a white head, and white brows, and white lashes to his eyes, and he wore dark circles of glass to protect those eyes from the sun, but when the circles were taken away you could see that the eyes were enchanted, the golden eyes of an owl."

He stood up, shakily supporting his thin frame on one hand against the chair. Gwion lunged forward to help, but the king raised his other hand.

"He came running," he said, "he came running to me across the room there, and the sunlight was in his white hair and he laughed at me, and it was the first music of that kind that this castle has heard for so long, so very long." There was a softening in the grim-set features like a faint glimmer of sunshine in a cloud-grey sky. "He brought an end, but a beginning. He took away the haunting of this place. He kneeled down before me, in my dream, and he said—"

Bran laughed softly; Will could feel all the angry tension fall away out of him. The white-haired boy took a few quick steps forward and knelt before the king, and said, smiling up at him, "And he said, *There are five barriers to be broken to reach the crystal sword, and they are told in five lines that are written in letters of golden fire over the sword itself. Shall I tell you what they are?*"

The king stood looking down at him with a life waking in his eyes that had not been there before. "And I said, *Yes, tell me.*"

"And when I have told you," Bran was looking up into his eyes in a closeness like an embrace, no longer quoting now, "then that will be a falling away of the fifth barrier, Majesty, is not that so? For we have come through four of them already —the words are witness. And if I can break open your despair, which is the tomb of all your hope, then will you let me take the sword?"

The king said, his eyes fast on Bran, "Then it will be yours."

Bran slowly stood up before him, and took a breath, and in the Welsh music of his voice the words came out as a lilting chant.

> "I am the womb of every holt,
> I am the blaze on every hill,
> I am the queen of every hive,
> I am the shield for every head,
> I am the tomb of every hope—
> *I am Eirias!*"

And King Gwyddno let out a long, long sigh like the sound of a wave of the sea washing over sand, and with a sudden crash the carved wooden screen that stood against the wall of the dome fell apart in two pieces, and lay on the ground. And glowing in golden letters on the banded wall they saw the lines that Bran had just spoken aloud, clearly written, and below them on a slab of slate lay like a bright icicle a crystal sword.

The king moved slowly, stiffly, across the smooth rush-matted floor; on the back of the dark green surcoat he wore over his white robe they saw embroidered in gold the royal crest with its roses and leaping fish. King Gwyddno took the sword in his hand, and turned his melancholy drooping body towards them again. He ran one finger along the chased flat side of the sword blade, wonderingly, as if in disbelief that he could ever have made so lovely a thing. Then taking the sword by the cross-piece of its hilt, so that it hung pointing downwards, he held it out to Bran.

"Let the light go to the Light," he said, "and Eirias to its inheritor."

Bran took the sword by the hilt, turning it carefully so that it pointed now straight upward. Instantly he seemed to Will to grow somehow a little more erect, more commanding; the sunlight blazed in his white hair.

Somewhere outside the tower, from far away, there came a long low rumbling like thunder.

The king said expressionlessly, "Now let come what may."

He put his hand up to his head suddenly and rubbed his brow. "There was . . . there was a scabbard. Gwion? I made a scabbard for the sword?"

Gwion's smile lit his face. "You did, Majesty, of leather and of gold. And there must be a breaking of the emptiness, as you call it, in your mind—or you would not remember that."

"It was. . . ." The king's forehead creased, he closed his eyes as if in pain. Then abruptly he opened them again, pointing across the domed room to a plain chest of light-coloured wood, with the figure of a man riding a fish painted in blue on its side.

Gwion went to the chest, and put back the lid. He said

after a moment, "There are three things." A strange note was in his voice, of some emotion Will could not comprehend.

The king said vaguely, "Three?"

Gwion drew from the chest a scabbard and swordbelt of white leather set with strips of gold. "To mask the blaze a little," he said with a smile, holding it out to Bran.

"Bran," Will said slowly, listening to deep faint stirrings within his mind. "I think . . . you should not put the sword into the scabbard yet, not for a moment."

Bran, sword and scabbard in either hand, looked at him with raised eyebrows, and an arrogant tilt to his white head that had not been there before. Then he gave a quick shiver and was Bran again, and said merely, "All right."

Gwion said, still at the chest, "And there is—this." His voice shook, and his hand too, as he took out a small bright harp. He looked across the room at his king. "Not a few moments ago, my lord, I was longing to have my harp that I left in the City, so that I could play for you as I did in the old days."

The king smiled, lovingly. "That too is your harp, minstrel. Long ago I made it for you, in the first days in the tower when I was struggling against despair, struggling still to work. . . ." He shook his head, wondering. "I had forgotten, it is so long . . . I had chosen to be alone, so that all others were barred from this place by the wheel, yet I missed you and your music so greatly that I made the harp. For my Gwion, for my Taliesin, for my player."

"And I shall play it for you in a little," Gwion said.

"You will find it in tune," the king said, and his smile held an echo of the maker's pride in the thing made.

Gwion put down the harp and reached again into the chest; he brought out a small leather bag gathered at the neck by a cord. "This is the third thing," he said, "but I do not know what it is."

He pulled open the neck of the bag, and a stream of small blue-green stones tumbled out into his other hand, smooth, shiny, rounded as though by the sea. One of them fell to the floor; Will picked it up and rolled it round his palm, watching the pattern of colour in its sleek irregular shape.

The king glanced at the stones briefly. "Pretty, but worthless," he said. "I do not remember them."

"You meant to work with them once, perhaps." Gwion poured the stones back into the bag; Will held out the one that had fallen.

Gwion smiled at him suddenly. "Keep it," he said lightly. He picked out another stone and held it to Bran. "And one for you, Bran. Each of you should have a talisman. A piece of a dream to take away with you, from the Lost Land."

The king said softly, vacantly, "Lost . . . lost. . . ."

The distant deep rumbling came again outside, louder than before. All at once the sunlight shafting in through the banded roof faded, and the dome seemed much darker.

Bran looked around. "What is it?"

"It is the beginning," the king said. His thin voice was stronger now, more alive as his face was more alive, and though the resigned acceptance in it was very plain, there was no hint now of the dreadful black emptiness of despair.

Will said, on instinct, "We must not stay under this roof."

Gwion sighed. He looked at Will with wry affection, and Will never afterwards forgot the look: the humorous wide mouth drawn almost into sadness by the lines of experience running down from nose to jaw; the bright eyes, smiling; the crisp curly grey hair, the odd dark stripe in the grey beard. He said to Gwion in his mind: *I like you.*

"Come," Gwion said. With the harp in one crooked arm he went to a part of the curved wall that seemed no different from any other part, reached up, and with one strong pull slid a whole wedge-shaped section of it to one side. The opening gaped like a triangular door. Outside, they saw the sky a dark, dark grey.

Gwion stepped out, down to a balcony. Following him, Will saw a golden balustrade, and realized that this too was identical with the balcony that ran round the dome of the Empty Palace, in the City. But as he looked out from the tower all thought dwindled away.

Westward over the sea, a gigantic bank of dark cloud was massing: heavy, mounded, yellowish-grey. It seemed to writhe, growing and swelling as if it were a live thing.

Will's fingers curled tightly round the strap of the golden shield that he still held on one arm. Bran came out on to the balcony behind him, and last of all came the king: frail now, supporting himself on the side of the opening in the roof, breathing suddenly faster as though the keener outside air were something his lungs had not felt for a long, long time.

The low, distant rumbling still filled the air, coming in like a mist from the westward horizon, where the great clouds rolled. Yet it was not the rumbling of thunder; it was a deeper, more insistent sound, like nothing Will had heard before.

"Be ready," Gwion said softly, behind him.

Will turned and found himself looking straight into the smile-creased dark eyes. He saw calm determination there, and self-possession, but beneath all else a flicker of dreadful blank fear.

"What is it?" he whispered.

Gwion took his harp and drew a series of soft beautiful arpeggios from the strings. He said, as lightly as if it were a casual joke, his eyes imploring Will to ignore the terror behind them, "It is the death of the Lost Land, Old One. It must come, when the time comes." His fingers began patterning the notes into a gentle melody, and the king, leaning against the shining wall of the dome, murmured with pleasure.

The rumbling from the western horizon rose. A wind blew against their cheeks, and stirred their hair: a strange warm wind. Will raised his head, sniffing; all at once the summer air seemed full of a smell of the sea, of salt and wet sand and green weed. The light was dying, the cloud spreading grey over the sky. He heard a faint sound like creaking over his head, and looked up sharply. On top of the dome the pointing golden arrow, still gleaming even in the murky light, was swinging gently round: turning, turning quite around, until it pointed inland, away from the sea. A brightness in the sky beyond it caught Will's eye, and he gasped, and saw that Bran was staring at it too.

Far away out there, on the far side of the Lost Land, over

the roofs of the City still dimly visible in the dwindling light, sudden sprays of light were springing up like fountains, to blaze for a second and vanish again. Like bursting stars, fireworks leapt, splashing the dark sky with brilliant red, green, yellow, blue: erupting over the City in joyous arches of light. There was a wonderful unafraid gaiety in all the sudden brilliance, as if children were flinging blazing branches out from a fire into a looming wild night. Will found himself smiling and yet close to tears; and in the same moment he heard, very faintly over the low roar filling the world now from the west, the high joyous sound of many bells ringing, somewhere out there, somewhere in the City. Gwion softly shifted the tune and the time of his melody so that his harp chimed in with the bells, and Will breathed fast as he stood on the balcony looking all round at the livid menacing sky and the dark sea and the brilliant gay fireworks challenging both. He was filled with a wild exhilaration that was terror and delight all in one: terror for the people of the Lost Land, delight in the contemptuous defiance they flung out to their doom.

Sea grew dark as sky; there was a new rumbling now as the waves grew, their angry tops visible far out, gleaming, throwing spray. The wind blew more strongly, whipping the king's thin hair across his face. Will put up his shield as a shelter. Gwion, still playing, moved back slowly towards the opening in the dome of the tower, moving so that the king moved before him, supported by the wall. And then with a great splitting flare of lightning the sky roared, and the sea seemed to cry out, and a huge wall of water came thundering towards them from the sea, over the sand and reedy marsh, swallowing trees and land and the lines of the river, spreading, swirling, wild. Bran gripped Will's arm with one hand, and Will saw, turning, that the sword Eirias was gleaming bluish-white as if from the inner heat of a fire.

In the dark sky over the City the fireworks suddenly ceased, and the sound of the bells became a long jangling confusion, wild over the lilt of Gwion's harp. Then they too abruptly stopped. But Gwion's music went on. The sea struck at the tower somewhere below; they felt it shake beneath their feet. Wave after wave came roaring, the sea rose higher, the king's light voice called out on the warm fierce wind, "Lost! Lost!" And out of the raging sea came sailing impossibly towards them, slantwise down the great waves, the chunky boat with its black-haired captain and single tight-filled brown sail, and from his place at the tiller the sailor reached out an arm to Will and Bran, beckoning, the deck of his vessel almost level for a moment with the balcony of the tower.

"Go!" Gwion shouted to them; he stood leaning sideways, his shoulder supporting the failing king.

"Not without you!"

"I belong here!" They saw only the last flash of a smile over the shadowy bearded face. "Go! Bran! Save Eirias!"

And the words hit Bran like a spur, and he seized Will and leapt with him into the boat tossing an arm's length away. The boat plunged down the side of a wave; for an instant they heard Gwion's harp sweet and faint through the thundering sea, until one single shattering blinding streak of brilliance came out of the sky and struck the tower, splitting the dome in two, and the golden arrow was driven from the roof as if it were suddenly a live malevolent thing and came hurtling over the waves down towards them. Out of an instinct not his own Will flung up the golden shield with both his arms, and the flashing arrow struck the shield and in a great flare of yellow light both vanished, flinging Will down on his back in the leaping boat.

His head rang, his eyes blurred. He saw Bran standing over him with the sword flaming blue in his hand, he heard the waves roar, he saw the lean dark face of the ferryman twisted with effort, as the man struggled to keep the boat heading away from harm. The world tossed and roared in a dark endless turmoil, with no count of time passing.

And then there was a lurch so violent that Will lost all consciousness, and when he opened his eyes he was in a world of grey light and soft sound, the gentle murmuring of small waves on a beach, and he and Bran were lying on a long stretch of sand, in a clear morning, with a whitish-blue sky overhead. The crystal sword gleamed white in Bran's hand, the scabbard lay at his side. The great beach reached far before them into the estuary of the River Dyfi; green sand-hills glimmered at its far edge, and beyond over the mountains and the grey roofs of Aberdyfi came the first golden edge of the rising sun.

PART FOUR
THE MIDSUMMER TREE

CHAPTER SIXTEEN

SUNRISE

JANE HAD GONE OUT before five, from the sleeping hotel. She did not wake her brothers. Irrationally but strongly she felt that when Merriman had said, "Be on the beach at sunrise," he had meant the words particularly for her. The boys, she thought, could follow in their own time.

So she slipped out alone into the grey morning, and crossed the silent road and railway track, hearing only the surf a distant thunder on the beach beyond. A dozen startled rabbits bounded away from her as she crossed the railway, their white scuds bobbing. Now and then a sheep's deep call floated down from the mountain. The morning was colourless and cold; Jane shivered, in spite of her sweater, and ran over the rolling golf course towards the high dunes. Then she was climbing through long wiry marram grass, with the dew-darkened sand sifting cold through her sandals, until the last step brought her breathless to the top of the tallest dune and the world opened before her in a great sweep of brown sand and grey sea, its flat horizon dissolving into mist where the arms of Cardigan Bay embraced the sea and the sky.

Something lay at her feet on the crest of the dune; looking down, Jane found a small brown rabbit. Its eyes were open and unblinking; it was dead. When she stepped over it she saw with a shock that its stomach had been torn open

209

and the guts ripped out, before the rest of the untouched furry body had been tossed casually aside.

Jane went on down the dune in long sliding steps, more slowly, wondering for the first time what she should expect to see when the sun rose.

She crossed the dry sand above highwater mark, scarred with the footprints of yesterday's holiday-makers and their dogs. Then feeling suddenly vulnerable she went on, out to the vast exposed sweep of sand that fills the Dyfi estuary at low water, and stretches for ten miles and more up the coast on either side. Nothing was before her but the grey sea and sky and the long soft-roaring line of the surf. Through the sandals her feet could feel the hard rippled pattern left on the sand by the waves.

Flocks of roosting gulls rose lazily as she reached the smooth wet sand nearer the sea. Dunlins swooped, piping. Round any tide-left heap of seaweed thousands of sand-hoppers busily leapt, a strange flurrying mist of movement in all the stillness. The record of other flurrying was written already on the hard sand: gouges and claw-marks and empty broken shells, where hungry herring gulls at dawn had seized any mollusc a fraction too slow at burrowing out of reach. Here and there an enormous jellyfish lay stranded, with great slashes torn out of the translucent flesh by the seagulls' greedy beaks. Out over the sea the birds coasted, peaceful, quiet. Jane shivered again.

She veered to the left and walked towards the great jutting corner of sand where the River Dyfi met the sea. A thin sheet of water spread rapidly towards her feet; the tide was coming in, advancing more than a foot every minute over these long flat sands. On the corner of the estuary Jane paused, isolated far out on the enormous beach, feeling small as a shellfish under the empty sky. She looked inland, to the village of Aberdyfi lying on the river, with the mountains rising on either side, and she saw that the sky over the huddle of grey slate roofs was pink and blue, mounded with reddish clouds. And then, behind Aberdyfi, the sun came up.

In a brilliant yellow-white glare the fierce globe rose out

of the land, and Jane swung round again, back towards the sea. All the greyness had gone. Suddenly now the sea was blue, the curling wavetops shone a brilliant white; seagulls gleamed white in the air and in a long roosting line on the golden sandbar in the mouth of the river, where they had not even been visible before. Her shadow lay long and thin before her on the sand, reaching out to sea. Each shell had its own dark clear shadow now, each strand of weed, even the ripples of the sand. Only the mountains across the estuary were dark and obscure, vanishing into cloud; at their feet a long white arm of mist shrouded the river. Overhead in the blue sky high bars of cloud were moving fast inland, row after row, but the wind that she could feel rising down here, cold on her face, was blowing from the land out to the sea.

Now in the sunlight Jane saw clearly the small hieroglyphs written by the feet of birds all round her on the sand: the arrowhead footmarks of gulls, the scutter of sandpipers and turnstones. A black-backed gull swooped overhead, and its yelping, yodelling cry faded into the wind, a long laugh ending in a husky croak. A high piping came from the sea's edge. The water ran in faster, faster, over the flat sand. All at once Jane too began to run, away from the sea, towards the sun. The clouds flew over her head faster than she, rushing eastward; yet into her face the rising wind blew, stronger and stronger, picking up the sand as it rose, in long streamers and trails. It blew into her eyes in a fine stinging mist; she ran more slowly, staggering against it, leaning into it, seeing only the flying streams of bright sand.

Voices called her name; she saw Simon and Barney rushing towards her from the dunes. She thought: *they came sooner than I expected. . . .* But something drove her to ignore them, to run on; even as they came up level with her she flung herself forward, eastward into the wind, with the boys at her side.

And then they stumbled as ahead of them two figures took shape in the flying sand, against the brilliant sun, like apparitions in a golden mist. The bars of cloud overtook the sun and the blazing light died, all colour dropping away, and before them stood Will and Bran. And bright against his white sweater and jeans Bran carried a gleaming sword.

Barney's yell was pure triumphant delight. *"You've got it!"*

"Hey!" said Simon, beaming.

Jane said weakly, "Oh goodness. Are you all right?" Then she saw the sword. "Oh Bran!"

The wind whistled softly past them on the beach, chill but more docile now, blowing gritty streamers of sand against their legs. Bran held out the sword toward them, slantwise, turning the two-edged blade so that even beneath the clouding sky its engraved surface glittered and danced. They saw that a thin core of gold ran down the centre of the crystal blade from the handle, a golden handle behind an ornate crosspiece hilt, inlaid with mother-of-pearl.

"Eirias," Bran said. "Yes, very beautiful." He was staring at the sword through narrowed eyes; his dark glasses were gone, and without them his face looked oddly naked and very pale. He turned inland slowly, the sword in his hand turning as if it were leading him. "Eirias, blazing. Sword of the sunrise."

"Reaching to the sunrise," Will said.

"That's right!" Bran looked at him quickly, in a kind of grateful relief. "It does, it turns to the east, Will. It—pulls, like." He pointed the sword high towards the glow in the cloud cover behind which the newly risen sun shone.

"The sword knows why it was made," Will said. He looked deeply tired, Jane thought: drained, as though strength had run out of him—whereas Bran seemed full of new life, vibrant as a taut wire.

The world brightened and filled with sudden colour as the sun shone out for a moment through a gap in the cloud. The sword gleamed.

"Sheathe it, Bran!" Will said suddenly.

Bran nodded, as if the same quick wariness had struck his own mind, and they watched in astonishment as he seemed to mime the raising and thrusting of the sword into an imaginary scabbard on an imaginary sword belt at his side. But as he thrust the sword down, it disappeared.

Jane, staring with her mouth open, found Bran looking at her. "Ah, Jenny," he said softly. "You can't see it now?"

She shook her head.

"So no other . . . ordinary person will either, I suppose," Simon said.

Barney said, "What about the Dark?"

Jane saw both Bran and Will glance up instinctively, warily, out at the sea. She turned, but saw only the golden bar and the white waves, and the blue sea creeping closer in over the long sands. She thought, *what's been happening to them?*

As if in answer Will said, "There's too much to tell. But it's like a race, now."

"To the east?" Bran said.

"To the east, where the sword leads us. A race against the rising."

Simon said simply, "What d'you want us to do?"

Will's straight brown hair was falling over his eyes; his round face was intent, concentrated, as if he were listening and speaking at the same time, repeating some inner voice. "Go back," he said, "and you will find things . . . arranged so that other people will not get in the way. And you must do what is arranged."

"By Great-Uncle Merry?" Barney said hopefully.

"Yes," Will said.

The sunlight died again, the wind whispered. Far out at sea the clouds were thicker, darker now, massing.

"There's a storm-front building," Simon said.

"Not building," Bran said. "Built, and on its way."

"One thing," Will said. "This now is the hardest time of all, because anything may happen. You have seen the Dark at work, you three. You know that although it may not destroy you, it can put you in the way of destroying yourself. So—your own judgment is all that can keep you on the track." He was looking at all three of them anxiously.

Simon said, "We know."

The wind was growing stronger; it began to tug at them again, lashing their legs and faces with sand. The clouds were solid over the place where the sun had disappeared, the

light as cold and grey now as when Jane had first come down
to the beach.

Sand whirled up in strange clouds from the dunes, flurrying, swirling, and suddenly there was a sound out of the
gold-brown mist, a muffled thudding like the sound of a heart
beating, but diffused all round them so they could not tell
where it began. Jane saw Will's head go up stiff and alert,
and Bran too turn in search like a questing dog; suddenly
the two of them were standing back to back, covering each
direction, watchful and protective. The thudding grew
louder, closer, and Bran suddenly swept his arm up holding
the sword Eirias, bright with a light of its own. But in the
same moment the muffled sound was a thunder all around
them, close, close, and out of the whirling sand came a
white-robed figure galloping on a tall white horse. The
White Rider sent his horse on one thundering pass beside
them, the white hood hiding his face, white robe swirling,
and at the last instant as they flinched away he leaned swiftly
sideways from the saddle, sent Simon sprawling on the sand
with one swinging blow, snatched Barney up into his grip,
and disappeared.

The wind blew, the sand scurried and leapt, and there
was no longer anyone there.

"Barney!" Jane's voice cracked. "Barney! Will—where is
he?"

Will's face was twisted with concern and an intent listening; he looked at her once, blindly, as if not sure who she
was. Waving back over the dunes he said hoarsely, "Go
back—we will find him." Then he was standing with Bran,
each of them with one hand on the hilt of the crystal sword,
Bran glancing sideways at him as if waiting for instruction;
and Will said, *"Turn,"* and without letting go of the sword
they disappeared in the blink of an eye as if they had never
been there. All that Jane and Simon had was the dark ghost
that is left inside the eye by a vanished bright light, for in
the last moment they had seen blue-white flame blaze up
and down the length of the sword.

"They'll bring him back," Simon said huskily.

"Oh Simon! What can we do?"

"Nothing. Hope. Do what Will told us. Aaah!" Simon ducked his head, blinking. "This damn sand!" And as if in retort the wind dropped suddenly down to nothing, and the whirling sand fell to the beach, to lie in utter stillness, with no sign at all of its manic blowing except the telltale little escarpment of sand sloping back from every exposed shell or pebble on the beach.

In silence they tramped back together toward the dunes.

Nothing took shape in Barney's mind but the whirling sense of speed, and then a dim growing awareness of restraint, of his hands tied before him, and a bandage over his eyes. Then rough hands were moving him, prodding him forward to stumble over stony ground. Once he fell, and cried out as his knee hit a rock; voices spoke impatiently in a strange guttural tongue, but after that a guiding hand was slipped beneath his arm.

He heard military-sounding commands, and the walking grew smoother; doors opened and closed, and then he was stopped and the covering pulled from his eyes. And Barney, blinking, found himself being studied by a weather-beaten dark-bearded face with bright dark eyes: wise eyes, deepset, that reminded him of Merriman. The man was leaning against a heavy wooden table; he wore trousers and jerkin of leather over a thick woollen shirt. Still gazing at Barney, eyes flicking from his face to his clothes and back again, he said something curtly in the guttural speech.

"I don't understand," Barney said.

The man's face hardened a little. "English indeed," he said. "The voice to match the hair. Have they reached such a pass that they must use children now as spies?"

Barney said nothing, since he felt he was spying indeed, peeping out of the corners of his eyes to discover where he might be. It was a low, dark room with wooden walls and floor and beamed roof; through a window he glimpsed outer walls of grey stone. Men who seemed to be soldiers stood grouped around; they wore only a kind of leathern armour over rough clothes, but each had a knife at his belt, and some carried bows as tall as themselves. They were looking at him with hostility, some with open hatred, Barney shivered suddenly, in fear, at the sight of one man's hand playing restlessly with his knife. He looked up desperately at the dark-eyed man.

"I'm not a spy, truly. I don't even know where I am. I was kidnapped."

"Kidnapped?" The man frowned, uncomprehending.

"Stolen. Carried off."

The dark eyes grew colder. "Stolen, to be brought to my stronghold, in the one part of Wales where no Englishman even of my allies dares set foot? The Marcher Lords are foolish, and do many stupid things in their rivalries, but none is quite as stupid as that. Try again, boy, if you wish to save your life. I can see no reason yet why I should not listen to my men, who are anxious to hang you by the neck in the next five minutes, outside that door."

Barney's throat was dry; he could scarcely swallow. He said again, whispering, "I am not a spy."

From the shadows behind the leader the man with the knife said something roughly, contemptuously, but another laid a hand on his arm and stepped forward, speaking a few soft words: an old man, with a heavily wrinkled brown face and wisping white hair and beard. He was looking closely at Barney.

Suddenly another soldier came hurrying into the room and spoke rapidly in the guttural tongue; the bearded leader let out an angry exclamation. He said a few brief words to the old man, nodding in Barney's direction, then swung preoccupied out of the room with men close around him. Only two soldiers remained, guarding the door.

"And where were you stolen from, boy?" The old man's voice was soft and lisping, with a heavy accent.

Barney said miserably, "From—from a long way away."

Bright eyes watched him sceptically through the wrinkles. "I am Iolo Goch, bard to the Prince, and I know him well, boy. He has had bad news, and it will not help his mood. When he comes back I advise you to tell him the truth."

"The Prince?" Barney said.

The old man looked at him coldly, as if Barney were questioning the title. "Owain Glyndwr," he said with chilly pride. "Prince, indeed. Owain ap Gruffydd, Lord of Glyndyvrdwy and Sycharth, Yscoed and Gwynyoneth, and now in this great rebellion proclaimed Prince of Wales. And all Wales is with him against the English, and Henry Plantagenet cannot catch him, nor hold even his English castles here or the towns they are pleased to call English burghs. All Wales is rising." A lilt came into his voice, as if he were singing. "And the farmers have sold their cattle to buy arms, and the mothers have sent their sons to the mountains, to join Owain. The Welshmen who work in England have come home, bringing English weapons with them, and the Welsh scholars at Oxford and Cambridge have left their books, to join Owain. And we are winning. Wales has a leader again. And Englishmen will no longer own Welsh lands and despise and rule us from Westminster, for Owain ap Gruffydd will lead us to set ourselves free!"

Barney listened helplessly to the passion in the frail voice, his uneasiness growing. He felt very lonely and small.

The door crashed open, and Glyndwr was there again among his men, scowling, silent. He glanced from Barney to Iolo Goch; the old man shrugged.

"Listen to me now, boy," said Glyndwr, his dark-bearded face grim. "There is a comet in the sky these nights, to show my coming triumph, and on that sign I shall ride. Nothing shall stop me. Nothing—least of all the thought of tearing apart a spy from King Henry who refuses to tell his sending." His voice rose a little, quivering with control. "I have just heard that a new English army is camped the other side of Welshpool. You have one minute remaining to tell me who sent you into Wales, and whether that army knows I am here."

Only one thought sang through the fear loud in Barney's head now: *He may belong to the Dark, don't talk, don't tell him who you are. . . .*

He said, choking, "No."

The man shrugged. "Very well. I have sent to speak once

more with the one who brought you to me. The light-voiced one from Tywyn, with the white horse. And after that—"

He broke off, staring at the door, and as Barney turned his head the whirling seemed to be back, the speed and the turning, turning. . . .

. . . and turning, turning, Will and Bran, each holding the gleaming crystal sword, found themselves suddenly still now. A heavy wooden door before them burst open, and inside in a low-roofed dark room they saw a group of armed men. One stood separate, a dark bearded man with an air of authority, and before him was Barney standing very small and tight-faced. Several of the men lunged forward in shouting confusion, and the bearded one snapped one sharp word and they fell back instantly like startled dogs, swift but reluctant, looking at their leader with an astonishment that was almost suspicion.

Will's senses as an Old One were vibrating like a harpstring. He stared at the man with the beard, and the man stared back for a moment and then gradually the grim lines of his face were relaxing, changing, becoming a smile. An unspoken greeting in the Old Speech came into Will's mind, and aloud the man said, in halting English, "You are come to a wild time, Sign-seeker. But welcome, if my men do not take you for another English informer such as we have here."

"Will," Barney said huskily, "he keeps telling me I'm a spy and they want to kill me. Do you know him?"

Will said slowly, "Greetings, Owain Glyndwr."

"The greatest Welshman of all." Bran was gazing in awe at the bearded man. "The only one ever to unite Wales against the English, through all the quarrelling and feuding."

Glyndwr was looking at him with narrowed eyes. "But you . . . you. . . ." He glanced uncertainly at Will's blank expressionless face, and shook his head crossly. "Ah no, nonsense. No place for dreams in my head, with the last and hardest battle waiting us. And the bloody English coming up like ants in spring." He turned to Will, waving a hand at Barney. "Is the boy with you, Old One?"

"Yes," Will said.

"That explains much," Glyndwr said. "But not his stupidity in failing to tell me so."

Barney said defensively, "How was I to know you weren't part of the Dark?"

The Welshman put back his head with a curt incredulous laugh, but then straightened, looking with something like respect. "Well. True. Not badly done. *Sais bach*. Take him now, Sign-seeker." He reached out one strong arm and propelled Barney backwards as if he had been a toy. "And go about your purposes in my land in peace, and I will give you any support you need."

"There will be great need," Will said grimly, "if it is not already too late." He pointed to the sword that Bran was already holding out before him, in wonder and alarm; the blade was flickering again with blue light, as it had done at the destruction of the Lost Land, as it had done at the rushing descent of the Dark that had carried Barney away.

Glyndwr said abruptly, "The Dark. But this is my stronghold—there can be none of the Dark here."

"There are many," said a soft voice at the door. "And by right, since you let the first of them in."

"*Diawl!*" Glyndwr sprang upright, instinct pulling a dagger from his belt; for in the doorway, between two armed men frozen helplessly out of movement, stood the White Rider, a robed figure with eyes and teeth gleaming out of the shadows of the white hood.

"You sent for me, Owain of Gwynedd," the Rider said.

"Sent for you?"

"*The light-voiced one from Tywyn, with the white horse,*" said the White Rider mockingly. "Whom your men welcomed so warmly for the gift of a spying English boy." The voice hardened. "And who claims in return now another boy, of more significance, and with him the sword he carries."

"You have no claim over me," Bran said with contempt. "The sword brings me into my power and out of your reach, in this time or any other."

Owain Glyndwr looked at Bran, at Will, and back at Bran:

at the white hair and the pale face with its tawny eyes, and the sword-blade flickering with blue flame.

"The sword is two-edged," the White Rider said.

Bran said, "The sword belongs to the Light."

"The sword belongs to no one. It is in the possession of the Light only. Its power is the power of the Old Magic that made it."

"Made it at the command of the Light," Will said.

"And yet also the tomb of every hope," said the Rider softly, masked still by the white hood. "Do you not remember, Old One? It was written. And there was no word as to whose hopes should be entombed."

"But they shall be your own!" Owain Glyndwr said suddenly, and he snapped some words in Welsh to his men and sprang towards the back wall of the room, reaching for something. Soldiers flung themselves at the white-robed form of the Rider. None managed to touch him; they fell sideways, backwards, colliding with some hard invisible wall, and the Rider lunged forward at Bran. But Bran swept the sword Eirias to and fro before him as if writing in the air, and the sword left a sheet of blue flame hanging and the Rider fell back with a shriek. Even as he moved he seemed to change, to multiply as if suddenly there were a crowd with him; but Owain was calling, urgently and Will dared not wait to see, but followed the rest through a doorway they had not seen before.

Then leather-clad Welsh soldiers were pushing them on to the backs of a string of sturdy grey mountain ponies, and past slate cliffs and stone walls and through green lanes they trotted swiftly and silently where Owain led. The roar and confusion of the Dark rose behind them, and with it the clash of swords and the song of arrows from long bows, and voices shouting in English as well as Welsh. Will said nothing, but he knew that another battle as well as their own was beginning there, the reason for the Dark's choice of this time for their new hostaging, and that Owain was not in the place where he must have ached to be.

Only when they reached a mountain path where the land

rose very steeply, and Owain motioned them to dismount and to follow him on foot, did Will look openly back—and saw smoke rising from the grey roofs they had left, and flame leaping.

Owain said, bitterly, "The Norman rides always on the back of the Dark, as the Saxon did, and the Dane."

Barney said unhappily, "And I'm all those things mixed up, I suppose. Norman and Anglo-Saxon *and* Dane."

"In what century?" Glyndwr said, pausing to stare ahead up the mountain.

"The twentieth," Barney said.

The Welshman stopped very still for a moment. He looked at Will. Will nodded.

"*Iesu mawr,*" Glyndwr said; then he smiled. "If the Circle spreads that far forward, it is not so bad to find failure here, for a time. Until the last summoning of the Circle, outside all Time." He looked down at Barney. "No worry about your race, boy. Time changes the nature of them all, in the end."

Bran said from above them, urgently, "The Dark is coming!" In his hand Eirias was burning a brighter blue.

Owain looked down the mountain the way they had come, and his mouth tightened. Will turned too, and gasped; a sheet of white flame was moving steadily towards them up through the bracken, without sound or heat, remorseless in its pursuit of those it sought to destroy. A troop of Glyndwr's soldiers stood directly in its path.

"It is not so bad as it seems," the Welsh leader said, watching Will's face. "Glyndwr has the tricks of an Old One, be assured." The white teeth flashed in his dark face, and he clapped Will on the shoulder, pushing him. "Go," he said, "go up that path, and you shall shortly be where you are meant to be. Leave me to take the Dark on a dance into these hills. And if my men and I shall seem to be kept in these hills forever, that will not be such a bad thing, for it will prove to my people that the Lord of the Dark was wrong, and that hope does not lie dead in a tomb but is always alive for the hearts of men."

He glanced at Bran and raised his dagger in a formal

salute. "*Pob hwyl,* my brother," he said gravely. Then he and his men were gone, darting back down the mountain, and Will led the way up the path on which he had been set. It wound between bleak points of grey rock, narrower and narrower, until they came to a sudden turn where the rock overhung the path and each of them had to bend his head to pass beneath a low natural arch. And at the moment when all three of them were in line, on that piece of the path which lay under the rock, there was a whirling and a turning of the air about them, and a long, strange, husky shrieking in their ears, and when the giddiness went out of their minds they were in a different place and a different time.

CHAPTER SEVENTEEN

THE TRAIN

SIMON AND JANE had left the dunes and crossed the golf course, coming to the wire fence edging the railway track, when they heard the strange noise. It rang out over their heads on the wind: a clear startling metallic clang, like the single blow of a hammer on an anvil.

"What was that?" Jane was very jumpy still.

"Railway signal. Look." Simon pointed to the lonely pole standing beside the track ahead. "I never noticed it was there before."

"Must be a train coming."

Simon said slowly, "But the signal's gone to 'Stop'."

"Well, the train's already been by, then," Jane said without interest. "Oh Simon, I wish we knew what's happening to Barney!" Then she broke off, listening, as a long, shrieking, husky whistle came on the wind, from a long way off towards Tywyn. They were standing close to the railway fence now. The whistle came again, louder. There was a humming in the rails.

"There's the train coming now."

"But such a funny noise—"

And they saw in the distance, against the growing grey clouds, a long plume of white smoke, and heard the rising roar, closer and closer, of a fast-moving train. Then it came into sight, round the distant bend, and grew clearer, rushing

at them, and it was like no train they had ever seen there before.

Simon gave a great whoop of astonished joy. "Steam!"

Almost at once there was a sudden hissing and groaning
and scraping as the train came closer to the signal and the
driver flung on his brakes; black smoke belched from the
funnel of the enormous green locomotive harnessed to the
long train—longer than any normally on that line, a dozen
carriages or more, all gleaming as if new in two colours,
chocolate brown below and a creamy almost-white above.
The train slowed, slowed, its wheels screeching and whimpering on the track; the vast engine came slowly past Simon and
Jane standing wide-eyed at the fence, and the driver and fire-
man, blue-overalled, dusty-faced, grinned and raised hands
in greeting. With a last long whish of steam the train stopped,
and stood still, hissing gently.

And in the first carriage, a door swung open and a tall
figure stood in the doorway, with one hand outstretched,
beckoning.

"Come on now! Over the fence, quickly!"

"Great-Uncle Merry!"

They clambered over the wire fence and Merriman hauled
them one by one up into the train; from the level of the
ground the door was almost as high as their heads. Merriman
swung the door shut with a solid crash; they heard the clang
of the signal again as its arm went down, and then the
locomotive began to stir, a slow heavy chuffing rising in
speed and sound, with the dunes slipping past outside, faster
and faster, swaying, rocking, clicketty-clacking, the wheels
beginning to sing.

Jane choked suddenly and clutched at Merriman.

"Barney—they've taken Barney, Gumerry—"

He held her close for a moment. "Quietly, gently now.
Barney is where we are going."

"Truly?"

"Truly."

Merriman led them to the first compartment in the swaying
train, its long plush seats quite empty. He closed the sliding

glass door behind them, and they collapsed on to the padded cushions.

"That engine, Gumerry!" Simon, an expert railway-fancier, was lost in admiring wonder. "King class, from the old Great Western, ages ago—and this old-fashioned carriage—I didn't think they even existed any more, outside a museum."

"No," Merriman said vaguely. Sitting there he looked the same rumpled figure who had wandered occasionally into their lives for as long as they could remember; his long bony frame wore a nondescript dark sweater and trousers, and his thick white hair was tousled. He was staring out of the window; the little compartment was suddenly dark, lit only by a dim yellow bulb in the ceiling, as the train dived into a succession of short tunnels and came out beyond Aberdyfi, running again along the river. A small station whisked by.

"Is it some special train?" Simon said. "Not stopping at stations?"

"Where are we going?" said Jane.

"Not too far," Merriman said. "Not very far."

Simon said abruptly, "Will and Bran have the sword."

"I know," Merriman said. He smiled proudly. "I know. Rest now a little, and wait. And—do not show surprise at meeting anyone on this train. No matter who it may be."

Before they could wonder what he might mean, a figure stopped in the corridor outside their compartment. The windowed door slid open, and John Rowlands stood there, swaying with the motion of the train. He looked spruce and unfamiliar in a dark and rather baggy suit; he was staring at them in amazement.

"Good day, John Rowlands," Merriman said.

"Well fancy that now," John Rowlands said blankly. He smiled slowly at Jane and Simon, and nodded; then he looked at Merriman, a strange look, wary and puzzled. "Funny places we do meet in," he said.

Merriman gave an amiable shrug.

"Where are you going, Mr. Rowlands?" Jane said.

John Rowlands grimaced. "Shrewsbury, to the dentist. And for Blod to do a bit of shopping."

The train's whistle shrieked, and another small station flashed by. They were deep in the hills now, travelling through cuttings, with little to be seen outside the windows but high grassy banks blurred by speed. In the train corridor someone approached John Rowlands; he straightened, standing back.

Simon said politely, "Hallo, Mrs. Rowlands."

Jane heard the warm Welsh voice.

"Well here is a nice surprise then! I wondered who John was talking to. Not having seen anyone we knew get on the train at Tywyn."

There was a faint question in the words, but Simon rode over it.

"Isn't it a marvelous train? Steam!"

"Just like in the old days," John Rowlands said. "Must be some sort of anniversary, revival, whatever. I thought I was back thirty years when she came into the station."

"Won't you come and sit in here with us, Mrs. Rowlands?" Jane said.

"That would be very nice." Smiling, Blodwen Rowlands moved into the doorway, so that she could see Jane; her eyes flickered past to Merriman.

"Oh," said Jane. "Mrs. Rowlands—this is our great-uncle, Professor Lyon."

"*Sut 'dach chi?*" said Merriman's deep voice, expressionless.

"How do you do?" said Blodwen Rowlands, nodding, still smiling. She added, to Jane, "I will just get my bag," and disappeared along the corridor.

"I didn't know you spoke Welsh," Simon said.

"On occasion," Merriman said.

"Like a native," said John Rowlands. He came into the compartment and sat down next to Simon. Two figures passed in the corridor, then another, without looking in.

"Is the train full?" Jane said, looking after the last retreating back.

"Filling up," Merriman said.

Mrs. Rowlands came back with her handbag and hesitated in the doorway.

"Would you like the corner?" said Jane automatically, moving up the seat towards Merriman.

"Thank you, my dear." Blodwen Rowlands gave her the astonishing smile that made her face glow with warmth, and sat down next to her. "And where are you all going?" she said.

Jane looked into her eyes, so friendly and close, and paused. A great sense of strangeness swept over her; there seemed to be no light in Blodwen Rowlands' eyes, as if they were not rounded but flat. She thought: *Don't be silly;* blinked, looked away and said, "Great-Uncle Merry's taking us out for the day."

"To the Marches," Merriman said in the deep unemotional voice he used for strangers. "The Border country. Where all the battles so often began."

Blodwen Rowlands took some knitting from her bag, a bright red bundle, and said, "Very nice."

The train swayed and sang. A large man passed slowly in the corridor, paused, looked in, and gave a courteous half-bow towards Merriman. They all stared at him. He had indeed a striking appearance; his skin was very black and his thick hair snow-white. Merriman inclined his head gravely in return, and the man moved away. Jane became conscious of a rapid clicking sound; Mrs. Rowlands had started knitting very fast.

Simon said in a fascinated hiss, "Who was that?"

"An acquaintance of mine," Merriman said.

Down the corridor in the same direction, limping, leaning on a stick, came an elderly lady in an elegant but old-fashioned coat, with a toque-like hat set at a dashing angle on her head and a certain wild wispiness about her pinned-up grey hair. She nodded in at Merriman. "Good day, Lyon," she said, in a resonant, imperious voice.

Merriman said gravely, "Good day, madam," and the lady's sharp eyes flickered over them all and then she was gone.

Four small boys ran past, laughing, clattering, boisterous.

"What weird clothes!" said Jane with interest, leaning to peer after them. "Sort of tunics."

The train swayed and lurched, roaring round a bend, and she sat back again rather suddenly.

Simon said thoughtfully, "Some kind of uniform, maybe."

Mrs. Rowlands took out a second ball of wool from her bag, yellow, and began knitting it together with the red.

"A busy train," John Rowlands said. "If there were more like this they might not be talking about closing the line."

Simon stood up, steadying himself against the door jamb. "Excuse me a moment."

"Certainly," Merriman said. He began an amiable conversation with John Rowlands about the necessity for railway services, while Mrs. Rowlands listened, rapidly knitting, and Jane watched the purple-brown sweep of the mountains and the close grassy banks alternately flashing by. Simon disappeared for a long time, then stuck his head in the door.

"Show you something," he said casually to Jane.

She went out with him; he closed the door and drew her to the end of the corridor, where a locked door ended the coach.

"This is the front end of the train," Simon said in a peculiar voice. "There's nothing this side of our compartment."

"So?" said Jane.

"So if you think about all those people who've been coming past—"

Jane gasped; it came out as a sort of hiccup. "They came from this end! All of them! But they couldn't have!"

"But they did," Simon said. "And I bet you there'll be more after we go back. The train's pretty full already, as far as I went. With the most peculiar mixture of people, in all different clothes. All kinds and colours and shapes. It's like the United Nations."

They looked at one another.

Jane said slowly, "Better go back, I suppose."

"Look normal," Simon said. "Concentrate."

Jane was trying so hard to concentrate that she went past the door of their compartment to the next. A man sitting in the corner there facing her looked up as she approached, and smiled through the window a sudden warm broad smile of recognition. He was an oldish man with a round, weather-beaten face and wiry grey eyebrows; his hair fluffed out in a grey tonsure round a bald head.

"Captain Toms!" Jane said joyfully, and then she blinked, or the air seemed to blink, and there was no one there.

"What?" Simon said.

"I thought—" Jane said. "I thought I saw someone we used to know." She looked hard at the empty seat; there was nobody in the compartment at all. "But—I didn't."

"Normal, now," Simon said. He opened the sliding door of their own compartment and they went back in.

They sat in silence, while voices eddied round them and Mrs. Rowlands' needles furiously clicked. Jane leaned her head back, looking out of the window, letting the rhythm of the wheels carry her mind. They clattered and clacked, merging with the needles' sound; with a twitch of nightmare she felt they were chattering: *into the dark, into the dark, into the dark—*

Then all at once Jane's mouth was dry, and her fingers clutched at the seat. Like a mist she could see in the fields outside a group of horsemen riding, galloping, leaping hedges, and though the train was rushing at full speed, yet they were riding as fast as the train. . . .

In troops and streams they rode, some all in black and some in white. And as the massing grey clouds came rolling in from the west the horsemen were galloping now through the clouds, through the sky, as if the clouds were great grey mountains and hills.

Wide-eyed, Jane hardly dared move. She edged one hand along the seat towards Merriman, and before it reached him his own strong hand was holding hers for a moment.

"Don't be afraid, Jane," he said in her ear. "This is the Rising, yes, the last pursuit. And the danger will grow now. But they will not touch this time-train of ours, for we carry on it something of their own."

The train, thundering, rocked furiously along the track. The compartment grew dim as the sky outside darkened with cloud and rushing figures; the rhythm of Mrs. Rowlands' busy needles faltered, and Jane saw the bright colours waver as her fingers slowed. The sound of the train began to change; the beat of its wheels fell off, the pitch of its fast song dropped; there was a sharp muffled report under the wheels somewhere a little way ahead, and then another, and the train began gradually to slow down.

"Maroons!" John Rowlands said in astonishment. "The old maroons going off, that they used to put on the track for fog warnings." He looked out of the window. "And indeed that sky is so grey it might well be fog, now."

The brakes skirled at the train's wheels; the flying landscape slowed, and suddenly the whirling riders were lost in the cloud; grey cloud was everywhere, and swirling mist. Hissing, rattling, the train slowed to a crawl, and all at once a little station was slipping up to them outside the windows. Simon jumped up, pulling Jane out into the corridor; they peered out. The station seemed to be a single platform in the middle of nowhere, without a name, and only a single arch-like structure indefinite in the mist. Beyond, dimly visible through a gap in the cloud, a long hill rose on the horizon ahead. Then slowly, gradually, three vague forms emerged from the arch.

Simon stared at them. "Quick! Jane, open the door!" He lunged past her and turned the long handle, thrusting the door outward, reaching down. And Bran and Will and Barney climbed into the train.

"*Oh!*" Jane said, quite unable to say anything else, and she gave Barney a quick hard hug, and to her surprise Barney hugged her back. The train began to move. In clouds and swirls the mist came swooping round the platform and the dim arch, as if all were dissolving into emptiness, and from the compartment behind them Blodwen Rowlands' musical voice said in pleasure, "Well Bran, *cariad,* how lovely! Are the trials in Shrewsbury, then? John never said—"

"I was telling Blodwen yesterday," John Rowlands' deep careful voice broke in, before Bran could speak, "about you boys going to help Idris Jones ty-Bont with getting the sheep to the sheepdog trials. His turn to supply them for the heats, it is, having no dogs of his own entered this year. I think he is chairman, isn't it, Bran?"

"Yes," Bran said smoothly, as they crowded into the compartment. "And we had to pick up a few more sheep out here, so no more room for us on the lorry, and Mr. Jones put us on the train. A surprise to see you, now."

"And the little one going too, now there's fun for him," said Mrs. Rowlands, smiling at Barney as if it were the most natural thing in the world for him to be helping herd sheep.

Barney smiled dutifully back, said nothing, but slid into the space beside Simon. The train swayed and sang, rushing at full speed again; the mass of the long low hill was rising ahead now like a wall. The grey clouds swept overhead. Hollow-throated, Jane saw the riders again, crowds and streams of them, flying through the sky. Panic gripped her; where were they riding to, where was the train rushing, where—?

"Sit by me, lovey," said Mrs. Rowlands to Bran, an affectionate tug at his arm bringing him down abruptly to the seat between her and Jane. Hastily making room, Jane wondered if the sword were still in the scabbard unseen at Bran's side.

Will stood swaying in the doorway, one hand at either side of the door-frame. He said, looking at Merriman as if at a stranger, "Many people on the train?"

"It is really quite full," said Merriman with the same stiff politeness.

And suddenly the engine gave a great shriek, and the train dived under the hill. In one gulp a tunnel swallowed it, and darkness was all around, a low roaring close in their ears, the sulphurous train-smell filling the air they breathed. Jane had a quick glimpse of apprehension on Mrs. Rowlands' pleasant face. Then she forgot it in the overwhelmingly vivid sense of the way they were driving into the earth, through the mountain, under tons and fathoms of rock, as the train's track carried them inexorably on.

Gradually she began to feel that they were no longer in a

train at all, that the bounds of the small boxlike room in which they sat were beginning to fade. Everyone was there still; the figures sitting, and Will surveying them from what had been the doorway; but now a strange glow had begun all around them, as if it were their speed made visible, as if the glow itself were whirling them along. She felt that they were rushing through the earth, riding on some power of their own, and a great company of people with them, all flying helter-skelter eastward. The glow of light around them grew and grew, became bright; they were contained in brightness, as if they rode on a river of light.

Jane saw wonder and incomprehension on John Rowlands' strong weather-lined face. Blodwen Rowlands gave a sudden whimper of fear; she scrambled to her feet, dropping her knitting on the floor, and lurched over to sit by his side. Rowlands put a comforting arm around her, the support of long affection. "There now, *cariad*," he said. "There now, don't be afraid. Just rest easy, and trust them. Will's Mr. Merriman will keep us out of harm."

But both Will and Merriman now, Jane saw in astonishment, were on their feet and standing before Blodwen Rowlands; both motionless, yet giving an impression of immense silent menace, the menace of accusation. Behind them, Bran stood up slowly, and with the same curious play-acting gesture that Jane remembered from the beach, he drew the invisible sword from the invisible scabbard at his side. And suddenly the sword was there, terrible, naked, gleaming, and the length of its crystal blade was flickering with blue fire.

Blodwen Rowlands shrank back, pressing against her husband's side.

"What is it?" said John Rowlands in angry distress, staring up at Merriman's silent towering form.

"Keep them away from me!" Mrs. Rowlands cried. "John!"

John Rowlands could not stand up, with the weight of her pressing him back, but he seemed to grow more upright as he stared up at them, accusing, reproachful.

"Leave her alone now, you people, whatever you are doing. What has she to do with your concerns? She is my wife and I will not have her frightened. Leave her alone!"

Bran stretched out the tip of the sword Eirias, with the blue flames dancing up and down all its length, and held it so that the tip was between Will and Merriman, pointing at Blodwen Rowlands' contorted face.

"Cowardly it is," he said in a cold adult voice, "to shelter behind those who love you, without giving love in return. Very clever, of course. Almost as clever as being in the right place to help the growing up of a strange pale boy out of the past—and making sure he never does or says or thinks anything without your knowing all about it."

"What is the matter with you, Bran?" said John Rowlands in anguished appeal.

The brightness carried them on, singing like the train, hollow in the hill.

Merriman said in his deep voice, expressionless, "She belongs to the Dark."

"You're mad!" John Rowlands' hand tightened on his wife's arm.

"Our hostage," Will said. "As the White Rider of the Dark took Barney hostage thinking to get Bran and the sword in exchange. A hostage for our safe running, now."

"Safe running!" Blodwen Rowlands said in a new soft voice, and laughed.

John Rowlands sat very still, and Jane winced at the horrified disbelief beginning to dawn in his eyes.

Mrs. Rowlands' laughter was cold, and her voice was all at once oddly different, soft and sibilant but with a new force behind it. Jane could not believe that it was coming from the familiar warm friendly face she could still see.

"Safe running!" said the voice, laughing. "You run to your destruction, all of you, and the sword will be no saviour. The Dark is massed and waiting, with your hostage here to guide it. Risen and waiting, Lyon, Stanton, Pendragon, risen and waiting. And not all your Things of Power will help you to the tree, when you rush out of the earth in a moment now and the Dark force falls upon you."

233

She stood up, John Rowlands' hand dropping limp away from her, to lie on the seat like a discarded glove while he sat there appalled and staring. She seemed to Jane taller, gleaming in the misty brightness with a light of her own. Deliberately Blodwen Rowlands moved toward the point of the sword Eirias, and Bran slowly put up the sword, letting the point rise so that it would not touch her, and Will and Merriman moved aside.

"Eirias may not destroy the Lords of the Dark," Blodwen Rowlands said triumphantly.

"None but the Dark may destroy the Dark," Will said. "That is a part of the law that we have not forgotten."

Merriman took one step forward. Suddenly he was the focus of everything around them; of all the Six, of all the power and intention of the Light driving, driving through the stone and the land towards its mysterious goal. He stood tall in the brightness, his white hair gleaming above the long cloak of dark blue that he wore now, and he raised one arm and pointed at Blodwen Rowlands.

"The Light throws you from this stream of Time," he said, his voice ringing as the song of the train had rung through the hollow land. "We drive you before us. Out! Out! And save yourself as best you can, when you fly forth ahead of this great progress, and the terrible force of your Dark falls upon you thinking to ambush the Light."

Blodwen Rowlands gave a thin cry of rage, the sound of it clutching Jane by the throat with horror; and she seemed to spin round, and change, and whirl away into the dark space around them as a white-robed form on a galloping white horse. Leaping high, caught up in fury and fear, the White Rider rose out of the brightness in which they travelled and was gone, ahead of them, into a misty darkness where nothing could be seen.

CHAPTER EIGHTEEN

THE RIVER

THE GREAT formless vehicle of the Light rushed on through the mountain as if it were a vessel carried along by an underground river. John Rowlands sat still and silent with a face like stone, and they did not look at him for more than an instant; it was not bearable.

At last Jane said, *"The tree.* Gumerry? What did she mean? She said, *Not all your Things of Power will help you to the tree."*

Merriman stood tall and imposing in his dark cloak, its hood falling like a cowl over his neck. His white hair gleamed in the brightness all around, and so did Bran's, beside him; they looked like two figures from some unknown race.

"The midsummer tree, in the Chiltern Hills of England," Merriman said. "The tree of life, the pillar of the world. . . . Once every seven hundred years it may be seen in this land, and on it the mistletoe that will bear its silver blossom on that one day. And whoever shall cut the blossom, at the moment when it opens fully from the bud, shall turn events and have the right to command the Old Magic and the Wild Magic, to drive all rival powers out of the world and out of Time."

Barney said, almost whispering, "And we're going to the tree?"

"That is where we are going," Merriman said. "And so is the Dark, following the path it has been planning all along, to make the final moment of its last and greatest rising the moment when the silver is on the tree."

"But how can you be sure we shall cut the blossom, and not the Dark?" Jane could see nothing but the rushing brightness all around them, but for an instant she had a fierce image of the grey sky filled with riding Lords of the Dark, with Blodwen Rowlands, the White Rider, laughing long cold laughter at their head.

"We have the sword Eirias," Merriman said, "and they do not. And although it is two-edged and may be possessed by either Light or Dark, yet it was indeed made at the command of the Light. If Bran can keep the sword safe, and if the Six and the Circle can keep Bran safe, then all will be well. *And where the midsummer tree grows tall,*" his voice deepened with the lilt of the verse, "*by Pendragon's sword the Dark shall fall.*"

Will glanced automatically at the crystal sword, glinting in Bran's hand. The blade was clear now, the blue flickering fire gone. But as he looked, it seemed to him that on the very point of the blade the dancing blue fire again began to grow —very faint and dim at first, but growing, creeping inch by inch up the blade towards the golden hilt. And the movement of the rushing river of light about them began to change; it became more pronounced, as though they were indeed tossing upon a river. They seemed to be in a boat, the six of them and John Rowlands; Will knew it even though he could see nothing tangible around them at all.

His eye came to Barney, and stopped, and he smiled to himself. The younger boy was sitting oblivious to anyone around him, grinning a private grin of pure pleasure in the sensations swirling through his mind. The fear put into him by Glyndwr's men had evaporated, and there was no ounce of nervousness in him now, but only wonder and astonishment and delight.

Barney looked up suddenly as if he knew Will was looking at him; the grin widened and he said, "It's like the best kind of dream."

"Yes it is," said Will. "But don't . . . relax into it. You can't trust what will happen."

"I know," Barney said equably. "Honest. I know. But all the same . . . *woo!*" It was a head-back, beaming, yelping shout of joyful excitement, spontaneous and startling, and every face turned; their apprehensiveness faded for a moment, and even Merriman, stern for the first instant, laughed aloud. "*Yes!*" he said. "We need that as much as the sword, Barney."

And then suddenly they were out into the day, into grey skies with a watery sun trying in vain to break through thickening cloud, and they could see that their boat was a long high-prowed deckless vessel set with thwarts, and that there were other boats before and behind them of the same shape, filled with figures who could not properly be seen. The mist hovered about them again, and with it a wavering of the air like the tremor of heat, though there was no heat. Will heard a faint familiar music in the air, delicate and fleeting. He looked out at the water and saw glimmering wavelets and an indistinct shore, with green fields beyond, and the shadowy figures of men and horses. For an instant the mist parted, in drifting tatters, and he saw hills rising behind, and the smoke of fires, and an army gathered there waiting, rank after rank of men, many of them on horseback, on small sturdy muscular animals that looked as tough and dark and determined as the riders they bore. It was a cavalry armed with glinting swords, waiting, tense. Then the mist closed again and there was only grey-white space.

"Who are they?" Simon said hoarsely.

"You saw them, then?" Will glanced round; the three of them were grouped beside him, with Bran and Merriman standing remote in the bow of the boat, and John Rowlands a grim hunched figure in the stern.

"Who are they?" Jane said. All three Drews seemed deeply intent, staring vainly into the mist. Will could see Barney's hands convulsively opening and closing, as if longing to be put to use.

Sounds came out of the greyness suddenly, vague, confused, from every direction at once: the clash of weapons,

the neighing of horses, the shouts and screams and triumphant yells of men fighting. Simon spun about, his face
twisted with frustration. "Oh where are they, what is it?
Will!" It was a cry for help, pleading.

Merriman's deep voice said from the bow, with an ache
of the same desperation, "You may well yearn towards it. It
is the first making and breaking of your land, this long-
worked land so many centuries on the anvil. It is *Mons
Badonicus,* the Battle of Badon, where the Dark comes rising and. . . . *How goes the day?*" The voice rose into a
searching shout, a question asked of no one visible, thrown
at random into the grey mist.

And out of the mist as if in answer a long shape loomed: a
boat longer and larger than their own, taking shape nearer
the bank as they drifted towards it on the stream. It was
decked with weapons, filled with armed men, with plain
green flags flying at stem and stern; it seemed the boat of a
general, rather than a king. But there was the bearing of a
king in the figure at its prow: a square-shouldered man with
sunburned face and clear blue eyes; brown hair streaked
with grey, and a short grey beard. He wore a short blue-green
cloak the colour of the sea, and beneath it armour like that
of a Roman. And round his neck, half-hidden but glittering
with a light like fire, he wore Will's linked circle of Signs.

He looked at Merriman, and raised a hand in triumphant
salute. "We go well, my lion. We have them, now, at last;
they will go back to their own lairs and settle, and leave us
to live in peace. For a while. . . ."

He sighed. His bright eyes moved to Bran, and softened.
"Show me the sword, my son," he said.

Bran had been gazing at him, unwavering, since the boat
had first appeared. Now without a flicker of change in his
intent gaze he drew himself upright, a slim pale figure with
his colourless face and white hair, and raised the blue-flaming
blade of Eirias in a formal salute.

"And still it flames for the Dark. Still the warning." The
words were another sigh.

Bran said fiercely, "But in this time too we shall drive out
the Dark, my lord. We shall come before them to the tree,

and then drive them out and away, out of Time."

"Of course. And I must return something that was brought to my aid, and that has served its purpose and must now serve yours." He put back his cloak and lifted the linked Signs from around his neck. "Take them, Sign-seeker. With my blessing."

Will came to the edge of the boat and took the gleaming chain from the strong brown hands; he put it about his own neck, feeling the weight pull at his shoulders. "Thank you, my lord."

Mist whirled round the two boats on the grey river; lifted for a moment to give a glimpse of the crowded armada of shades behind and before; then fell again, leaving all indefinite and vague.

"The Circle is complete, but for the one," Merriman said. "And the Six are strong together."

"Indeed they are, and all is well done." The keen blue eyes flickered over Jane and Simon and Barney, standing silent and awed, and Arthur gave them a nod of greeting. But his head turned again to Bran, as if by compulsion, back to the pale vulnerable figure standing there holding the sword Eirias, his white hair sleek in the mist and the tawny eyes creased a little against the light.

"And when all is done, my son." The voice was soft now. "When all is done, will you sail with me in *Pridwen*, my ship? Will you come with me to the silver-circled castle at the back of the North Wind, where there is peace beneath the stars, and the apple orchards grow?"

"Yes," said Bran. "Oh yes!" His pale face was alight with joy and a kind of worship; Will thought, looking at him, that he had never seen him fully alive before.

"And it will be an easier rest than the last, and without end. Unlike the other." Arthur looked away into the mist, his bearded face sorrowful, looking at the time past from which he spoke to them. "For our great victory against the Dark at Badon does not last so very long. We British stay untroubled in our own parts of these islands, and the English peaceably in theirs, and the Pax Arturus thrives for a score of years. But then the Saxons come again, those bloody pirates, a trickle and then a flood, battering westward through our land, from Kent to Oxford, from Oxford to the Severn. And the last of the old world is destroyed, our cities and our bridges and our language. All vanishes, all dies."

There was anguish in the voice now; it was a long aching lament. "Lost, all lost. . . . The savages bring in the Dark, and the servants of the Dark thrive. Our craftsmen and our builders leave, or die, and none replace them except to deck out barbaric kings. And on our roads, on the old ways, the green grass grows."

"And men flee westward," Merriman said gently, out of the bow of their vessel, "to the last corners of the land where the old tongue lives, for a while. To those places where the Light waits always for the force of the Dark to ebb, so that the grandsons of the invaders may be gentled and tamed by the land their forefathers despoiled. And one of those fleeing men carries a golden chalice called a grail, that bears on its side the message by which a later time will be able better to withstand the last and most menacing rising of the Dark—when it will rise not through the spilling of blood but through the coldness in the hearts of men."

Arthur bent his head in a kind of apology. The mist blew round him; he seemed fainter now, the sea-blue cloak less bright. "True, true. And the grail is found, and all the other Things of Power, by the six of you, and the Light thus fortified so that all of us in the Circle may come to its aid at the end. I know, my lion. I do not forget the hope promised by the future, even though I weep for the pain suffered by my land here in the past."

The river began to swing the boats apart; the sound of battle and of triumphant shouting rose again from the mists around them. Arthur's voice grew distant, rising in a last call.

"Sail the river. Sail on. I shall be with you in a little while."

And the ship and its flags and armed men were gone into the bright mist, and instead a darkness came whirling around them, on both sides of the gleaming stream, a darkness as deep and vast as the sea, battering at their minds, rising, enveloping.

John Rowlands rose slowly to his feet in the stern of the boat where he had been silently sitting. Will could see him only as a vague shape; he could not tell how much Rowlands saw of what was happening.

Rowlands reached out an arm into the darkness, standing pressed against the gunwale of the boat, and with fear and longing in his voice he called out something in Welsh. And then he called, "Blodwen! *Blodwen!*"

Will closed his eyes at the pain in the voice, and tried not to hear or think. But John Rowlands came stumbling up the boat towards them, his head turned for guide towards the blue-flaming blade of the sword in Bran's hand, and when he reached them he put out one hand and grasped Merriman by the shoulder.

Light glimmered round them as if they carried the moon in their vessel, sailing through clouds, yet the light came only from the sword, burning like a cold torch. John Rowlands said, taut with anguish, "Was she always so? Always . . . from outside the earth, like yourself?" He was gazing at Merriman like a man begging for his life, pleading. "Was not one part of it ever real?"

Merriman said unhappily, "Real?" For the first time since Will had come to know him, his voice was without authority, seeking, lost. "Real? When we live in your world as you do, John, those of the Light or those of the Dark, we feel and see and hear as you do. If you prick us, we bleed, if you tickle us, we laugh—only, if you poison us we do not die, and there are certain feelings and perceptions in us that are not in you. And these in the last resort have dominion over the others. Your life with your Blodwen was real, it existed, she felt it just like you. But . . . there was another more powerful side to her nature as well, of which you never had sight."

John Rowlands flung out one arm and struck the side of the boat a fierce blow that his hand did not seem to feel. "Lies!" The word was a shout. "That is all it was, a deceiving, a pretending! Can you deny that? I have been living my life on a lie!"

"All right." Merriman's broad shoulders drooped for a moment, then slowly straightened. His voice seemed to Will to hold a great weariness. "I am sorry, John. Do you blame the Light? Would it have been less of a lie if you had never discovered the Dark?"

"The hell with both of them," John Rowlands said bitterly. He stared coldly at Merriman, at Bran, at Will, and his voice rose in anger and misery. "The hell with all of you. We were happy, before any of this. Why couldn't you leave us alone?"

And while the words rang in the air, to all of them on the boat a figure appeared immediately out of the whirling misty darkness as if riding on the echoes of the angry voice: a dark shape, riding. Each of them saw it in a different way, this towering figure, cloaked, the hood put back from the arrogant head.

Bran saw the Lord of the Dark who had hounded Will and himself through the Lost Land, in wild pursuit through the City, in wait beside the Castle, in roaring fury at their achieving of the sword.

Jane and Simon and Barney saw a figure they had hoped to forget, from days earlier in their lives when they had been caught up in a search for the grail of the Light: a black-haired, black-eyed man named Hastings, fierce and powerful, and in the end raging with the urge for revenge.

Will saw the Black Rider, riding his black stallion in a whirling cloudy turret of the Dark, with one side of his face turned awry out of sight. He caught the glare of a blue eye beneath glinting chestnut hair, and the sweep of a robed arm as the Rider turned in his saddle, pointing at Bran. The tall horse reared up over them, hooves glinting, eyes white and wide. Beside him, Will saw Jane instinctively duck.

"A challenge, Merlion!" the Black Rider called. His voice was clear but faint, as if muffled by the surrounding dark. "We claim there is no place for the Pendragon, the boy, in this flight and this quest. A challenge! He must go!"

Merriman swung round, turning his back in contemptuous dismissal. But the Rider did not move, but stayed by them, his spinning dark tower of cloud rushing with them down the misty river—yet moving gradually more slowly, slowly, just as the boat on which they themselves travelled, Will realised, was slowing now. Soon it was motionless, resting on the still water. For a moment there came a break in the misty darkness ahead, as if a watery sunlight were breaking through; they saw hints of green fields, of swelling green hillsides and the darker green of trees, all hung about still with ragged mist so that nothing was properly distinct.

And then through the mist came flying a pair of swans, their great white wings beating the air so that the wind sang through the feathers. They flapped slowly overhead, now visible, now gone, now bright again, through the patches of mist, and then both dived and came awkwardly down, on either side of the boat, skidding into the river, settling, long necks taking back their peaceful graceful curve. And in the moment of raising his eyes from the two handsome birds, Will saw as if standing high on the prow of their boat the figure of the Lady.

She was neither old nor young, now, her beauty ageless: she stood a straight upright figure with the wind blowing round her the folds of a robe blue as an early morning sky. Will leapt forward, overjoyed, reaching out a hand in welcome. But the Lady's fine-boned face was grave; she looked at Will as if she did not properly see him, and then at Merriman, and then at Bran. Her gaze flickered over the others, with a hint of a pause for Jane, and then came back to Merriman.

"The challenge holds," she said.

Will could not believe what he heard. There was no emotion in the musical voice; it stated merely, without expression but with utter finality. Merriman took one quick unthinking step forward and then stopped; Will, not daring to look up, could see the long fingers of one gnarled bony hand curve tight into a fist, the nails cutting into the palm.

"The challenge holds," the Lady said again, a faint quiver in her voice. "For the Dark has invoked the High Law against the Light, claiming that Bran ap Arthur has no rightful place in this part of Time, and may therefore not take the journey to the tree. That challenge is their right, and must be heard.

For without the hearing, the High Magic will let nothing go further forward in this matter."

The beauty of her face was a grave sadness, and she reached out one arm, graceful as a bird's wing in the falling folds of the blue robe, and pointed the five fingers of her hand toward Bran. For an instant a breeze blew on the still river, and there was a hint of a delicate music in the air; and then the blue light died out of the blade of Eirias, and in a strange slow movement without a sound the sword fell to the deck of the ship. And Bran stiffened and then stood motionless, upright, his arms at his sides, a slim dark-clad figure with the face almost as white now as the hair, caught out of movement as if out of all life. A misty brightness took shape and hovered all about him, like a cage of light, so that he was still in their company and yet kept separate.

The Lady looked out into space at the hovering figure of the Black Rider in the cloudy dark.

"Speak your challenge," she said.

CHAPTER NINETEEN

THE RISING

T H E B L A C K R I D E R said, "We challenge the boy Bran, of Clwyd in the Dysynni Valley in the kingdom of Gwynedd, called Bran Davies for his father in the world of his growing, called the Pendragon for his father the Pendragon in the world from which he came. We challenge his place in this business. He has not the right."

"He has the right of birth," Will said sharply.

"There lies the challenge, Old One. You shall hear." The Black Rider could not now be seen; his voice came hollowly out of the dark turmoil beyond the mist. Will had the sudden sense of an endless army of unseen forms behind him, out there in the dark; he looked quickly away.

The Lady's clear voice said, overhead, "Whom do you seek to judge the challenge, Lord of the Dark? For you have the right to choose, as the Light has the right to approve or deny your choice."

There was a deliberate pause. All at once the Rider was visible again, a distinct figure; his hooded head turned toward Merriman.

"We choose the man, John Rowlands," he said.

Merriman glanced down at Will; he said nothing, either aloud or in the silent speech of the Old Ones, but Will could feel his indecision. He was filled with the same vague suspicion himself—*what are they up to?*—but it fell back, like a wave that breaks over a rock, when he thought of John Rowlands and their long reasons for trusting his judgment.

Merriman nodded. He lifted his wild-haired white head. "That is agreed."

John Rowlands was paying them no attention. He stood in the middle of the boat, with Jane, Barney and Simon grouped beside him on a thwart as if they had drawn close for comfort, though for whose comfort Will would not have cared to tell. Rowlands was gazing at Bran, his lean, lined brown face tight with anxiety. His dark eyes flickered to the tranquil, gleaming form of the Lady and then back to the bright mist enclosing Bran. "Bran *bach*," he said unhappily, "are you all right?"

But there was no answer, and instead the Lady turned her grave face to Rowlands and he was suddenly very still, looking up at her, a silent awkward figure with the dark formal suit sitting on his lithe frame as if it belonged to someone else.

"John Rowlands," the cool, musical voice said, "there will be things said to you now, by the Lords of the Dark and of the Light, and you must listen to each with good attention, and weigh in your own mind the merit of what is said by each. And then you must say which you think is in the right, without fear or favour. And the power of the High Magic, which is present in this place as it is everywhere in the universe, will put its seal on your decision."

John Rowlands stood there, still looking at her. He seemed caught in awe, but there were spots of colour on his high cheek-bones, and the finely modelled mouth was set in a straight line. Very quietly, he said, "*Must?*"

Will flinched, and carefully did not look at the Lady; he heard Merriman hiss softly between his teeth.

But the Lady's voice grew quieter, more gentle.

"No, my friend. This matter holds no compulsion. We ask a favour of you, to make such a judgement. For in this world of men it is the fate of men which is at stake, in the long run, and no one but a man should have the judging of it. Have you not said as much yourself, to the Old Ones, here and elsewhere?"

John Rowlands turned and looked at Will, without expression. Then he said slowly, "Very well."

Suddenly Will was conscious of a crowding of the Old Ones, an immense array of shadowy presences, all around him and behind him on the still, misted river; hovering in the unseen vessels like their own that he had glimpsed, just as they had travelled across the miles and years of the island of Britain in the vehicle that had taken the appearance of a train. It was as if he heard the murmuring of a great crowd, as he had heard the whole Circle of the Old Ones gathered twice before in the course of his life; yet there was no sound, he knew, but the whispering of the wind in the trees that edged the river. Holding in his mind the sense of their attendance, and his awareness of Merriman's tall blue-robed form at his side, he looked hard and openly at the whirling black mist of the Dark as he had not dared look before. The voice of the Rider came strong and confident out of it.

"Judge then. You know that the boy Bran was born in a time long past, and brought into the future to grow there. His mother brought him, because she had once in her own time greatly deceived her lord and husband Arthur, and although the boy was his true son she feared that he would not believe that was so."

John Rowlands said emptily, "Men may be deceived indeed."

"But men forgive," the Rider said swiftly, smoothly. "And the boy's father would have forgiven, and believed Guinevere, if he had had the chance. But a Lord of the Light took Guinevere through Time, at her asking, and so there was no chance and the boy was taken away."

Merriman said, soft and deep, *"At her asking."*

"But," the Rider said, "and mark this, John Rowlands— but, not to a *time* of her asking."

Will felt a coldness creeping into his mind: a dreadful misgiving, like a tiny crack that grows in a great secure dike holding back the sea. Merriman's robe rustled, beside him.

The Rider's voice was quiet and confident. "She came to the mountains of Gwynedd, with her child, without thought of the time to which she came. And a man of the twentieth century, called Owen Davies, fell in love with her, and took her and reared her child as his own when she vanished away again. But that century was not of her choosing. She went where the Lord of the Light took her, she did not care. But the Light had great care."

Suddenly his voice rose, and became harsh and accusing. "The Light chose, and made sure that Bran ap Arthur, Bran pen Dragon, came to this time to grow into the right place at the right moment for the working of the quest of the Light. Thus all the old prophecies have been fulfilled only by their manipulation of Time. And that is a twisting of the terms of the High Magic, and so we claim that the boy Bran, who is here only through the craft of the Light, should go back to the time in which he belongs."

John Rowlands said thoughtfully, "Send him back more than a thousand years? And what language were men speaking here then?"

"Latin," Will said.

"He has very little Latin," John Rowlands said, looking out at the dark mist beyond the river.

"You are frivolous," the voice out of the darkness said, curtly. "He may be taken out of Time merely, as he is now, so long as he plays no part in this present matter."

"Not frivolous," John Rowlands said, softly still. "I am simply wondering how a boy can be said to belong to a time whose language he does not even speak. Just wondering, sir, in order to judge."

Merriman said, without moving from his place at the stern of the boat, "Belonging. That is the answer to this challenge. Whether it was the boy's mother or the Light who chose the time into which he came to grow up, or whether the choice was random, nevertheless he has attached himself to that time. He has bound himself by love to those with whom he has lived there, most particularly Owen Davies his adopted father, and Davies' friend—John Rowlands."

"Yes," Rowlands said, looking up in the same swift anxiety as before to the strange cage of misty light in which, dimly, they could see Bran held motionless.

"Such loving bonds," Merriman said, "are outside the control even of the High Magic, for they are the strongest thing on all this earth."

But then out of the darkness beside them, over the still water, from no direction that they could tell, a frightened voice cried urgently, "John! John!"

John Rowlands' head jerked upright, wary and yet longing.

"That's Mrs. Rowlands!" Jane whispered.

"Where is she?" Barney swung all round, for the voice had seemed to come out of the air.

"There!" Simon was pointing. His voice trailed away. "There. . . ."

They could see only her face, dimly lighted in the churning darkness beside the boat, and her hands, out-stretched. She was gazing imploringly at John Rowlands, and her voice was the soft warm voice they had known in the beginning, and it was full of fear.

"John, help me, help—I have no hand in all these things, I am possessed. There is a mind of the Dark that comes into my own, and then . . . I say things, and I do things, and I do not know what they are. . . . John, we too have loving bonds of our own. *Shoni bach,* you must help, they say they will let me go free if you will help them!"

"Help . . . them?" John Rowlands seemed to speak with difficulty; his voice sounded slow and rusty.

"Set right the balance," the Black Rider said curtly. "Give us the proper decision, that the Light is not entitled to the help of the boy Bran. And we will leave the mind of your wife Blodwen Rowlands, and give her back to you."

"Oh please, John?" Mrs. Rowlands reached out her arms to him, and the appeal in her voice was so poignant that Jane, listening, could hardly bear to keep still. The things she had learned about Blodwen Rowlands vanished totally from her mind; she could hear only the unhappiness and yearning of one human being cut off from another.

"Possession." There was the same odd creaking quality in John Rowlands' voice, as if he were forcing the words out. "It is like the possession by demons, you mean, that they used to speak of in the old days?"

The Black Rider gave a low bubbling laugh, a cold sound.

Blodwen Rowlands said eagerly, "Yes, yes, it is the same. It is the Dark taking over my mind and making me into something else while it is there. Oh John *cariad*, say what they want, so that we can go home to the cottage and be as happy again as we have been all these years. This is all a terrible dream—I want to go home."

John Rowlands' fists clenched tight as the plaintive musical voice rose in appeal; he gazed at his wife's face long and closely. Turning, uncertain, he looked up at Merriman and Will, and last of all at the high remote form of the Lady, but each one of them looked back at him expressionless, without any sign of threat or appeal or advice. John Rowlands looked again at Blodwen—and suddenly Jane felt a hollow feeling of shock at the pit of her stomach, for the look that she saw on his face now was like a sad farewell for something that is forever gone.

His voice was low and gentle, and they could barely hear it over the soft whimpering of the breeze on the riverbank.

"I do not believe any power can possess the mind of a man or woman, Blod—or whatever your name should really be. I believe in God-given free will, you see. I think nothing is forced on us, except by other people like ourselves. I think our choices are our own. And you are not possessed therefore, you must be allied to the Dark because you have chosen to be—terrible though that is for me to believe after all these long years. Either that, or you are not human, wholly a creature of the Dark, a different creature whom I have never really known."

The soft deep voice hung over the misty river, and for a moment there was no sound or movement anywhere, from the indistinct flotilla of the Light or the teeming black emptiness of the Dark. Blodwen Rowlands' glimmering face was there still, and the towering figure of the Rider.

John Rowlands' deep whisper went on, as if he were speaking his thoughts to himself. "And as to Bran, that is a matter of a boy whose choice at first was not his own, but who has lived his own life since then. Which is all that you can say of most of us, in the end. He has indeed made loving bonds for himself, with his father—adopted father, if you like. And with me, and with the others who have watched him grow up on Clwyd Farm. Though not with my wife, as I had thought." His voice husked to nothing, and he swallowed and was silent for a moment.

Jane was watching Blodwen Rowlands' face; she saw it begin gradually to harden. The longing dropped away like a mask, leaving indifference and a cold rage.

"If I am to judge," John Rowlands said, "then I judge that Bran Davies belongs to the time in which both he and I live our lives. And that since he is not separate, as I am, but has thrown in his lot with the Light and risked much for them— then there is no reason why he should not be free to help their cause. As . . . others . . . are free to help the Dark if they choose."

He looked up at the Lady. "There's my judgment, then." His voice seemed deliberately rough and rural, as if he were trying to isolate himself.

The Lady said clearly, "The High Magic confirms it, and thanks you, John Rowlands. And the Light accepts that this is the law."

She turned a little towards the bank of the river, to the churning darkness behind the mist; the brightness seemed to grow around her, and her voice rose. "And the Dark, Rider?"

The wind was rising, tugging at her long blue robe; somewhere far off, faint thunder rolled.

The Black Rider said in quiet fury, "It is the law." He came a little way out of his dark refuge, and put back his hood, and his blue eyes glinted in the scarred face. "You are a fool, John Rowlands! To choose to destroy your home, for the sake of a nameless cause—"

"For the sake of a boy's life," John Rowlands said.

"He was always a fool, always!" Blodwen Rowlands' voice came out of the darkness, strident, stronger than before; it was again the voice of the White Rider, and suddenly, listening, Will knew that he had always heard the likeness of the two but never thought to add them together, and he saw from Jane's face that she had in her mind the same fearful parallel.

The thunder rumbled again, closer.

"A soft one, *yn ffwl mawr!*" Blodwen Rowlands cried. "A shepherd and a harp-player! Fool! Fool!" And her voice rose high into the whine of the rising wind and was carried away into the darkening sky. All around them the mist was darkening now, and the sky above was solid with clouds so dark a grey as to be nearly black.

But the Lady raised her arm and pointed the five fingers of her hand at Bran, where he stood motionless in his cage of bright mist. There was a hint of music in Will's ears, though he did not know if anyone else heard, and then Bran was standing there clear, with the sword Eirias in his hand, and the blade of the sword was flaming with cold blue light.

Bran raised Eirias in the air like a brand. Swelling behind him and all around, Will felt the company of the Light advancing, driving on, and he saw that their boat was moving again, the water lapping past the bow, choppier now, with small waves raised by the rising wind. He knew that the other vessels of their shadowy fleet were moving too. But at the same time the sky was growing darker, darker yet, filled with great billowing clouds.

The wind gusted suddenly higher; he saw the Lady's robe swirl round her slender form and Merriman's dark cloak billow out like a spinnaker over the bow. And then for an instant all light was blotted out around them, as with a roar the whirling tornado of the Dark rose into the sky, travelling over and before them, circling the horizon to collect its final strength.

Only one streak of light still glowed. Standing in the bow of their boat, Bran swept the crystal sword before him in a blue line cutting the air, and the dark mist parted in a ragged, widening gap. They saw green fields rising before them, and suddenly they were all standing on a smooth green slope, on grass, with the river no more than a distant murmur in their ears.

"Stay close, all Six," Merriman said. He led them up the grassy slope. The chain of Signs rang musically round Will's neck. He could feel the myriad shadowy forms of the Circle all about them, shielding them, pressing them on. John Rowlands moved beside the Lady, blank-faced, as if in a trance. Thunder growled overhead.

Then the last of the mist blew away, and in the dim light beneath the lowering sky they saw a line of trees before them, a wood of beech trees capping a round chalk hill—and, gradually appearing on the slope in front of the wood, a single huge tree. It took shape under their eyes, a shadowy outline becoming steadily more solid and real; it rose and filled out and its broad leaves rustled and tossed in the wind. Its trunk was as thick as ten men, its branches spread wide as a house. It was an oak tree, more vast and ancient than any tree they had ever seen.

Overhead, lightning ripped one of the dark clouds, and the thunder came thumping at them like a huge fist.

Barney said, whispering, "Silver on the tree . . . ?"

Bran pointed Eirias up into the tree, in a sweeping triumphant gesture. "See, where the first branch divides—there!"

And through the swaying branches they could see the mistletoe, the strange invading clump of a different green than the green of the oak: the twining stems and the small leaves, growing upon the tree, glimmering a little with a light of their own. Will gazed at the plant and seemed to see it changing, flickering; he blinked in vain to make out something in the middle of the clump.

Merriman's dark cloak blew round him in the rising wind. "There will be one spray of blossoms only," he said, his deep voice rough with strain. "And we shall see each bud break, and when every small bright flower on that spray is in bloom, only then do we cut the spray. Then, and not before and not afterwards, but only in that one moment, does the great spell have force. And in that moment too, he who cuts the mistletoe must be kept from attack by the Six, each with one of the Signs."

He turned his deep-shadowed eyes on Will, and Will reached to his neck to take off the gold-linked circle of the Signs.

But before he could touch them, white lightning suddenly

flashed far closer than before from the dark cloud-base overhead. Will saw Merriman's tall form stiffen, facing the great tree. He too turned, seeking the mistletoe, and saw all at once that a glint of light fierce as fire came from the middle of the strange green clump. The moment was coming; the first bud on the spray of the mistletoe flowers had broken into bloom.

And with it, the Dark came rising.

Will had never, by any enchantment, known what it would be like. Long afterwards, he thought that it must have been like what happens to a mind that goes instantly and totally mad. And worse, for here the world went mad. Like a soundless explosion the immense force of the Dark's power rocked everything round him, rocked his senses; he staggered, reaching blindly for support that was not there. The appearances of things ran wild; black seemed white, green seemed red; all flickering and throbbing as if the sun had swallowed the earth. A great scarlet tree loomed over him against a sky of livid white; the others of the Six, flashing in and out of sight, were like negative images, blurred forms with black teeth and empty white eyes. The endless dull roar of thunder filled his ears and his mind; he felt sick and ill, cold and hot at once, his eyes closing to slits, a constriction growing in his throat.

Unable to move any limb, he saw through leaden eyelids that Simon and Jane and Barney had collapsed to the ground; moving with tremendous effort, as if held down by weights, they struggled in vain to get up. Darkness loomed over them; slowly turning his heavy head, Will saw in sick horror that half the sky, half the world, behind him was filled with the whirling black tornado of the Dark, spinning between cloud and earth, more vast than his senses could comprehend. He saw Bran, staggering, holding up a blue streak of flame as if for support. Bright blue, he thought, I've never seen a brighter blue, except the Lady's eyes. *The Lady, where is the Lady?* And he could not move to look for her, but crumpled to his knees while the world wove to and fro in his spinning gaze. It was only by simple accident that his feeble hand hit the circle of Signs hanging from his neck.

Then all at once he could see clearly, and wonder caught him as he saw. Down across the storming sky, cleaving the monstrous grey-black clouds, came six horsemen, riding. Three on either side they came, silvery-grey glinting figures on horses of the same strange half-colour: galloping, cloaks flying, with drawn swords in their hands. One of them wore a glinting circlet about his head, but Will could not clearly see his face.

"The Sleepers ride!" Bran called to him. Will saw him leaning back in an intent curve, staring upward, clear against the green grass with his white hair and blue-flaming outflung sword. "The seven Sleepers, changed now to Riders, just as I said they would be!"

"But still I remember there were six Sleepers," Will said softly to Merriman, so softly that he knew Bran could not hear. "Six Sleepers, oldest of the old, that once we woke out of their long sleep beside the lake, with the golden harp."

Merriman neither moved nor spoke, but stood looking at the terrible sky. And as Will gazed up at the wheeling Riders of the Light, a long brightness began to glow in the east. And like a white sun rising, another figure came leaping across the sky: a different rider of a different shape, like no shape ever born on the earth.

He was a tall man riding a brilliant white-gold horse, but his head was horned like the head of a stag, with shining antlers curving out in seven tines. As Will gazed, he raised his great head, yellow light flashing from tawny round eyes like the eyes of an owl, and he gave a call that was like the halloo a huntsman blows on the horn to call up hounds. And through the sky after him, belling and baying, came flowing an endless pack of huge ghostly white hounds, red-eared, red-eyed, fearsome creatures running inexorable on a trail no living power could turn. They milled round the feet of the Huntsman's horse, high up there in the sky, as he laughed dreadfully over them in delight of the chase; they thronged round the silver-grey horses of the Sleepers waiting restlessly to join their hunt.

And then the Huntsman in a wild shout gave the call to

let loose the chase, and he and the ghost-grey swordsmen, seven riders, were leaping through the clouds with the Hounds of Doom flooding after them, red eyes burning, a thousand throats giving tongue like the whickering of migrant geese: the Wild Hunt, in full cry against the Dark for the last time.

The vast storm-cone of the Dark lashed and thrashed about the sky as if in agony, and its tip seemed to split away. A horrible flailing filled the sky, until with one last convulsive lunge that seemed to bring half the clouds in the heavens down to the earth, the huge tornado-like black pillar rushed away and upward, out into nowhere, with the Sleepers and the Wild Hunt in howling merciless pursuit.

But great Herne the Hunter reined in his white-gold mare, leaping high in the heavens with the force of her arrested speed, and he turned seeking through the torn and rushing clouds with his tawny wild eyes. And in sudden new terror Will saw what he sought, the peak of Dark power that would never flee: the two huge figures, indestructible now in their full power, of the Black Rider and the White Rider of the Dark, curving out of the sky on a long rushing lunge down to the grassy Chiltern hill and the enchanted tree.

Will heard Simon shout from beside the tree, the first sound any one of the Six had made in all their breathless watching, and he turned back to see flashing on the tree new small brilliant points of light as more buds on the green patch of mistletoe burst into their magical bloom. His hands went to his neck, in the same instant that he heard Merriman's silent cry of command in his mind, and he tore off the circle of Signs. High in the sky the Riders, grown now to huge size, came rushing closer towards the earth. Will shouted to Simon and Barney and Jane, *"Six Signs shall burn!* Take one for each, and circle the tree!"

They were at his side, eager, reaching, and in the gold-linked chain each Sign in turn came easily away from the rest as the gold seemed to melt and vanish like wax. Simon took the smooth black Sign of Iron and rushed with it to the tree, to stand against the gnarled enormous trunk holding it high in challenge; Jane followed with the gleaming Sign of Bronze,

Barney with the rowan-born Sign of Wood. There they stood, brave and quivering, staring terrified at the monstrous Riders galloping headlong down from the high clouds, down to consume them. Swiftly Merriman joined them with the brilliant gold Sign of Fire, Bran holding the crystal Sign of Light with the Sword, to leave Will swinging round last of all with his back to the tree, holding up in defiance the glittering black flint Sign of Stone. And the Riders were upon them, with bright lightning and deep thunder that came from no cloud but out of the dark air; their huge horses reared up, screaming, lashing out with wild deadly hooves. Herne's great horned figure rode at the Dark Lords in attack from above, and the force of all the unseen shades of the Circle was holding, barring, wrestling them below, with the Lady as its shining focus, but the strain was near to breaking-point. And in a burst of brilliance, the last flower on the mistletoe burst into bloom.

Bran reached up, his white hair flying, swinging Eirias over his head to cut the spray; but with the Sign of Light in his left hand he had only one arm for the long crystal blade, and his balance would not hold. He cried out in desperation. The Black Rider's eyes blazed blue as sapphires and he lunged forward in triumph, straining to break through the strength of the Circle and reach the shining bloom with his own sword. But suddenly John Rowlands was at Bran's side, pale and grim; he seized the Sign of Light and thrust it out against the rearing attack, the shimmering crystal circle frail in his big brown hand.

And Bran, free now to use both arms, swung the glittering blade of the sword Eirias at the green mistletoe within the oak, and cut the stars of bright blossom from the tree. As the spray parted Merriman turned, tall and triumphant, and caught the blossom before it fell; he swept round, blue cloak billowing, and in a swift breathtaking movement flung it up into the sky. And the mistletoe blossom changed in that instant into a white bird, and the bird flew up into the sky and away, away through the broken white clouds scudding now across the blue, away into the world.

Each of the Signs held there in each of six hands blazed

suddenly with a cold light like fire, too bright for eyes to watch, and with two mingling voices crying out in fear and despair the great rearing figures of the Black Rider and the White Rider of the Dark fell backwards out of Time and disappeared. And each of the six hands suddenly was empty, as each Sign burned with its cold fire into nothing and was gone.

CHAPTER TWENTY

ONE GOES ALONE

THEY STOOD IN SILENCE about the tree, unable to speak.

High up where a last few tatters of storm cloud blew dark across the sun, Herne the antlered Hunter put back his fierce head and gave a long triumphant cry, the gathering call that is lifted up by the horn when the quarry is slain. His white mare leapt across the sky, whinnying high and clear like the singing of the wind on the hill, curving down to a place where a stream of high wind-blown cloud lay like a river across the sky.

Out and down the Hunter leapt, and in the very instant that he seemed to plunge into the river of the sky and disappear, instead they saw sailing out from that same point the great ship *Pridwen,* graceful and high-prowed, with the green standard of the Lord Arthur rippling out at bow and stern. Closer and closer she came, sailing on the wind, and among the Six beside the tree Will saw Bran slowly raise the sword Eirias and thrust it down into the scabbard visible now at his side. It was a strange reluctant gesture that Will could not interpret. He stared at his friend, at the pale face and the tawny eyes beneath the white hair, but he could see no expression there as Bran watched the long ship sail towards them, down the sky. He found himself reflecting instead, not for the first time, that Bran's golden eyes were curiously like those of the Wild Huntsman, Herne.

And then the ship *Pridwen* was upon them, and he was looking instead at the blue-grey eyes and weathered, brindle-bearded face of the leader-king, Arthur.

Arthur was looking past him, at the fragile slim blue-robed figure of the Lady, standing a little apart from them all. He stepped from the prow of the boat where he stood, and down to the land, and he knelt on one knee before the Lady and bent his head. "Madam," he said, his voice as warm with the pleasure of living as when Will had first heard it, "your boatman awaits."

Will stood with his head singing in bewilderment, feeling the baffled awe of the three Drews beside him.

The Lady came forward to the boat, with a beckoning touch on Arthur's arm in the casual closeness of those who belong to the same family. "It is done," she said. Suddenly there was a deep weariness in the music of her voice, that spoke of great age in spite of the calm ageless beauty of her fine-boned face. "Our task is accomplished, and we may leave the last and longest task to those who inherit this world and all its perilous beauty."

She looked back at them all, and as if in farewell she smiled at Barney, at Simon, and more lingeringly at Jane. Then she looked at John Rowlands, standing empty-eyed and stiff beside the broad oak tree, and she moved swiftly to him and took both his hands.

Rowlands looked at her, his dark Welsh face drawn down by lines at nose and mouth that had never seemed so marked before.

"John," the Lady said softly. "In all this great matter you have done more for your world than any of us, even before your courage at the end—for you could have retreated into an unseeing happiness of your own and yet gave it up. You are a good and honest man, and for a time now you must be an unhappy man. But—it is only for a time." She released his hands, but still gazed commandingly into his eyes, and John Rowlands looked back at her without awe or subservience, and shrugged. He said nothing.

"You have made a hard choice," the Lady said, "and lost

the pattern of your life thereby. I cannot give you back your Blodwen, that ambitious fallen figure. But I can give you another chance gentler than the first. In a moment you will be back in your own world and time, and there you will find that the . . . appearance of your wife has had some tragic accident, and died. It is for you to decide whether or not, in that moment, you want still to remember all that has happened to you. You may indeed remember the hard truth about the Light and the Dark, and the true nature of your wife, if you wish."

John Rowlands said, expressionless, half to himself, "It is very strange, there was one thing she would never tell me. It was a joke with her—she never would tell me where or when she was born."

The Lady reached out a hand in pity, then let it fall. "Or," she said gently, "instead you may forget. You may, if you wish, forget all that you have seen ever of the Lords of the Dark and the Light, and although you will then have perhaps a deeper grief at the loss of your wife, you will mourn her and remember her as the woman you knew and loved."

"That would be living a lie," John Rowlands said.

"No," Merriman said from behind him, very strong and deep. "No, John, for you did love her, and all love has great value. Every human being who loves another loves imperfection, for there is no perfect being on this earth—nothing is so simple as that."

"It is for you to choose," the Lady said. She moved to the boat and paused beside it, looking back.

John Rowlands stood facing them all, still without visible emotion; then he turned his dark eyes to the Lady and a warmth came into them. "I cannot choose, this time," he said with a wry smile. "Not such a choice as that. Will you by your grace do it for me?"

"Very well," the Lady said. She raised her arm, pointing. "Walk away from me, John Rowlands, and when you turn you will find a path at your feet. Follow it. In the moment that you pass the one tree, you will be gone from here and instead be on another path in your own valley, that you know far better than this. And whatever is in your mind then will be whatever choice I have made for you. And—we wish you well."

John Rowlands bent his head for an instant; then looked from one to another of them with a half-smile that held no happiness, but great affection. He looked last at Bran. *"Mi wela'i ti'n hwyrach, bachgen,"* he said. Then he turned and walked away towards the immense spreading oak, on a path that no one else could see, and as he drew level with the tree he was no longer there.

The Lady sighed. "He shall forget," she said. "It is better so."

Arthur put out a hand to her, and she stepped down into the boat. A rising wind blew, rocking *Pridwen* on the river of the sky, and suddenly Will had the sense once more of a huge throng, and knew that all the Old Ones of the Circle were making their way aboard, to sail with the Lady and the king. At the ship's mainmast now the vast sail rose, square, billowing, marked with the cross within a circle, the Sign of the Light. He heard the cries of sailors; timbers creaked, halyards clattered against spars.

Will glanced at the three Drews beside him, and saw on their faces the beginning anguish of loss, and a long emptiness. But he could not keep his eyes for more than a moment from the great ship. He looked back, and in the ghostly throng of beings on her decks he saw in one quick flash after another the faces of those he had known, on this journey and on other journeys, in this time and other times. A tall burly figure in a smith's apron raised a long hammer in salute; he saw a bright-eyed small man in a green coat wave to him, and an imperious grey-haired lady, leaning on a stick, make him a formal little bow. He had the flash of a smile from a stout brown-faced man with a tonsure of white hair; he saw Glyndwr, and the frail form of the King of the Lost Land; and then with a jerk of his heart he saw Gwion, looking at him, smiling his brilliant smile. Then the wind began to grow stronger out of the clouds, and the sail billowed and flapped as if impatient, and the faces merged into the misty crowd.

Chapter Twenty   ONE GOES ALONE

Arthur stood in the prow, his bearded head outlined against the sky, and held out his hand to Bran. His warm voice rang out, triumphant and welcoming. "Come, my son!"

Bran came quickly towards him; then paused. He was close to Merriman, his white hair and pale face almost luminous against Merriman's deep-blue cloak. Will looked on sadly, knowing it would be for the last time, seeing in Bran's face a mixture of longing, and determination, and regret.

"Come, my son," said the warm deep voice again. "The long task of the Light is over, and the world is freed of the peril of dominion by the Dark. Now it is all a matter for men. The Six have performed their great mission, and we have fulfilled our heritage, you and I. And now we may have rest, in the quiet silver-circled castle at the back of the North Wind, among the apple trees. And those we leave behind may think of us in greeting each night, when the crown of the North Wind, the Corona Borealis, rises above the horizon in its circlet of stars."

He reached out an arm again. "Come. There is a tide in this matter which is almost at the full, and I do not sail on the ebb."

Bran looked at him in yearning, but he said clearly, "I cannot come, my lord."

There was a silence, into which only the wind softly sang. Arthur let his arm come slowly down to his side.

Bran said, stumbling, "It is what Gwion said, when the Lost Land was to be drowned and he would not leave it. *I belong here.* If it is a matter for men now, as you say, then the men are going to have a hard time of it and perhaps there are things, later, that I might be able to do to help. Even if there are not, still I . . . belong. *Loving bonds,* Merriman said. That is what I have, here. And he said"—he was looking up at Merriman, beside him—"that those bonds are outside the High Magic, even, because they are the strongest thing on the earth."

Merriman stirred; from his mind Will could feel something like awe.

"That is true," Merriman said. "But consider well, Bran. If you give up your place in the High Magic, your identity in the time that is outside Time, then you will be no more than mortal, like Jane and Simon and Barney here. You will be the Pendragon no longer, ever. You will remember nothing that has happened, you will live and die as all men do. You must give up all chance of going out of Time with those of the Light—as I shall go before long, and as one day long hence Will will go too. And . . . you will never see your high father again."

Bran turned sharply toward Arthur, and as he watched the two stare at one another, Will saw again the tawny eyes of Herne the Hunter in Bran's face, and yet a look of Arthur too, as if all three were one and the same. He blinked, wondering.

All at once Arthur smiled, proud and loving, and he said softly, "Go where you feel you should go, my son Bran Davies of Clwyd, and my blessing go with you." He stepped down over the side of the boat again to the grassy bank, and held his arms open, and Bran ran to him and for a moment they stood close.

Then Arthur stepped back, smiling, and Bran, looking up at him all the while, drew Eirias white and gleaming from the scabbard at his side, slipped the swordbelt over his head, and held out both sword and scabbard to his father. Will heard Merriman sigh gently, as if in release, and found his own fists unwittingly clenched. And Arthur took Eirias in one hand and the scabbard in the other, and sheathed the sword. He looked for a moment past Bran to Merriman, and his eyes smiled, though his mouth was serious now. "I will see you in a little while, my lion," he said, and Merriman nodded his head.

Then the king stepped back into his ship *Pridwen,* and the broad sail filled and bellied out, and with all the host of shades of Light looking back, without sign of farewell or any ending, the ship sailed across the sky. Small sunlit clouds lay scattered there, so that the blue sky was like a sea scattered with small islands, and there was no telling whether the ship was in sea or sky when it disappeared.

Bran stood watching until there was no ship to watch, but

Will could see no regret on his face.

"That must have been what John Rowlands meant," Bran said quietly.

"John Rowlands?" said Will.

"In Welsh. When he left. He said to me, *See you later, boyo.*"

Jane said slowly, "But—he didn't know you would come back."

"No," Bran said.

Merriman said, "But he knows Bran."

Bran looked up at him, very young and vulnerable suddenly, with his pale eyes unprotected, and the astonishing burden of the sword Eirias taken from his side. "Was it the right thing to do?"

Merriman threw back his awesome white-maned head as impulsively as a schoolboy, and let out a hoot of breath that was the most unguarded sound they had ever heard him utter. "Yes," he said, sobering suddenly. "Yes, Bran. It was the right thing, for you and for the world."

Barney moved at last, from the place on the grassy slope where he and Simon and Jane had been standing close for a long time, watching in a wondering silence. He said anxiously, "Gumerry? Are you really going away, or will you stay too?"

"Oh Barnabas," Merriman said, and Jane found herself turning to him in swift motherly concern, there was such weariness in his tone. "Barnabas, Barnabas, time passes, for the Old Ones even as for you, and though the seasons turn in every year much as in the one before, yet the pattern of the world is different in every year that goes by. My time is done, here, my time and the time of the Light, and there will be other work for us to do elsewhere."

He paused, and smiled at them, the weariness fading a little from his bony deep-lined face, with the fierce hawk-like nose and the shadowed eyes. "Here now are the Six," he said, "together for the first and last time in the place that was destined for us, on a chalk hill in the Chiltern Hundred of Buckinghamshire, where centuries ago men fleeing from the

Dark tried vainly to hide their treasures, and gave prayers to the sky for safety. Look at it now. Look well. Keep a little of it alive."

So, wondering what he might mean, they looked hard and long, at the slope of smooth green grass with tiny orange-yellow toadflax growing here and there, and small blue butter-flies fluttering. They looked at the copse of beech trees cap-ping the hill, and the broad mysterious oak tree standing just below the wood; at the clear blue sky scattered with puffy white clouds.

And then, although Merriman made no move, each of them blinked suddenly as their vision seemed to blur; and they staggered a little, with a singing in their ears and a gid-diness taking away their balance. They saw everything about them shiver strangely, as if the air were dancing in the heat of a fire. The outlines of the giant oak wavered, grew dim, and disappeared; the green of the hill darkened, and the shape of its slope was no longer a smooth arc. Though the sun still shone, there were darker patches on the hill now, of yellow-flecked green and brown and purple, where gorse and bracken and heather grew. Other shapes rose in the distance, faraway mountains misted grey and blue on a hazy horizon; and when they turned to look over their shoulders they saw spread below them a broad valley golden with sand, and the winding silver thread of a river making its way out to the immense blue sea. They could hear the erratic aimless call-ing of sheep, now and then in the silence, basso profundo answered by tenor; somewhere far below them a dog barked. And over their heads, gliding down from the Welsh hillside to the river and the sea, came a single seagull, keening its one repeated melancholy cry.

Merriman took a long gentle breath, and let it out again. He said once more, softly, "Look well."

Jane said in a very small voice, looking out at the bar of golden sand that the river had set as guard against the sea, "Shall we never see you again?"

"No," Merriman said. "None of you, except my Will the watchman there. That is the only right way."

There was a command and a clear strength in his voice that caught each of them into stillness, gazing at him, held by the bright dark eyes and the bleak face.

"For remember," he said, "that it is altogether your world now. You and all the rest. We have delivered you from evil, but the evil that is inside men is at the last a matter for men to control. The responsibility and the hope and the promise are in your hands—your hands and the hands of the children of all men on this earth. The future cannot blame the present, just as the present cannot blame the past. The hope is always here, always alive, but only your fierce caring can fan it into a fire to warm the world."

His voice rang out over the mountain, more impassioned than any of them had ever heard a voice before, and they stood quiet as standing stones, listening.

"For Drake is no longer in his hammock, children, nor is Arthur somewhere sleeping, and you may not lie idly expecting the second coming of anybody now, because the world is yours and it is up to you. Now especially since man has the strength to destroy this world, it is the responsibility of man to keep it alive, in all its beauty and marvellous joy."

His voice grew softer, and he looked at them with the far-away dark eyes that seemed to be looking out into Time. "And the world will still be imperfect, because men are imperfect. Good men will still be killed by bad, or sometimes by other good men, and there will still be pain and disease and famine, anger and hate. But if you work and care and are watchful, as we have tried to be for you, then in the long run the worse will never, ever, triumph over the better. And the gifts put into some men, that shine as bright as Eirias the sword, shall light the dark corners of life for all the rest, in so brave a world."

There was a silence, and the small sounds of the mountain drifted back into it: the faint calls of sheep, the humming of a distant car, and far above, the cheerful trilling of a lark.

"We'll try," Simon said. "We'll try our best."

Merriman gave him a quick startling grin. "Nobody can promise more than that," he said.

They looked at him mournfully, unable to grin in return, weighed by the melancholy of parting. Merriman sighed, and swept his midnight-blue cloak around him and back across a shoulder.

"Come now," he said. "The oldest words have it the best— *be of good cheer.* I go to join our friends, because I am very tired. And none of you will remember more than the things that I have been saying now, because you are mortal and must live in present time, and it is not possible to think in the old ways there. So the last magic will be this—that when you see me for the last time in this place, all that you know of the Old Ones, and of this great task that has been accomplished, will retreat into the hidden places of your minds, and you will never again know any hint of it except in dreams. Only Will, because he is of my calling, must remember—but the rest of you will forget even that. Good-bye now, my five companions. Be proud of yourselves, as I am proud of you."

He embraced each one of them in turn, a brief hug of farewell. They were grim-faced, and their eyes were wet. Then Merriman went up the mountain, over the springy grass and the outcrops of slate, through the browning bracken and the yellow-starred gorse, and paused only when he was at the very top, outlined against the blue sky. They saw the familiar tall figure, standing very erect, with the fierce-nosed profile and the springing shock of white hair, blowing a little now in the wind that had risen out of nowhere. It was an image that would flicker in and out of their dreams for the rest of their lives, even when they had forgotten all else. Merriman raised his arm, in a salute which none of them could bear to answer, and then in a subtle inflection of movement the arm stiffened, the five fingers spread wide and pointed at them—

And a wind whirled on the hill, and the slope against the sky was empty, and five children stood on the roof of Wales looking out over a golden valley and the blue sea.

"It's a terrific view," Jane said. "Worth the climb. But the wind's made my eyes water."

"It must blow like anything up here," said Simon. "Look at the way those trees are all bent inland."

Bran was gazing puzzled at a small blue-green stone in the palm of his hand. "Found this in my pocket," he said to Jane. "You want it, Jenny-oh?"

Barney said, gazing up over the hill, "I heard music! Listen —no, it's gone. Must have been the wind in the trees."

"I think it's time we were starting out," Will said. "We've got a long way to go."

When the Dark comes rising, six shall turn it back;
Three from the circle, three from the track;
Wood, bronze, iron; water, fire, stone;
Five will return, and one go alone.

Iron for the birthday, bronze carried long;
Wood from the burning, stone out of song;
Fire in the candle-ring, water from the thaw;
Six Signs the circle, and the grail gone before.

Fire on the mountain shall find the harp of gold
Played to wake the Sleepers, oldest of the old;
Power from the green witch, lost beneath the sea;
All shall find the light at last, silver on the tree.

AND HERE ENDS THE SEQUENCE NAMED
THE DARK IS RISING

SUSAN COOPER

Susan Cooper was born in Buckinghamshire in 1935, and read English at Oxford. For seven years thereafter she was a staff writer for the *Sunday Times* of London. She then married an American scientist and moved to the United States, where she now lives near Boston. She has two children and three stepchildren, and has written nine books and several hundred newspaper articles. Her books for children are DAWN OF FEAR and, in the sequence named "The Dark Is Rising," the following titles: OVER SEA, UNDER STONE; THE DARK IS RISING; GREENWITCH; THE GREY KING, and SILVER ON THE TREE, the last book in the sequence.